MURDER
AT THE
MANSION

ALSO BY SHEILA CONNOLLY

MURDER
AT THE
MANSION

A Victorian Village Mystery

Sheila Connolly

St. Martin's Paperbacks

This is a work of fiction. All of the characters, organizations, and events portrayed in this novel are either products of the author's imagination or are used fictitiously.

MURDER AT THE MANSION

Copyright © 2018 by Sheila Connolly.
Excerpt from *Killer in the Carriage House* copyright © 2019 by Sheila Connolly.

All rights reserved.

For information address St. Martin's Press, 120 Broadway, New York, NY 10271.

ISBN: 978-1-250-21278-8

Our books may be purchased in bulk for promotional, educational, or business use. Please contact your local bookseller or the Macmillan Corporate and Premium Sales Department at 1-800-221-7945, ext. 5442, or by e-mail at MacmillanSpecialMarkets@macmillan.com.

Printed in the United States of America

Minotaur Books hardcover edition / June 2018
St. Martin's Paperbacks edition / June 2019

St. Martin's Paperbacks are published by St. Martin's Press, 120 Broadway, New York, NY 10271.

10 9 8 7 6 5

To Clara Barton, my very distant cousin,
who was a far more interesting woman
than I ever suspected

Acknowledgments

This book was inspired by a trip to Boonsboro, Maryland, where I strolled around the small town and realized that the buildings on the main street had changed very little since the nineteenth century, except for a thin skin of later siding. It was easy to envision peeling off that skin to reveal the original town beneath.

I am grateful to my editor, Hannah Braaten at St. Martin's Press, who saw the potential in this new series and whose comments made this a better book. Many thanks also to my tireless agent, Jessica Faust of BookEnds, who put me together with Hannah.

I've been published for ten years now, and I never would have made it this far without the steady support and encouragement of the mystery writers community, and I can't begin to count the friends I have made there. The national organization Sisters in Crime, along with my local New England chapter, have been mainstays. The same goes for my blogger colleagues from Mystery Lovers' Kitchen, Killer Characters, and Wicked Cozy Authors, where we all share our writing and publishing ups and downs.

And I have to add a nod to the Massacusetts Barton family from which I am descended. They have provided a wealth of interesting plots, and I simply borrow them and drop them into my books.

I stopped in the doorway of the second-floor restaurant at the Oriole Suites Hotel in Baltimore, where I'd worked for the past five years, looking for Lisbeth. She'd called out of the blue and asked to meet me for lunch, but she'd been very secretive about why, which led me to think it was more than just a "hey, how are you, what have you been doing for the past ten years?" kind of lunch. Still, we'd been good friends in high school then sort of drifted apart. As far as I knew, she'd stayed in Asheboro ever since, going to the local community college, marrying a local guy, having a couple of kids. Unlike me: I'd headed out of state for college and never looked back. Not that there was anything wrong with Asheboro, Maryland. It was a nice small town—with emphasis on the "small"— but I'd always had bigger plans. Most of what I knew about Asheboro now had come from holiday cards from the few people I'd kept in touch with, like Lisbeth.

She spotted me standing in the doorway and waved enthusiastically. I smiled and wove my way through the tables until I reached hers. When she'd called me, I'd made the reservation for us, and made sure there was a nice view of Baltimore Harbor. Working for the hotel had a few perks.

"Katie, you look great!" she exclaimed, standing and hugging me. "Love your outfit. But then, you work in a city, so I guess you have to look good. I had to dig into the back of my closet to find something to wear that wasn't jeans or sweats. I'm so glad you could meet with me!"

"It was great to hear from you," I told her, as we took our seats. "How long has it been?"

"I think you came to Jeffrey's christening. He's eight now."

"Wow, that long? But since my folks moved to Florida, I haven't had much reason to visit Asheboro."

"They bailed out early, didn't they? What are they, fifty-something?"

"Yes. But they always figured they'd head south eventually, and they decided to go while they were still mobile enough to enjoy it. They didn't want to get stuck in one of those old-folks towers on the beach. They've got a nice small cottage that suits them, and I get to visit when I want."

"Sounds great!" Lisbeth said, although I sensed a false note in her voice. "Anything new with you? A guy? Or lady? Kids?"

"No to all of those," I told her, smiling. "I'm married to my job, and that's enough for me."

A waiter appeared. I smiled at him; I knew Tony pretty well, since I often dropped into the restaurant to pick up something to eat. He handed us menus, and we ordered iced tea.

"What's good here?" Lisbeth asked Tony, staring in awe at the multipage menu.

"If you want some local flavor, the crab cakes are great."

"Okay, I'll do those." She shut the menu with a firm slap

and handed it to Tony. "How long have you been working at the hotel, Katie?"

"About five years. I don't remember when I last updated you, but you already know I went to college, worked for a while, decided I wanted to be in management so I got an MBA, worked at a big chain hotel in Philadelphia for a couple of years. Then this hotel opened up in Baltimore, and I snagged a really good job in administration, and here I am."

"I'm surprised you came back to Maryland," Lisbeth said. "Didn't you want to travel, see other places? Los Angeles? Chicago? London?"

"I thought about it, but this was too good a job to pass up and I was given a free hand, since the hotel was new."

Waiter Tony delivered the tea and slipped away again. "What exactly is it you do here?" Lisbeth asked.

Since I'd more or less created the position, it wasn't easy to explain. "A little of everything. I'm in charge of customer satisfaction. I know, that sounds vague, but it's kind of a catch-all job about making sure that everything goes smoothly. No, more than that, really: that everything is comfortable but memorable. Appearance, cleanliness, responsiveness of the staff, even the quality of the food and the polish on the silverware and glassware. We want people to go home talking about this place, sending their friends here, coming back themselves."

"You always were a little OCD," Lisbeth said. When I looked startled, she spoke quickly to explain. "In a good way, of course. I mean, you were always really well organized. You turned in your assignments on real paper, not just something torn out of a notebook. You always spell-checked everything twice. When we were on the soccer team, you always knew all the rules, and you even argued with the refs now and then. Now you just do it on a much bigger scale. I mean, you've got a whole hotel here!"

Had Lisbeth really seen me that way, years ago? "Yes, but you can still break it down into smaller tasks, like service staff, restaurant, website, reservations, and so on. I won't bore you with it all. What about you? What have you been doing?"

Tony brought our lunch dishes and refilled our water glasses, then disappeared discreetly once again. While we ate Lisbeth nattered on about her husband, and her kids, and how smart they were (all of them), and how wonderful, and what a busy life she led—what with the PTA and the annual school fund drive, and her daughter's Brownie troop and her son's softball team. I listened with half an ear and tried to summon up my memories of Asheboro: small town, one main street, one stoplight in the center. Surrounded by pretty rolling country (although for all I knew it was nothing but strip malls now) and near a lot of Civil War battlefields, but most history buffs just passed right through, since there was no reason to stop in town. One elementary school, ending with eighth grade, and one high school—or maybe now there was a regional high school—I wasn't exactly on their email list for updates. One old factory that had been closed since long before we were born. Maybe it had fallen down by now. Parents had warned us to stay away from it, but there were always a few guys who couldn't resist a dare. Yet I couldn't recall that anybody had ever gotten hurt there. I had no recollection of what the old factory had made.

My hometown was sounding really dull, even to me—and I'd been more or less happy growing up there. So I hurried to recall a few good points: no violence, no poverty, no pollution.

It was a safe, quiet town, like so many others. It was also a place I hadn't wanted to stay, but that didn't mean that good people didn't go on living happy lives there. People like Lisbeth, who seemed to have thrived in that setting.

I noticed that Lisbeth kept darting nervous glances as me. Did she have another motive that she hadn't mentioned? "So, what brings you to Baltimore, Lisbeth? Don't tell me it's just to have lunch with me and catch up. Are you leaving your husband? Looking for a job?"

She giggled nervously. "No, no, nothing like that. Phil and I are fine. He's got a great job. The kids are healthy and happy. I keep busy with volunteering, like I told you, and we're doing okay financially."

She wasn't answering my question, so I pressed on. "You wanted a mini-vacation? Come on, Lisbeth, there's something you aren't saying. Isn't there?"

She sighed and looked out at the sparkling harbor, the clusters of people passing by, the boats on the water—anywhere but at me. "I have a favor to ask. Or we do. And it's a big one."

We? "You mean, you and Phil? And what's big?"

"No, actually, I mean the town." She took a deep breath. "We want you to save Asheboro."

Well, that was something I didn't expect to hear. "What on earth do you mean?"

"It's kind of complicated. You have time?"

"After a request like that, I'll make time. Start at the beginning."

Tony appeared again. "Would you ladies care for anything else?"

"Just coffee for me, please," Lisbeth told him. I asked for coffee too, but I also requested one of the petit fours plates to share for dessert. The restaurant had a great chef and baking staff, and I'd asked that they create a plate of small bites for those patrons who didn't want anything heavy to end their meal. It had proved very popular, even for people requesting room service, and I was proud of it. Attention to detail in the hospitality business was important.

My mind was wandering. Was I stalling for time? Lisbeth was staring at me with an odd expression on her face, but she stayed silent until Tony reappeared with the pretty platter of goodies and set it carefully between us, then retrieved the polished coffee carafe and filled our cups. Then he retreated silently.

I looked her straight in the eye. "Have a strawberry tartlet and then tell me what the heck is going on, Lisbeth."

She reached tentatively for the silver-dollar-size pastry and took a bite—and smiled. "Ooh, this is good."

"I know it is. What is it you want me to do?"

Lisbeth finished the tartlet with a second bite. "I'm what I guess you'd call an emissary, although I was the one who brought your name up, and volunteered to come talk to you. When was the last time you visited Asheboro?"

I had to stop and think. "I know I was there to help my folks pack for the move—that must have been at least three years ago. Other than that I have no reason to go back. I haven't been to a high school reunion. Why?"

"You heard about that big storm a couple of weeks ago?"

"I saw it on the news, but they didn't mention Asheboro." Now she was beginning to worry me. "Was the town in its path?"

"No, not directly, but close enough. There was a lot of damage, mostly superficial rather than structural. You know, high winds blowing shingles off, or siding. But a lot of people had been putting off fixing things the past few years, so things were loose, you know? And people, mainly the store owners, were cutting back on their insurance, because it just cost too much. They may not be able to make all the repairs they'd like to, so they might just pack up and go somewhere else."

I still didn't see where I fit in this. "Can't the town help? There must be some municipal funds for emergencies."

"Well, yes, there would be, normally. But . . . you remember the old Barton place, outside of town?"

"Sort of. Did it blow down?"

"No, not at all. It was built to last. You probably don't remember the history of the place. It was built by some Civil War veteran who moved to Asheboro and made a mint with the factory in town, and poured most of it into making his house as grand as he could. But he never had kids, so when he died, nobody inherited. He created a trust to support it until a buyer came along, and the bank has been managing it ever since. But they couldn't manage to sell it—too big, too expensive, too far out of town, who knows what. So that's where things rested for quite a while. More than a century, actually."

"So what's that got to do with anything?"

Lisbeth helped herself to another pastry. "Well, last year a member of our town council proposed that the town buy it from the bank and turn it into something useful. She was really enthusiastic, not to mention persuasive, so she sold the rest of the council on the idea. The bank was happy to go along with it to get it off their books, so they expedited the paperwork and set a really reasonable price on it, and the town bought the place outright. Which used up whatever surplus money we had. If it's used for any commercial purpose, the town will get some of that back, in taxes, but right now our account is just about empty, so we can't help the businesses in town."

"Ambitious," I said, nodding, "but not a bad idea, if they can turn the place around. Which of course does not solve your immediate problem."

"It gets worse," Lisbeth said. "Turns out that board member had her own ideas for what to do with it, but when she laid them out to the board, *after* the purchase had been voted on by the town and the title had been transferred, they pitched a fit and voted her idea down. She's royally pissed off. But nobody's got a better idea."

"Buyer's remorse, probably. And that's where you think I come in?"

Lisbeth nodded. "Yes. You're in the hotel business. You know how to run things. You know how to fix things up and make people want to visit them, like you said. We thought maybe you could come spend a little time in Asheboro and maybe come up with some new ideas?" Lisbeth looked at me like an eager puppy.

Obviously if the town had no money, there wouldn't be anything like a consulting fee in it for me. Did I really want to bail out a place I had deliberately left behind? Could I even do it? From Lisbeth's very brief description of the issues, nobody had any money to throw at the problem—and it was pretty clear that it would take money. And nobody had a clue which way to go. As I remembered the town, there really wasn't much there, and no way to dress it up—and that had been before this storm had swept through. I had to admit I had barely seen the Barton mansion, because it was surrounded by a substantial piece of property that kept it invisible from the roads. But if in fact it had been sitting more or less empty for decades, there had to be some major problems with it, didn't there? Even if it was gorgeous, could it be brought back?

"Say something. Please?" Lisbeth begged. "We're at the end of our rope, and you're our last resort. I wouldn't have come to see you if there was any other way out of this mess."

I thought about it for a moment. While I could see plenty of pitfalls, this project in Asheboro sounded like a real challenge. If I looked around and saw there was no hope for the town, I could tell them as much and walk away. Couldn't I? What the heck—why not?

"All right. But I have to see what's going on—what kind of damage the town has suffered, and what kind of shape that Barton place is in. Maybe talk to some of your town council. Will people be around if I come down this weekend?"

Lisbeth looked like the weight of the world had been lifted from her shoulders. "Of course! I'll make sure they are." She grabbed another pastry and ate half of it in a bite, beaming all the while. "We'll set up a meeting for you."

"Don't get too worked up about it, Lisbeth—I'm not promising anything. But I'll look things over and tell you what I think can be done. Or if it's hopeless."

"That's all I can ask. Thank you, Katie. You're a lifesaver."

"Don't say that until after I've looked at things." I glanced at my watch. "Look, I've got a meeting at two and a foot-high stack of paperwork on my desk. But how about I drive over on Saturday and you can show me around and connect me with the people I need to talk to?"

"Perfect. Thank you so, so much, Katie!"

"I go by Kate, mostly, these days."

"Oh, right, of course. But I'll always remember you as Katie."

I wondered just what I had let myself in for. Bailing out my old hometown? Yeah, right. But it was worth taking a look, if only to help an old friend. I hoped.

2

At the end of the day I headed back to my condo on the fringes of the city, and I found a message from my boss, George, on my answering machine. That was odd, since I'd been in the office all day except for my lunch with Lisbeth, and I was pretty sure he'd been somewhere in the hotel as well. In the message he asked to meet me early the next morning when I came in, but didn't leave any explanation. George and I got along well so I hoped it might be good news. I'd have to wait and see.

The next morning I was in my office at Oriole Suites early, in advance of the meeting with my boss. I still had no idea what it was about: as far as I knew, everything was going smoothly, and our stats looked good. A few minutes ahead of schedule I presented myself to George's executive assistant, who said quickly, "He's expecting you. Go on in." Then she looked away.

"Good morning, George," I greeted him as I walked in. "Is this about the refurbishment of the penthouse?"

"Sit, please, Kate," he said, his expression somber. He sat

back in his chair and steepled his hands. "We've worked together for some time now, so I'll get right to the point: this hotel has been bought out by a Japanese conglomerate, one that owns quite a few hotels in multiple countries. As a business acquisition, it makes a lot of sense."

I hadn't seen that coming. I felt gut-punched. "And?"

"They want to bring in their own management team to run the hotel. They've decided that I'd be redundant, so I've been let go."

"Oh, George, I'm so sorry to hear that. You've done a great job here." I knew that for a fact: the hotel was running like a well-oiled machine, and bookings and profits had been up for the past two years. Which was probably why it had been a tempting target for a buyer. I sat back and waited for the other shoe to drop, because I was pretty sure there had to be one.

"As have you, Kate. It's hard for me to tell you that they don't want to keep you on either. It's no reflection on your work or your abilities. It's purely a business decision. There will be a generous severance package—at least a year's salary."

It took me a moment to wrap my head around what he'd just told me: I'd been fired. No matter how anyone dressed it up, I was out of a job. "When will this happen?" I finally managed to say.

"As soon as possible. The new managers are already onsite, and they'd like to speak with you."

And ask for all my records and pick my brains about the hotel and the city, before they booted me out the door. But I was determined to stay cool and collected, so I said, "I will certainly extend them all professional courtesies. How long have you known?"

"I was told about this last week, but I was asked not to share the news. I've enjoyed working with you, and you've done an impressive job here. Even made me look good." He smiled, but his heart wasn't in it.

"We've made a good team. Have you had time to make any plans?"

George shook his head. "No, not yet. I'm a bit older than you, and I have kids in college, so I have to think through what my options are."

George and I reviewed some of the corporate details that needed consideration, and when we were finished, I made my way to my office, shut the door, and sat in my swivel chair, staring into space. Poor George. I didn't want to add "poor me" but I was pretty sure I could see the handwriting on the wall: after the new owners had pumped me for any information they needed I was out the door. I hadn't been unemployed since I got my MBA.

I sat a moment longer to pull my thoughts together. Then I walked out of my office, told my administrative assistant that I had an unexpected appointment out of the office and wasn't sure how long I would be gone, but she could reach me on my cell with anything urgent. And then I retrieved my car and drove home.

What was I supposed to do now? I had enough money in the bank to get by for a while, and George had promised I'd get a generous severance payout. I had friends and colleagues in the hospitality industry up and down the East Coast. Or, I could do what Lisbeth had reminded me of my old dreams—I could take some time off and travel. I hadn't been to Europe since college, and now I could check out the high-end hotels instead of those ratty B&Bs of my early travels. I didn't have to make a decision any time soon, did I?

And I had promised Lisbeth that I'd come back to Asheboro and see what the heck was going on there and whether I could be of any help to the town. I certainly had the time for that now. And it might be a good distraction while I tried to figure out what I wanted to do next with my life.

I thought about cleaning out my office, but I rejected that because what I really wanted to do was go home and feel sorry for myself. When I did get home, what I found myself doing was cleaning my small apartment, something I'd seldom had time to do. I hoped chasing dust bunnies would keep me from thinking.

❦

It didn't. As I vacuumed under my bed I thought about Asheboro—as I had known it years ago. Lisbeth and I had been good friends in high school. Looking back, I'd come to think of us as the Invisible Girls. We weren't cheerleaders, but we weren't pond scum either. We were part of that amorphous middle: nice kids who didn't make trouble or get in trouble, who kept their grades up, who volunteered for things like library fundraisers and litter cleanup days. I'd lost touch with most of that friend group—in fact, all of them except Lisbeth. I'd left, made new friends in college (not that I was doing much better keeping in touch with them, but there was always the alumnae mag for that, and occasionally Facebook), and just kept moving.

It had to have taken a lot of guts for Lisbeth to come to Baltimore just to ask for my help. From what little I knew of her current life, she was pretty much a town mouse, next to my city mouse. I wondered just why she thought I was a miracle worker. Sure, I knew the town. Correction: I used to know the town, but a lot could have changed. I had no background in municipal management, for a town of any size. I could handle a hotel that held maybe a thousand people in full convention mode, but that was about my limit. Although, I reflected, maybe Asheboro didn't have more than a thousand people anymore.

The town wasn't unique in the problems it faced. Towns that had thrived in an earlier century, with industries and shops and agriculture, had been left behind by changing times through no fault of their own. Industries were farmed out to foreign countries. Ditto agriculture. New businesses, particularly in the tech industry, could be managed from anywhere and didn't necessarily need brick-and-mortar headquarters anymore, except for show. And I had real trouble visualizing Asheboro—at least, the Asheboro I remembered—as the hub of any sort of commercial enterprise. Its location was all right: near major cities, with an airport close by and highways for easy access, and moderate weather as well. But it was just a shade too far away to qualify as a bedroom community for Baltimore, although that boundary kept moving farther out. But then, Asheboro didn't have a lot of housing.

Funny how when you live in a place you don't really see it. My mom and dad had lived in a modest post–World War II colonial house, but I didn't harbor any particular nostalgia for it—it had been bland and functional. The main street in town had had some basic shops, and there had been a supermarket on the fringes of town, along with a gas station or two. But nobody had ever built a mega-mall anywhere in the area, and since Internet shopping had ballooned, now a lot of malls were dying too. So, bottom line, the town now had a damaged main street that had been subpar to begin with, a white elephant of a crumbling mansion outside of town, a defunct factory, and no money. Not a whole lot to work with.

I thought about all of this as I drove west out of the city to meet Lisbeth in Asheboro. I'd be the first to admit that it was pretty country—I'd had little reason to travel west from the city recently, and I'd forgotten. It wasn't spectacular—mostly low, rolling hills, with tidy farms tucked in the shallow valleys. The near-empty highways sported signs for towns even I recognized as historic, mainly for Civil War battles. I'd never taken much interest in history. In school, I'd memorized all the names and dates and done well on tests—and then promptly erased all the information from my brain as soon as I got my diploma. It was hard for me to visualize armies numbering in the thousands crawling over these gentle hills and killing each other. But then, I'd seen some parts of Europe where centuries of bloody wars had been fought, and now they were serene and studded with delightful small hotels and restaurants, as if all that violence had never happened. Those towns had faced unimaginable horrors and moved past them. They'd survived for centuries. Why shouldn't Asheboro, whose problems were much less dramatic?

I arrived in Asheboro before lunch. It always surprised me that it took me little more than an hour's drive to reach the place from my current Baltimore home, since it felt like traveling to a different world, or going through a time warp. I drove slowly down the one and only street—creatively labeled Main Street—and pulled into a parking space in the center. Lisbeth hadn't described the storm damage to me in detail, and it looked both better and worse than I had expected. All the buildings were still standing, though a few here and there sported broken windows; some of the street-level plate-glass windows were covered over with sheets of plywood. The roofs were all in place, although quite a few had lost some shingles. Modern-day aluminum and plastic siding hadn't fared well, peeled back like a second skin to reveal the brick-and-stone structure beneath. Heaps of trash were still stacked by the curb, waiting for pickup. Hadn't it been something like two weeks since the storm had done its damage? Nobody in town seemed to be in a hurry to fix things up.

I pulled out my cell phone and called Lisbeth. She answered on the fifth ring. "Katie! Please don't tell me you're canceling on me!" She must have put her hand over the phone, because I heard muffled orders to various family members.

When she came back to the phone, I said, "No, I'm sitting in my car in the middle of Asheboro. You want me to meet you at your house?"

"Uh, no, this place is a mess. I'll tell Phil to take Jeffrey to practice, and Melissa's got a play-date and sleepover with a friend, so I have to drop her off. I could meet you in half an hour?"

"That's fine. I can look around a bit. Where do you want to meet?"

"Is McDonald's okay? I know it's not what you're used to, but it's close and easy to find."

"Hey, I'm here to look at the town, not to sample fine dining—I get plenty of that in the city. Where is it?"

"About half a mile from the town center, on the west side. It'll be on your right." She turned away again, apparently, and I heard her yell, "Melissa! Get your overnight stuff together!

We're leaving! Phil, don't forget Jeff's glove!" When she returned to me, she said, "See you at Mickey D's." Then she hung up. I almost smiled: her crises and mine were so very different. She worried about misplaced baseball gloves, while at the hotel I had to track down international shipments of high-priority documents and make sure they reached the right people.

Since I had a half hour to fill, and a five-minute drive to our lunch spot, I decided to walk around and get a feeling for the place. After a few steps I realized I felt like I was seeing double: I remembered what used to be there, and I saw what had replaced it, but I was kind of seeing both at once, one laid over the other. Once there had been a drugstore on the corner; now it was a store that sold outdoor wear. The genteel little gift shop next to it had morphed into a three-chair beauty salon. And so on. Had everybody moved on since I'd lived here? And who had moved in? As I strolled I started paying attention to the structure of the buildings themselves. I didn't see anything new—most buildings looked like they'd been built in the later nineteenth century, maybe 1900 at the latest. They were uniformly two or three stories tall, and originally made of brick or stone. Fake siding had been slapped over most of them, in an effort to modernize, but it didn't look like it had been very successful, and now it had been trashed by the storm. The bank building looked pretty much as I remembered it. It wasn't large, hardly wider than the shops next to it, but the front façade appeared to be granite. The old library at the end of the street was about the right vintage to be one of the many Andrew Carnegie libraries of the era, probably built around 1900, but it was pretty plain. At least it seemed to be functioning as a library still.

That took care of one side of the street, and the opposite side looked much the same. My overall impression was that the whole place looked shabby and neglected. I checked my watch, then turned around and headed for my car, picking up my pace. I arrived at McDonald's at the same time as Lisbeth.

"Did you beat me?" she panted as she approached.

"Nope, just got here myself. Let's grab a table and some food and we can talk."

Three minutes later we were settled in a corner, which gave us a little privacy. I was surprised at how empty the place was, given that it was a Saturday. "Where is everybody?" I asked, waving at the vacant seats.

Lisbeth shrugged. "Games, practices, rehearsals, whatever. But to be honest, it's not very busy on the best of days. You know what it costs to feed an adult and two growing kids here?"

"Can't say that I do." I tried to remember the last time I had eaten in a chain restaurant like this and failed.

"Too much. We bring our kids here as a treat, not as a regular thing. So, what do you think?"

"About Asheboro?" I paused, searching for the right words. Lisbeth still lived here, and she'd told me she was happy, so I didn't want to be too harsh. "It kind of feels like whatever was happening here stalled about a century ago."

Lisbeth's mouth quirked. "You've got that right. I think it peaked around 1915, with a small surge in housing after World War II."

"Why do you stay?" I asked.

"In a nutshell, Phil has a good job, between here and Baltimore. The schools are decent, it's safe for the kids, and parents in the neighborhoods look out for their own and others. It's home. That probably doesn't make sense to you anymore."

"Not really. It was a fine place to grow up, but I didn't want to live here forever. I don't mean to criticize your choice."

Lisbeth smiled gently. "I'm not offended. I know its flaws. But I don't want to see it just wither away and die. Sure, we could live somewhere else, but we wouldn't have the memories, the sense of belonging somewhere."

Which were things I'd given up almost without thinking. Did I regret not having that? I didn't think so. There were still plenty more places I wanted to see, wanted to spend a year or two in. I had deliberately chosen a career that gave me those opportunities. It wasn't for everyone, but it worked for me. "What is it you think I can do for you, for Asheboro?" I asked, grabbing up a French fry. And then another. Those things were good.

"I don't know." Lisbeth studied her Quarter Pounder, looking for the best bite. "Other places have reinvented themselves, or found a way to attract new business, new people. Can we do that here?"

"To be honest, based on my quick walk-through earlier, you don't really have anything here to attract people. Now if some huge company decided to move here and hire a couple of thousand people, you'd have a chance, but I don't see that happening. You have no natural wonders, like caves or waterfalls. You're near a lot of historic sites, of course, but so are a lot of other towns, and they've gotten their acts together faster to accommodate the visiting history buffs. Any famous people born here? Any gruesome murders in the past century?"

"Like Lizzie Borden, you mean? Nope. Nothing important has ever happened here. It's never been more than an average town."

"What did the factory make, back in the old days? I don't remember anyone ever telling us. They just called it 'The Old Factory.'"

"I don't know. You should talk to our town librarian—I think there's a decent local history section."

Good point—*if* I decided to take on this seemingly bleak project and needed local resources. "I think it's a safe bet that whatever they made isn't coming back again. Anybody useful in the cemetery?"

Lisbeth shook her head. "Not that I know of. Oh, and the storm took down the steeple of the church, but it was ready to fall anyway. Luckily nobody got hurt."

"Maybe we could build a fence around the town and put up a sign saying "The Land That Time Forgot."

Lisbeth sighed. "I was afraid you'd feel like that. I don't take it personally, but I hoped . . ." She shook her head. "I don't know what I hoped. That you'd swoop in and fix things, I guess. Not exactly realistic, I know."

"Was there anything else you wanted me to see while I'm here?" I asked.

"Two things. One, you *have* to see the Barton place. I've gotten the key from the bank—the bank manager, Arthur Fairchild, is a friend of mine, plus he's on the council—so we could go this afternoon. Two, I asked the town council and managers to get together and sit down with us and kick around ideas, and that's on for tomorrow, since they're all free on Sunday. I want you to meet them. This isn't official—it's more like a brainstorming meeting."

"Do I know any of them?"

"Maybe. Some of them were a good few years ahead of us in school, so you wouldn't have known them back then. It's the older people and the retirees who have the time to dabble in community groups. And then there's Cordelia Walker."

That surprised me. "Cordy's on the board? I would have thought she couldn't get out of Asheboro fast enough." Cordelia had been student council president for three of my high school years. I didn't begrudge her that honor, but mostly she used it to boss other people around, and I was pretty sure she'd run for the office so she could play it up on her college applications.

"She did for a while, but then she kind of slunk back a few years ago. I think she decided that being a big fish in a small pond was better than battling all those sharks out in the bigger world. And she's the one who pushed the town to buy the Barton house."

"Didn't you say that the board turned against her after that went through?"

"It did, when she told them she wanted to open a swanky bed and breakfast in the place, and run it herself."

"What's wrong with that, as long as it brings in paying customers?"

"The thing is, she already has a small B&B in town, and she's had trouble filling that. Now she wants to move it into the big house for a nominal rent."

"Has anyone proposed another idea?"

Lisbeth shook her head. "Not really. A museum? We don't have any kind of collection to show off, and the library can accommodate most of that anyway. A private hospital? It would need too much work to refit it. A hush-hush conference center? There are plenty of those around here already. So, the short answer is no, there's no idea on the table that anyone thinks will work."

I wasn't surprised. But before I could consider any ideas, I had to see the place. "Then let's go see the Barton house now. Maybe then I'll have a better idea of the possibilities."

"Works for me. You finished eating?"

"I have." I pushed the few remaining fries away from me. "Let's hit the road. We'll take your car, okay? Unless you have to be somewhere or pick someone up."

"Nope, I told Phil he'd just have to cope. My afternoon is free."

"So let's go."

I

3

Lisbeth turned off the main street and headed . . . I didn't know which direction. I had seldom had any reason to go out of town this way, because there was nothing there except the Barton place, and that was off-limits to us as kids. As in the case of the factory, there were probably brave souls who had ventured to explore, but I couldn't remember anybody reporting the details. Oddly enough, it wasn't said to be haunted, which abandoned Victorian heaps were often accused of.

It was a bright sunny spring day. The leaves on the trees were still a tender young green, and there were early wildflowers scattered around. Fields were marked off with sturdy picket fences, and we passed a horse or two on our way. I couldn't remember the last time I'd treated myself to a day in the country, if that's what this was. It was nice to let someone else do the driving, so I could admire the landscape. But didn't people get tired of looking at fields and trees and barns? Didn't they want at least a little excitement in their lives? Restaurants, museums, theater?

After a couple of miles, we pulled up in front of a heavy pair of iron gates hanging slightly askew from a pair of massive stone pillars. A brick wall, whose height I estimated at eight feet, ran as far as I could see in both directions. Beyond the gate a paved driveway wound its way across a field and continued up a small rise before disappearing on the far side. If you didn't know it was there, you'd never think there was a house on the property.

"Just a sec," Lisbeth said, as she fished a large ring with an assortment of old-fashioned keys from her bag. One of them apparently opened the relatively modern padlock for the linked chain that held the gate shut; even from where I sat in the car I could tell the original lock was too rusty to function. Not a good introduction to the place. Lisbeth wrestled with the chain, then pulled back the panels of the gate. They moved smoothly and quietly, which told me that someone had oiled them fairly recently. She got back in the car and drove through, then got out again and pulled the panels together, but without reattaching the lock.

"Is there anything worth stealing?" I asked.

"We're more worried about vandals. Funny how kids like to destroy things, just for the heck of it. Thank goodness the bank installed a basic alarm system awhile back."

How long ago was that? I wondered. *Did the alarm system still function?* "Have there been problems?"

"Nothing significant. There was a raccoon that decided to make itself at home inside, and that gave the alarm company a few anxious moments."

If a raccoon was the worst threat they had faced, the town was lucky. I settled back in my seat, waiting for the house to appear. Lisbeth was driving slowly—trying to build up some drama?—until she reached the crest of the low hill and stopped. "There it is."

I looked through the windshield. "Holy crap! It's huge!" The sprawling building lay spread out in the valley below, and from this distance it was hard to estimate the actual square footage. My first impression was that anywhere the builder could stick a gable or a turret or a chimney or a porch or a railing or a mansard roof, he did. It was absurd: high Victorian taste at its best. Or did I mean worst?

I loved it on sight.

Lisbeth wisely said nothing and let me take it all in.

"Nobody wanted this?" I said incredulously.

"Seriously? It's kind of big for most people. Eight bedrooms, not counting the servants' quarters in the attic. Two formal parlors, plus a library and a dining room. A kitchen, of course. The latest in indoor plumbing—over a century ago."

I shut my eyes, then reopened them, to see if the gorgeous monstrosity had disappeared. It hadn't. "If we get any closer, will I see it's in abysmal condition? Or should we just sit here and admire the glories of yesteryear?"

I don't know what had come over me. I prized order and efficiency, and the Victorian style was anything but orderly. More like chaotic. I valued simplicity and precision, and in my condo in Baltimore I had created a spare precise space that worked well for me. No unnecessary clutter, and a place for everything. Serene and unencumbered with stuff. So why was I slavering over a Victorian heap?

"Had enough ogling?" Lisbeth asked with a smile, after a minute or so.

"I guess. Are we going in?" Would that make my instant obsession better or worse?

"Of course we are. And don't worry—it's structurally sound. The bank made sure of that, over the years." She put the car back in gear and we rolled down the hill toward the house. In front there was a wide semicircular drive, and in its center stood a fountain that had seen better days, surrounded by what might have been flowers once upon a time. Lisbeth pulled up in front of the main door and turned off the engine, then got out of the car and retrieved the key ring from her purse. I climbed out more slowly, absorbing details. Granite stoop, fully ten feet wide. Front door needed some paint but looked solid, and the brass fittings appeared to be original. Tall windows down to the floor, in the front, and some odd configuration of panes—did they open like doors?

Lisbeth finally found the right key and opened the front door. Like the gate it swung inwards silently. I noted original hinges, ornate, immense. The hall had to be twenty feet wide, with marble flooring. Ten-foot ceilings sat atop crown moldings a foot high. I felt like I had walked into an alternate universe. *No, that's absurd, Kate.* I looked around and realized I didn't see anything that dated from after 1900. How could that be?

When I found my voice I said, "There's got to be a story behind this, Lisbeth. I mean, nobody's touched it for more than a century, but it seems to be in good condition. That doesn't just happen by accident. Is this a portal to a time warp?"

Lisbeth laughed. "No, of course not. There's a resident caretaker, and always has been. There's a small apartment over the stable behind the house, and a succession of people have lived there in exchange for free rent. It's worked out well."

"But do they dust and polish and all that stuff? Turn the heat on in winter? Make sure the pipes don't freeze? Open the windows to air it out now and then?"

"Yes, actually, they do. When the bank took it over originally, years ago, it put together a checklist of things that should
be done regularly until the property was sold. I don't think
they expected to wait this long, but as the saying goes, If it ain't
broke, don't fix it. You can see the results—it worked."

"And now the town owns it. They've kept up the same arrangement with a caretaker?"

"So far. But it's only been a couple of months, and nobody's
made any plans going forward. Yet."

I stood in the middle of the hallway and made a 360-degree
turn. Heavy, ornately carved wooden doors with intricate
knobs led off on both sides. A staircase with intricate spindles
and a wide mahogany rail led to the second story. "What's the
layout?" I asked.

"Two parlors on the right, with pocket doors between. On
the left, the library's in front, with a small sitting room beyond
it—that gets some nice sun. The dining room is behind the
library, and the kitchen and the pantry are at the back."

"And you said eight bedrooms?"

Lisbeth nodded. "Well, one is pretty small—we figured it
was meant to be a nursery originally. There's only one closet
per room, and they're all pretty skimpy. And there's only one
bath on the second floor."

"For eight bedrooms?" I asked, unbelieving.

Lisbeth nodded. "Chamber pots. Remember, they had servants to empty them."

"Heating?"

"Coal furnace originally, but the ductwork reaches only
the first floor, with some passive heat by way of the staircase.
There are small coal-burning stoves in the bigger bedrooms,

which the servants were responsible for. No heat in the servants' rooms, of course."

"Well, of course," I said, then regretted my sarcasm. It had been a different way of life, and the "girls" had no doubt been poor immigrants who'd have been glad to have a job and a roof over their heads.

We drifted toward the kitchen at the back of the building, where there was a massive stove—wait, was that a coal burner too?—and deep slate sink and a wood-clad icebox. Farm to table had a whole different meaning in 1900. "Lisbeth, when did the original owner die?"

"Henry Barton? 1911, I think. He outlived his wife and they had no children, so there was no one to leave the place or its contents to. He had a couple of brothers, I think, but they were well established, around Boston if I recall, and they didn't want a place in Maryland, and neither did their offspring, not that there were many of those either. Maybe there was some fighting among them about what to do with this place, and in the end, they just signed away their rights. Hard to believe, isn't it? The bank has managed it ever since, thanks to a generous trust."

"What a waste," I said. But tastes had changed, and by the early twentieth century the ornate Victorian style had become passé. "Can we look at the bedrooms?"

"Sure," Lisbeth said. "Follow me. There's a servants' stairway back here, but we'll go up the grand staircase."

I trailed behind her, gliding my hand over the smooth (and only slightly dusty) finish of the stair rail. On the second floor the trim was a bit less opulent, but it was still very, very nice. In one of the front bedrooms—the master bedroom?—there was an immense carved bed, the headboard standing at least six feet high. "You couldn't hope to get it out of the room now, without taking it apart."

Lisbeth didn't comment. "Let me show you the bath."

I tore myself away from the enormous bed and followed her down the hall. The bathroom proved to be almost as large as the bedroom, but the fixtures were . . . old. And weird. "Is that a metal bathtub?" I asked.

"Sure is. Nice mahogany casing, though."

"Does all this work?"

"I hope so. The caretaker's supposed to come through periodically and flush the toilet and run the taps. Probably cast-iron pipes in the basement, so I'd bet the water's kind of rusty."

I had to agree, looking at the reddish stains left by decades of slow drips in the sink.

"What about the attic?" I asked, after marveling at plumbing I'd never seen before, like a toilet with a tank (also mahogany-clad) mounted close to the ceiling above it, and a pull chain with a china handle. I'd read about those, but I'd never expected to meet one. I resisted pulling the chain just to see if it really worked.

"This way," Lisbeth said, leading the way down the hall to a door at the end. When she opened it, cool musty air rushed out, but I didn't smell anything like mildew or damp. The stairs were narrow—naked wood. Nobody had wasted any fancy details up here. At the top of the stairs Lisbeth waited for me, then pointed. "That side's attic storage, unfinished. There are two maid's rooms on the opposite side. Well, more likely a cook and a general servant."

"Show me." Lisbeth led me to the nearer room. It was small, with a dormer window on one side, and a row of hooks attached to the unpainted plaster wall. The rough board floor was covered with what I guessed was an early version of linoleum. There was still a single bed with a painted iron frame against one wall, and a small table beside it. Apparently nobody had bothered to clean out this space.

"The other room's pretty much the same."

"No heat up here, you said?" I asked.

"I gather the hired help weren't supposed to spend much time up here—they would be downstairs working all hours."

"Is that all?"

"You want to look at the basement? There's not much there except the furnace."

"I know nothing about furnaces from any era, so I guess I'll pass. But it really is like everyone just walked away from the place. Or, well, when this Henry of yours died, there was no one who cared. I'm guessing he died in the house?"

"Of course, although he had the best medical care available around here. Luckily his doctor stopped by once a day toward the end, so if you're wondering, he didn't lie here, uh, deteriorating for a while. And Henry had left everything regarding his estate in good order. I'd bet he was surprised when no one stepped up to claim the place. If only he'd left it directly to the town, our lives would be a lot easier."

"He wasn't involved in local affairs?" I asked.

"Not that so far as I know. He managed the factory as long as he was able, so I guess that was enough."

We went back downstairs and toured the parlors and the sun room and the library, but by the end I was feeling overwhelmed by the sheer opulence of the place. Finally Lisbeth led me out the back door. The stable was set back behind the house about a hundred feet, with tall sliding doors in front.

"Anything inside there?"

"Stalls. I think I remember an old carriage, but that might have fallen apart by now. Nothing so modern as an automobile. The caretaker has a small apartment above."

I surveyed the landscape from this view: rolling hills again, trees, a fence or two. Not a sign of the modern world. "Did they grow their own vegetables here?"

"I think so. There's what looks like a fenced plot behind the stable—wouldn't want to sully the view from the house, right? You'd need the fence because there are a lot of deer around here. Seen enough?"

I nodded. We strolled around the house, and I admired the ornate brickwork of the chimneys on the side. The chimneys and the foundation, also brick, looked like they could use some repointing, but overall they were in decent condition. Whoever had built this place had built it well and apparently had spared no expense.

We both looked up at the sound of another car approaching. When Lisbeth and I reached the front of the house, we saw a tall fortyish man emerging from a battered car parked in the driveway. Lisbeth leaned toward me and whispered, "That's the caretaker."

When I'd first heard him mentioned, I'd assumed it would be some down-on-his-luck local person happy for a free room, or maybe a college student. This man was clearly neither: even in casual clothes, he looked like a professional of some sort. How had he ended up here?

He approached us without hurrying. "Lisbeth, what's up?" He gave me a glance that I wouldn't call friendly. "This isn't one of Cordelia's, uh, colleagues, is it?"

Apparently there was no love lost between the man and

Cordelia. I stepped forward. "No. I'm Katherine Hamilton, and I grew up in Asheboro. Lisbeth and I go way back. She asked me here to see if I could help the town with its problems."

"And how is an old pal supposed to solve the town's financial crisis?" he said.

I didn't like his tone. "I manage a hotel in Baltimore, so I know something about the hospitality industry."

"So you *are* one of Cordelia's flunkies," he said.

"*No*," I said more firmly than I might have intended. "I don't know the full story, but from what little Lisbeth has told me, what Cordelia thinks she's planning would destroy the place."

"You disagree with her grand scheme?" he said, his tone a shade less hostile.

"In principle," I replied. "Look, I've only just heard about the whole mess, so I'm not up to speed." I decided not to mention that I'd known Cordelia most of my life, and I wasn't exactly a fan of hers. "We may have gotten off on the wrong foot, so let's try again. Hello, I'm Katherine Hamilton, former resident of Asheboro, more recently a hotel manager in Baltimore, called in by Lisbeth and the town council to consult on what options are open to the town of Asheboro to revitalize its economy." I extended my hand and almost by reflex the man shook it. It was a start. "And you are?"

He almost smiled. "Joshua Wainwright, history professor at Johns Hopkins, currently on sabbatical so I can finish a book on post–Civil War industrialization. Henry Barton played a larger role in that than most people are aware of. Call me Josh—when I hear Joshua I think of some character from the Bible."

My professional ears pricked up: maybe there was something in Henry Barton's story that could be useful. "I'd love to hear more about that. So I take it that you oppose Cordelia's plans?"

"I do. She has no sense of history, and what she wants to do would seriously devalue this place as an asset to the town, and to local historians."

"I agree, even without even having seen her plans. But as I understand it, the council needs an alternate plan if there's any hope of stopping her from going forward."

The man's expression relaxed. "I have some ideas about that. We should talk. Unfortunately I have a prior engagement. Do you have a card? We can set up a time later."

"Of course." I fished in my bag and found a business card, which I handed him. "I stopped by today just to get a sense of the place. Let's wait a day or two—I still have to process what I've seen and heard here today. But I think I see some possibilities." To my own surprise I meant it.

"Great." He smiled, and his face was transformed. "I'll call you, then. Lisbeth, good to see you." With that he turned and strode toward what must be his lodgings over the former stable.

I turned to see Lisbeth grinning at me. "No, he's not married. Or gay," she said gleefully.

"And I'm not looking," I replied, a bit more tartly than necessary.

"Uh-huh," Lisbeth said, as she leaned against her car. "You want to go find an early dinner, or do you need to go home?"

"I'm thinking maybe I should go back home now and do some online research. We can have lunch tomorrow after the meeting, if that works for you. We may have things to talk about by then."

"Sounds good to me. I'll warn Phil that he'll be on kid duty for most of the day."

"I don't mean to disrupt your life, Lisbeth."

"Hey, this is important, and you're doing us a huge favor just looking at what we've got to work with in Asheboro and helping us figure out what we can and can't do."

She really seemed to mean it, and I hoped I could come up with some kind of good news to repay her faith in me. "I'll do the best I can. We're meeting with the town council in the morning, right? We'll have time to talk afterwards."

Impulsively she laid a hand on my arm. "Does eleven work for you? That's after church around here, so the council members will be around. And remember, this isn't an official meeting, and nothing is binding. We're looking for ideas."

"Where's the meeting?"

"Town Hall, in the conference room."

"How many people will be there?"

"Eight or ten? Depends on how people feel about the old Barton place, and how committed they are to the town. I'll admit there are those who'd like to walk away entirely, although I'm pretty sure they have no idea what the outcome would be. I've heard of big cities wrestling with bankruptcy, but a small town? If everyone just packed up and left, what would happen?"

"I'm not the person to ask, Lisbeth," I told her. "Used to be that plenty of ghost towns happened that way, but I have no clue about the legal aspects. Does the town have a lawyer?"

"Yes—Jim something-or-other. I don't know him well."

I racked my brain for other information I needed to ask about. " Do you have a town utility, or are you on a grid?"

"That's a story of its own. Local utility, but maybe not the best solution."

I filed that away for the future—if there was one. "Water?"

"The lake, same as always. Don't worry—it's clean. We have a water purification plant for the town. We do test it regularly."

"Property taxes?"

"Too low. We haven't done an assessment for over a decade. I'd worry about saddling homeowners with any more costs, but then, the property values may not have gone up at all. Kind of a lose-lose situation."

She painted a very bleak picture for Asheboro. From what I was hearing, maybe the best option was to let the town die a natural death. It might also be the least expensive, in the long run. If it was legal. That was outside my area of expertise. I sighed. "It would be helpful if you gave me a quick rundown of who's who at this meeting, and where they stand. If you've got the time now."

"No problem. Let's sit on the steps, because this might take a few minutes." We sat, and once again I admired the view, which probably hadn't changed since the house was built. Lisbeth began, "I already told you about Cordy. She's an elected member of the town council. She's miffed at everyone, but she can't just walk away. I don't think she would even if she could—she wants to keep an eye on what everyone else is doing. There's the mayor, of course—that's Skip Bentley—and the deputy mayor, Howard Short, and three other elected members. The bank manager, Arthur Fairchild, is on the council, and then there's the town manager, Megan Conroy, and the town engineer, Brian Anthony, and that's all. I'll introduce you all tomorrow. Again, this is not a formal meeting and it's not binding. Nobody's taking minutes or voting on anything. We're just kicking around options. Feel free to be frank with us—at least you can wash your hands of us after the meeting."

"I can handle it. I really am sorry the town is having such problems." I might have left it in my rearview mirror years ago, but I didn't wish it any harm. "I'll help if I can, but don't get your hopes up."

"Don't worry—we're scraping bottom. Thanks for helping us out, Katie. I really do appreciate it."

"Hey, it's my hometown. It's the least I can do." Did I believe that? Did it matter? It was an interesting problem, whether or not I had a personal stake in it.

❧

I waved as Lisbeth pulled away, and then I drove home.

Which gave me too much time to think. Why did it have to be the Barton house? The place loomed large in my memories of Asheboro, but for the wrong reasons. I'd buried them deep, only to have them thrust in my face again now. Well, I was a big girl, so I could deal with it, right? But the situation was made worse by the role of my nemesis, Cordelia. Well, "nemesis" was probably too strong a word. I had barely made a dent in her consciousness back then.

Lisbeth and I had been best friends in high school. The last time we'd gotten together was when I'd been back to help my parents pack up and move a few years ago. Since high school, I could probably count the times we'd seen each other face to face on my fingers, leaving out the thumbs. Her wedding, of course, and the christening of her older child, Jeffrey. I couldn't even remember if I'd been invited to the christening of her second one—a girl, I knew. What was her name? Melissa?

But I didn't think about Asheboro much.

But that mansion . . . offered some intriguing possibilities—if I could just set aside what I remembered about it. The house had been spectacular in its day, and based on what little I'd seen, no expense had been spared in its decoration. Even in my brief walk-through, I'd seen light fixtures that screamed "Tiffany Studios" and wallpaper that could well be original William Morris patterns. If you liked Victorian style, it would be a treasure. Not my style, of course. My condo was kind of the antithesis of the Victorian style, wasn't it? I seemed to be a subscriber to the "less is more" philosophy. The Victorians preferred "more is better."

Still, the idea of Cordy and her team of renovators ripping down that wallpaper and tearing out the original woodwork made me sick to my stomach.

I arrived back at my condo by nine o'clock, and entered my uncluttered space with a sigh of relief. The home I had created for myself: orderly, easy to manage, and everything in its place. I didn't have a pet or a plant because my job sometimes required quick trips to somewhere else on a moment's notice, not to mention industry conventions—and pets and plants needed attention. I didn't bring back souvenirs from my various excursions, because that was just . . . stuff. I had pictures, didn't I?

It was neat and tidy and . . . totally lacking in personality. Why had I chosen to live like this? And why had I fallen for the Barton mansion on first sight, when it was everything I had convinced myself that I disliked?

I told myself I was just tired and drained by wrestling with a past I thought I'd left behind.

4

Maybe I shouldn't have driven home. Maybe I should have stayed and chatted about this and that with my old friend and her husband, whom I barely knew, and her two children, whom I'd hardly met. It would have been a great distraction, and I could have stayed in a crappy local motel after a bit too much wine and awakened bright and early, in time for lots of coffee and then the secret council meeting about saving Asheboro.

Why hadn't I done that? Because, well, like a wounded animal I wanted to crawl back into my cave and lick my wounds. I was trying to ignore the fact that I'd been fired, but the reality was that I'd been dumped without warning from a job that I loved and was good at, and it hurt. Even if my head was saying that things like that happen all the time, I was grieving. It was going to take some alone time to get over that.

And there was that council meeting looming. I'd always been the good girl who got all her homework done, as Lisbeth had reminded me, and I wasn't going to walk into that meeting cold without having done a little research. Not that there was much I could do in a few hours, but I wanted to try, so at least I could present a general concept to the council. I knew there were other examples of places that had somehow transformed themselves into living history sites, but I wasn't sure whether that would fit Asheboro's needs. Not everyone in a small town wanted to dress up in quaint clothes and pretend to pull taffy or braid rugs, or whatever people in a small rural town did around 1900. Plus I wanted to find out why Henry Barton had been such an enigmatic figure, hiding in the shadows inside his opulent mansion. Was there anything from his story that I could use? Josh Wainwright had hinted there might be something there.

But my experience—and my gut—was telling me that the mansion alone, lovely and untouched as it might be, was not going to be enough to lift the town into financial stability. There had to be something more to the package in order to attract visitors. The factory was still an unknown quantity, but who would detour from visiting battle sites to wander through an antique widget factory? But somewhere lurking in my brain was a glimmer of an idea, if I could just unearth it.

I reached home without any grand "Aha!" or "Eureka!" moments. I parked and unlocked the door to my uncluttered condo, and turned on a couple of lights. It was neat and tidy and . . . totally lacking in personality. Why had I chosen to live like this? And why had I fallen for the Barton mansion on first sight, when it was everything I had convinced myself that I disliked?

I changed into some comfortable raggedy sweats, poured myself a glass of wine, and sat back on the oatmeal-colored couch and started at the ceiling. If the mansion was not enough, what could be added to make it more appealing? Cordy's proposal was still on the table, but I doubted that she could survive financially with only eight bedrooms, especially if she was going to have to add modern amenities like more plumbing, and it wouldn't really help the town—just Cordy. Okay, if I was honest with myself I would really, really like to snatch the project away from her greedy hands and make something impressive out of it. But how?

Mentally I reviewed the sad and shabby Asheboro I had seen earlier in the day. It had no redeeming features. It looked like exactly what it was: a failing town with no hope for the future. But then I realized what I had seen in my brief tour. The modern town was pathetic, but from what little poking around I'd done, I guessed that the bones of the Victorian town were still intact under the cheap modern siding and windows and asphalt shingles. What if, what if . . . we made the whole town the attraction?

I sat up straighter, thinking hard. Say instead of repairing the recent storm damage, we simply peeled off all the later ticky-tacky and repaired the underlying original structures? Made Main Street look like Main Street 1900? With era-appropriate shops, and maybe a stable–slash–harness maker, and an old inn, and . . . It *could* work. I could make it work, with help. It didn't have to be very expensive, and I was pretty sure I could find some outside funding for some parts of it.

I looked at my watch and realized it was getting late. I didn't want to get too invested in my scheme to make the whole town an attraction, and I needed to do my homework. I could already see a lot of obstacles, but there were also a lot of plusses, if Lisbeth's feelings for the town were any indication. If there were more people like her in the town, they'd want to see their town survive, wouldn't they? Would the town council be willing to put some time and effort into making that happen? At least I could ask. Fine: I would put the idea to bed for now, and toss it on the table tomorrow at the council meeting and see who took the bait. If it flopped, they weren't any worse off than they were now. If it flew, it could be an exciting challenge. And it would be *my* project, not Cordy's.

✦✦

Sunday morning I drove back to Asheboro for the council meeting, with my nighttime ideas still churning in my head. Was the whole concept simply impossible? Would the people of the town get behind it? Did I have enough information, gleaned from a quick Internet search, to make a convincing case? And was I going to have to face off against Cordy, with a half-baked idea?

It wasn't hard to find the town hall, which was on Main Street, where it had always been. It was a squat Victorian cube built of red brick, with a few incongruous boxy air conditioners hanging precariously out of windows. It had a small parking lot on one side, and that's where I parked. There weren't many cars in the lot. Had the town leaders carpooled, or had they decided to skip this meeting?

Lisbeth was leaning against one of the cars, talking on her cell phone. "I'll be home as soon as the meeting is over, Phil, and I think Kate and I are going to have lunch. I told you that. Surely you can handle the kids that long, can't you?"

I didn't need to hear the other end of the conversation to know that Phil wasn't happy about dealing with the kids on his own, for the second day in a row.

Libby looked up and saw me approaching, and pocketed her phone. "Hi, Katie. You ready for this? Any big ideas that came to you in your sleep?"

"Actually, maybe, but it's pretty preliminary, and I want to find out if the council is interested before I dig into it. Do we go in now, or do you want to make a grand entrance once everyone is assembled? I warn you, I left my white horse at home."

"What? Oh, I get it. I'd like to see that, though. We might as well go in. If someone's not here by now, they're not coming."

I followed her through a side door that was unlocked, and down a rather dim corridor with ancient brown linoleum on the floor. At the back of the building Lisbeth stopped and opened the door to what was clearly a conference room, with a long table surrounded by chairs. A few of them were occupied, and some other people were standing around chatting. Everyone stopped talking and turned to look at Lisbeth and me when we entered.

"Hi, everyone," Lisbeth began, sounding artificially chirpy. "I bet a lot of you have met Katie in the past, but let me introduce you in case she doesn't remember you."

"Kate, please," I said firmly before she could go any further.

Lisbeth faltered. "Oh, right, Kate. All right, at that end"— she waved vaguely to her left—"you've got Mayor Skip Bentley, and next to him is our deputy mayor, Howard Short. We have a total of five council members, but only four of them are here: Arthur Fairchild, the president of the Asheboro Savings and Loan, Janeen Logan, Barbara Metzler, and Bridgette Connors." Each nodded in turn. I wondered where the power lay.

Lisbeth was still talking. "I also asked our town manager, Megan Conroy, to attend, since she knows the most about the day-to-day stuff of running the town. I didn't ask the tax collector or the water and sewer clerk to sit in, but that guy at the other end is Brian Anthony, who's our town engineer and handles planning and zoning." Brian gave me a curt nod. I returned it.

"So the people in this room are the ones who keep Asheboro going," I said, pasting on a polite smile. "I'm happy to meet you all, and I apologize if we knew each other back in the day and I've forgotten you. But aren't we missing someone, Lisbeth? What about Cordelia?" I asked.

"She doesn't seem to be here," Lisbeth said, looking surprised. "Has anyone heard from her? Did she say she was coming?"

Most heads turned toward Mayor Skip, who said sheepishly, "I don't know how much Lisbeth has told you about our current situation, but Cordelia is a strong advocate for one particular plan. We asked you here to explore other ideas, and I think we can go forward without her. This is not an official meeting, merely an exploratory one."

"She's hoping we all change our minds without looking at any other ideas," one of the councilwomen said bluntly. "Not happening."

"I don't think we need to air our dirty laundry in front of Kate here," Town Manager Megan protested.

I had to admit that secretly I was relieved, both that I wouldn't have to deal with Cordy today, and that at least some of the council members appeared willing to consider other ideas. "I'm afraid you do," I said firmly. "If there's anything to be done to keep this town alive, it's going to take everybody's participation, particularly the council's. If you send a mixed message, it's not going to work. So if there's something dividing you all, I'd rather hear about it now than be surprised later."

"I take it Lisbeth filled you in about Cordelia's scheme?" the mayor asked.

"Only the barest details—Skip, right? Look, let me tell you what I think I know, and then you can correct me and fill in the gaps. All right?"

After everyone nodded and we had all taken a seat, I proceeded to give a shortened version of what Lisbeth had told me over the last couple of days and what I'd seen for myself. It didn't take long: I wrapped it up in about five minutes. "Is that a fair representation of the current status?"

Most of the people there were sitting in stunned silence. They must be masters of self-delusion: Had they never heard the case stated quite this baldly? No wonder the town was having problems. It boiled down to this: no money, plus no people, plus no businesses equals no town. Simple.

Finally Skip the mayor spoke. "Kate, I wish I could contradict what you've just said, but it's pretty much on target. I appreciate your honesty. You must think we're all a bunch of ostriches with our heads stuck in the sand."

Much as I agreed with him, I couldn't tell him so. "And you have every right to think I'm a know-it-all who's got a swelled head after living in the big city. The question is, can anything be done about the situation? The answer is, maybe, and I have an idea I want to run by you. Look, I was here briefly yesterday. I took a look around at the town, and I have to say Asheboro looks a lot worse than I remember it, and I haven't been gone that long. Lisbeth also took me to see the Barton mansion, which I think we'll all agree is an asset—but only if handled properly. So I've had some time to think about what I've seen, and what I think is possible, and here's what I've arrived at." I proceeded to give them a quick outline of the ideas I'd come up with, for both the mansion and the town. It didn't take long because I had few details to offer, just an ambitious vague concept—and a growing enthusiasm, it seemed.

When I finished, I looked around the table. Everyone seemed stunned, but I might have seen a hint of optimism in their expressions, which gave me hope. "Lisbeth told me that Cordy—Cordelia—had presented a plan to you and you'd turned it down. Can you tell me why?"

One council member who had remained silent snorted now. "Because it benefited Cordelia first, last, and in-between. She wanted a free ride to run her business at the Barton place, and it wasn't clear that the town got anything out of it, except maybe some tax dollars down the road. And she wasn't open to negotiation." The woman looked at her companions before adding, "Cordelia is pretty used to getting her own way. She does not like to hear the word 'no.'"

That fit with what I remembered about Cordelia. "I knew her in high school here, and I think I know what you mean. But you've got enough votes to override her, right?"

"We do," Skip said. "But we need a plan to vote on. Maybe I shouldn't say it, but Cordelia has made it clear that she has some big guns backing up her plan—people with money—and if her numbers work, we won't have an excuse to turn it down."

"Tell me why you said no, then," I prompted quickly.

"Because her vision of the place was not one we shared," Skip said, in a decisive voice. "Look, you grew up here. You know it's a sleepy little town filled with decent people. We simply can't see a glitzy hotel for rich folk fitting here. Or maybe what I mean is, we don't see it as contributing anything positive to the town and we think that matters."

I nodded. "Good, because I agree with you. What's your time line?"

"Fast. We need to make repairs to the damaged buildings in town sooner rather than later, but if we're going to be making changes to those buildings, we need to know going in—you know, whether it's preservation or reconstruction. How fast can you turn a proposal around?"

"A week?" I was guessing but I'd done it before. "You have a regularly scheduled council meeting coming up?"

"We do—a week from tomorrow. If you could pull something together by the end of the week and send us a draft, we'd be good to go—we could review it over the weekend." He glanced at the people seated around the table, and most nodded yes.

They really did want to move fast. "I think I can manage that. And if you don't like the ideas I propose, I won't complain. I know it won't be easy, but this could make a real difference to the town."

Skip stood up, followed by the other members of the council. "Kate, thank you for coming, and thank you for your efforts. I think I speak for the group when I say you've given us hope, and we appreciate it."

The meeting broke up quickly after that, with a lot of handshaking all around. If nothing else, I'd made this group of people happy, at least for a short time.

Lisbeth came up to me, beaming. "Kate, that was terrific! And I think they like the idea."

"Don't get too excited yet—there are a lot of hurdles, and a lot of things that could go wrong. Listen, I'm starving. Where should we go for lunch?"

"Heck, let's celebrate. We can go to the hotel—they've got a decent restaurant."

"There is no hotel in Asheboro."

"Exactly—it's the next town over. Please? What with the kids, I don't get to go out for a nice meal very often."

"Sure, why not?

We took both cars, and I followed Lisbeth as she drove back toward Baltimore, pulling off the main road at a pleasant-looking but undistinguished modern hotel. We parked and went in, and Lisbeth guided me to the restaurant. It looked much as I would have expected, based on the exterior of the building, but Lisbeth seemed excited to be there, and I wasn't going to rain on her parade. We had to wait a few minutes for a table, but once we were seated and had ordered, Lisbeth turned to me. "You think you could really make this happen?"

"Frankly I don't know. If I didn't make it clear at the meeting, I'm not picturing a quaint theme park. Asheboro has to remain a living city, with people and jobs. But there's only the one main street, and I think it could be remodeled to meet both historic standards and modern needs. Of course, the good people of Asheboro would have to be involved, and it may not be for everyone. But then, they're not exactly thriving as it is, so they don't have much to lose. If some people are unhappy serving as re-enactors of a sort, I'd guess there are people who would like to step in. But right now there are more questions than answers."

"Well, I'm excited," Lisbeth said firmly. "So let's pretend this is our mini-celebration and enjoy lunch." Which we did, accompanied by one glass of wine each, and wrapped up with a ridiculously rich dessert.

At the end of the meal Lisbeth said with regret, "I hate to

abandon you, but Phil will be going nuts by now, so I should head home. What are you planning to do?"

"Don't feel guilty—go. Me, I may walk around Asheboro a bit more, maybe look at it more critically. And I want one more look at the Barton place, to see how it could be connected with the town in some way."

"I gave the keys back to Arthur—I didn't think you'd need them again."

I grinned at her. "I know the back way in."

"No!" Lisbeth said. "And did you . . ."

"Almost," I told her. "Once I get inside the fence, I'll look around for Josh—he could let me in. But that's not important—mostly I want to get a feel for the place."

"Let me get the check," Lisbeth said.

"No way!" I told her. "It's on me, and if things work out, it will be a business expense for me."

"Shoot, nobody ever talked about paying you for your time."

"Don't worry about it—we can all talk about that later, when and if this project goes forward."

"Thank you, Kate. For all of it. It means so much to a lot of people."

"And to me, Lisbeth," I replied, surprising myself.

5

I decided to skip looking at the town, and half an hour later I pulled up behind the Barton property, near the not-so-secret entrance that plenty of high school kids had known about. I hoped nobody had barred it yet. Heck, I could always go over a wall, although I was dressed for "meeting with the council" rather than climbing. But nothing ventured, nothing gained. Nobody had added any new houses on this side to observe my efforts at trespassing. I persuaded myself that I could have called Josh Wainwright and asked to be let in, but I didn't have his number, and he could have been anywhere. I was going to tackle this on my own.

The foliage had grown up since the last time I had attempted this. In high school. With Ryan Hoffman. It had been dark then, and we had been . . . in lust. He had brought a flashlight, and he had lent me a hand when I needed it—not because he was a gentleman, but because he was really eager to get inside and get into bed. From the looks of things, nobody had come this way recently. I wondered briefly where kids these days went to "do it." By now there must be some sort of alarm or security system. Henry Barton had had the foresight to leave a pile of money to take care of his place, although I doubted he had expected it would have to last for a century, but he hadn't anticipated the invention of surveillance equipment. As I clambered through the bushes—damn thorns!—I reminded myself that I ought to look at the details of the financial arrangements Henry had made. If there was any money left, after paying maintenance and most likely a stipend for the caretaker, what would happen to it? Would it make its way into some philanthropic organization's coffers? Or would there be some way to divert it to the ongoing care or even improvement of the property? Was I going to need to involve a lawyer in this, one for the estate rather than the town? *One step at a time, Kate.*

I emerged from the shrubbery and dusted myself off, then set off toward the building. It had been carefully situated in a dell, which was why it couldn't be seen from any direction. Maybe Henry had valued his privacy, or maybe it was a strategic decision to minimize the impact of adverse weather, not that that was a large problem in this area. I realized again how little I knew about Henry's background beyond the fact that he had fought in the Civil War and decided to settle here. Was he trying to hide? Himself, or his obvious wealth? Where had he come from, before the war?

I reached the top of the rise that had concealed the building, and paused to catch my breath—obviously I didn't do much cross-country hiking these days. I spotted one car toward the back of the property, so most likely Josh was there. I decided I should gather my wits before going any farther, so I sat down and studied the scene laid out below, looking at it as a potential luxury hotel. Lovely countryside, more or less well maintained—that endowment might not have stretched to a staff gardener, but at least the lawns near the house had been mowed. Only the one driveway, from the front. Limited parking: that could be a problem if there were going to be guests. How many bedrooms had Lisbeth said there were? Eight? Would that be enough to sustain a small luxury hotel? I couldn't see any way to add more space without spoiling the ambience. That small stable and presumably the caretaker's suite above it were too small to expand into bedroom space, and would be more useful for storage, or maybe a small spa. Maybe someone on staff could use the caretaker's rooms. No pool, no tennis court, no stable with horses—that might eliminate athletic guests.

I retreated to fantasizing about what I was beginning to visualize in my head: a true Victorian experience. Gas lighting inside. Fireplaces, kept lit and cleaned by servants. And that single bathroom that Lisbeth had mentioned—that wasn't going to work, period. I'd have to figure out a way to shoehorn in the bare necessities for modern guests. Back in high school Ryan and I hadn't bothered to explore all the rooms, but had headed straight to the master suite with its huge bed. When Lisbeth and I had taken our quick tour on Saturday, I hadn't been focused on how the place could work as a hotel, but now I had to think of the place in a different light. There was a large and opulent dining room, and it would certainly be possible to prepare authentic meals in the original kitchen, if I could find a chef willing to work with antique appliances. Unlikely: maybe there would be a way to camouflage the modern counterparts, or put the real kitchen in the basement. Which, I reminded myself, I hadn't seen yet. Finding authentic china and silver and glassware would be no problem, if Henry's were long gone, but what about cookware? Maybe I should binge-watch *Downton Abbey* to get a feeling for the kitchens of the era.

I jumped a foot in the air when a branch cracked behind me. I turned to find Josh Wainwright looming over me.

"What are you doing here?" he asked, although he didn't sound exactly hostile—more like curious.

"Oh! You scared me. I wanted to see the house again. I don't have any of the keys. I figured you would have yours, but I couldn't get through the front gate because it's locked, and I couldn't call you because I didn't have your number, so I came around the back. I was going to look for you—I saw your car so I figured you were around somewhere." I took a deep breath to calm my breathing then went on the offensive. "What the heck are you doing here, sneaking around the grounds? Aren't you supposed to be hunched in your garret writing weighty scholarly tomes about—what was it, industrial history? Is patrolling part of your job description?"

"Not exactly. Actually I wasn't looking for intruders—I was probably doing what you were—trying to see the place from a different direction. Why did Henry Barton set it in a shallow valley, rather than planting it on a hilltop for everyone to see?"

"You know, I was wondering the same thing. I thought it could be due to weather conditions here, but this isn't exactly New England. Does it snow much? Big storms? You've been living here for a bit—are there howling gales in the night?"

"No. So maybe the man just wanted his privacy. Okay, your turn. What do you hope to learn?"

I realized he didn't know the details from the council meeting, so I filled him in. "The town asked me here to find a way to save this building and the whole future of Asheboro.

This place seems to be the biggest draw, although I don't think it's enough. It can be the centerpiece, but the whole project needs to be bigger. And I kind of proposed a larger project to them, or the kernel of one."

He raised one eyebrow. "Which is?"

"Promise you won't laugh—I kind of sketched this out overnight. I proposed that Asheboro re-create itself as an authentic Victorian village."

I sneaked a look at Josh's expression, but it remained neutral. "I realized when I walked around on Saturday that most of the changes to the town since Henry's day were cosmetic. The town is going to have to spend money on storm repairs, so why not divert that money to restoration instead?" I stared at him directly. "Say something."

"I hope you're not thinking of Disneyland."

"Of course not. More along the lines of Old Sturbridge Village, but eighty years later."

"Ah. A good model. So why are you here rather than poking around in town?"

"As I said, this is going to be the main draw. Plus I need to have ammunition to counter Cordelia's proposal, which is already on the table, and possibly with some outside funding in hand. I need to know more about Henry Barton—where he came from, why he came to Asheboro, what he did while he was here. I've heard it said that his wife died young and there were no children, but was that a romantic myth? If it's true, did the man just wander around this spectacular house all by himself? Did he entertain? Did he have any lady friends? A staff of twelve who played poker with him on Saturday nights?"

"So you want the story of Henry Barton," Josh said.

"Yes. Before you protest, I don't want to intrude on whatever your research is, although I can't imagine you writing that upon the premature death of his lovely wife he was devastated and spent the next year or five wandering around the echoing rooms, unwashed and unshaven, calling out her name. Were you planning to?"

He finally smiled. "God, no—sounds like a cheap romance novel, except that if it was, some lovely, kind, sympathetic, and no doubt beautiful replacement would have to show up in the last third of the book and they'd live happily ever after, wallowing in Henry's riches and popping out six kids."

"So why are you interested in Henry?"

"How much do you know about post–Civil War history?" he countered.

"Not a lot. Mostly what I learned in public school. I might have taken a few required history courses in college, but not about this particular era. Maybe you can give me a quick summary."

"For the whole war? Not right now. What you do need to know at the moment is that Henry and some of his brothers fought bravely in the war—"

"Hold on," I interrupted him. "I don't actually know which side he fought for. North or South? I seem to recall Maryland was kind of mixed."

"North, as did his brothers. Most of them survived, and obviously Henry did. He'd taken part in some of the battles around here, so when the war was over he decided to settle here."

To me it seemed odd to return to a place where an army of men had tried to kill you, but I'd never been in a battle. "Where'd he come from originally?"

"I think the family originated in New England, although they'd lived in several other states."

"And where'd the money for all this come from?" I waved my hand at the lush vista spread out below us, and the ornate mansion embedded in the middle of it.

"Now that is the interesting question. You know about the factory in town?"

"I know it's there. Lisbeth and I were talking about how we grew up with it in the background, but we never knew what it produced. Was it enough to generate income to support all this?"

"That, my dear Ms. Hamilton, is the key question. I haven't collected all the information yet, much less the original sources, but I'm beginning to find hints that Henry was a major player in the rebuilding of this region after the war. Possibly even more. But he was also one of the most self-effacing men I've ever come across. He really didn't like to draw attention to himself, publicly or privately."

"Interesting," I said. "Which might explain why he built this fancy pile but hid it. But why build it at all? For his wife?"

"Could be. She's about as enigmatic a figure as he is, although that's less surprising for a woman of her era."

"So, are you writing a survey of regional economic history, or a biography of Henry Barton?"

"That is what I'm beginning to wonder."

"How long have you got?"

"'Til classes start in the fall. For the research, at least."

"Ah. I haven't got anywhere near a plan for the town, with or without the mansion, but off the cuff I'd guess there's no way we could launch anything before fall, and then only in stages. So we're on the same time line. Are you and I competing for something?"

"I can be of use to you, if I find some interesting stories. What can you do for me?"

"You want to write a stuffy academic tome or a best seller?"

He cocked his head at me. "I'm an academic. What do you think?"

"I think if you add some human elements, it might sell better on both fronts. Maybe not to the audience you originally intended, though."

"And where do you fit in this new and improved warm and fuzzy approach to my *opus magnum*?"

"If I—and the town—go ahead with this ambitious project, we'll either go down in flames or we'll be a hot ticket in the preservation community for at least a few years. Either way there'll be a lot of publicity—I've got contacts around the region and you can believe that I'll tap them all. You can ride on my coattails, or you can give sorrowful comments to the press about how you tried to tell Asheboro and me that this was a terrible idea but we wouldn't listen. You're covered either way."

He actually looked like he was considering the idea. But he didn't answer directly. "Why don't we go take a look at the house? I know you went through it with your friend on Saturday—"

"And yesterday," I added.

He gave me an odd look but didn't comment. "—but you might not have been paying attention to the details. And you've had time to think about things. You may see things differently now."

"Is there a security system?" I asked abruptly.

"You mean like cameras? No. The most the trustees would

spring for was a motion-sensor alarm system. If there was any movement outside the building, a god-awful siren would go off, not that anyone except me would hear it—it's not connected to the local police station. I suppose I should be flattered that they believed that I could handle determined intruders."

"Were there any?" Certainly there hadn't been any alarms back when Ryan and I had been sneaking around the place, or somebody had figured out how to disable them.

"Not unless you count the occasional fox. I still had to drag myself over to the house and disable the noise each time."

I struggled to my feet—I was getting stiff. "Well, let's go check the place out while it's still light. The power is on, right?"

"It is, but the light bulbs are about as low wattage as possible. I suppose we shouldn't complain. If the bank trustees hadn't been so thrifty, the funds might have run dry a while ago, and where would you and I be then?"

6

Since we were already behind the building, we went in through the kitchen entrance at the rear. I thought briefly about making notes as we walked through, but decided I'd rather just get a general feeling for the place and worry about specifics later. We headed slowly through the dining room toward the main hallway. I paused long enough to admire (once again) the ornate built-in china cabinets, brimming with what appeared to be matched sets of bone china. For twelve. Did Henry and his wife entertain, or was this standard issue for the upper classes? "Do you know, I've never learned what Henry's wife's name was—she's always 'the wife.'"

"It's Mary," Josh said.

"Ah. Have you spent much time in the house?" I asked.

"Not really. Actually I've been remiss—I should be examining whatever documents survive."

"There are documents in the house?" I asked. "Nobody ever cleared them out?"

"There was nobody who cared. I supposed we should be thankful that nobody ever did buy the place, or they might have gotten rid of everything. So, short answer, there are boxes and trunks of I-don't-know-what in the attic. In my own defense, I arrived in the fall, and the attic is unheated, with about two hanging light bulbs, so it was not an appealing place to spend time in winter. I intend to delve into all that now that it's warmed up a bit."

"Can I help?" I said. "I did get a peek at it, with Lisbeth."

"Don't you have a day job?" he countered.

I supposed that I might as well confess—I'd have to at some point. I cleared my throat and said formally, "I was informed on Friday that the hotel has been acquired by an international chain that wants to bring in its own staff, so it was, Thank you very much, and here's your severance."

"You didn't see that coming?" He seemed honestly concerned.

"No, I did not. My boss said he'd known for only a few days, and he's out too. So now my time is my own and at the disposal of the town of Asheboro, if the council approves my plan. But I haven't said anything to the town council about this yet. I wanted to get a better sense of the options—and the costs—before I agreed to anything. I may have a vision for the town, but that doesn't mean they can afford it, and I'm not about to start something and walk away leaving it half finished. If I decide it's hopeless, I'll tell them."

"I'm glad to hear that. So where do you want to start?"

"Let's start with the first floor and work our way up. I've already done a couple of walk-throughs. What I want to know from you is what kind of shape the systems are in. You know—plumbing, heating, that kind of stuff. You have kept an eye on those?"

"Kind of," Josh said, "but mostly to make sure nothing has

blown up or stopped working. So, in the kitchen: slate sink, hand pump next to it. Icebox—and that does mean ice, literally. A cast-iron coal-burning stove. There's also a pantry that could probably supply an army for a week, if it was filled. There's some old cookware on a few of the shelves, but I don't know if it's usable. Henry didn't splurge on the hired help."

"No wine cellar?"

"Maybe there's something like it in the basement. I haven't been inspired to explore down there—too many spiders. The best I've done is to check to make sure nothing is flooding—we are in a valley of sorts here."

"Well water, I assume," I said, almost to myself. There couldn't possibly be municipal water out this far from town.

"There's a cistern system too, actually. To trap rainwater."

"Really? Is that what you've been using out back?"

"Pretty much. My wants are few. Actually it's been a good experience—it gives me more insight into the impact of creeping industrialization. Lights, running water, basic sanitation. Things we all take for granted now."

"How quickly we forget. So we saw the kitchen. Let's check out the other side of the hall."

Before we left the dining room, I looked longingly at the magnificent mahogany dining table that occupied the center of the room. Above it hung an elaborate crystal chandelier that was lit with gas. "Where'd the gas come from?" I asked.

"I can't say I've given it any thought. Besides, it was superseded by the electric lights you see now."

"Where'd the electricity come from?"

Josh looked bewildered. "Uh, the town? I've never tried to rewire anything here so I haven't poked around. As long as my lights work I don't complain."

"You get wireless out back?"

"Yes, but it's kind of patchy. But I don't use it a lot. When I hit a thorny research question, or when I start talking to the birds, I take myself off to the library in town and catch up on news and actually talk to people. Why all the questions?"

"I'm trying to sort out the time line for the place, which means: how much is original, from the last quarter of the nineteenth century or earlier, and what Henry added, mainly later in the century. I'm sure I can find out when the town was electrified, but it's less clear when it would have extended out here. Although I suppose if Henry was rich enough to put all this together, he could have afforded to run his own line out this way—it's only a couple of miles. Okay, next?"

"Parlor one and parlor two. I've never quite understood the need for two. I suppose if you were a guest you could figure out where you stood with your host by which room he greeted you in. Nice original pocket doors between the two."

"Let's see them." I followed him into the nearer of the two rooms on one side. Again, high ceilings, ornate moldings, fancy hanging lights, plus a few gas-fed wall sconces. The carpets were long gone—I wondered if someone had parked them in the attic, or if the moths had gotten to them—but the floors seemed to be in good condition. How sad to think of two adults, and then only one, rambling around all this elegant space.

Josh wrestled with the pocket doors and finally pried them open. The front parlor was similar to the back one, save that it had a big bow window in the front.

"What's on the other side?" I asked.

"A very handsome spacious library–sitting room combo, and a glassed-in sun room on the far side. A few of the panes there are cracked, but basically it's intact. It faces north and gets indirect sun, so it doesn't get too hot."

I looked at him critically. "You really like this place."

"I do. It's as if it's frozen in time, and that's a rare thing these days. I will admit that I shudder at the idea of Cordy taking it down to the studs and starting over. It seems like sacrilege."

"I can understand that. What do you think she is really after? Money? Prestige? Power over the town? She is on the council, and she has her own business."

"Hey, I'm not from around here, and I don't hear much gossip. From what little I've heard, nobody on the council likes her, and her little business doesn't make any money. I'd guess she couldn't stand to see it fail, so she was hoping to move on to bigger and better things before that became too obvious. Somehow she got fixated on this place. To tell the truth, I'm amazed the council stood up to her as long as they did."

"You seem to have collected quite a bit of information in a short time."

"I'd meet for a beer or two with one or another of the council members occasionally. After two, people tend to get chatty."

"Did Cordy know you were going behind her back?"

"I'm not sure. I never saw much of her, and when I did run into her here, she treated me like the hired help. No one on the council went go out of their way to hide our meetings, but we didn't invite her to join us either."

I almost felt sorry for Cordy, until I reminded myself that she'd made her own bed, alienating people left and right for years. She knew what she wanted, but she apparently never learned the best way to get it. "Upstairs?"

We took the broad staircase to the second floor. The staircase was unquestionably gorgeous: four-foot-wide mahogany treads, ornate spindles, and a curving mahogany railing. The upstairs landing was wide, as was the hallway it led to. I was beginning to understand how there could be eight bedrooms up here. "Maybe we'd better start with the bathroom," I said dubiously.

"Because that might be your worst problem? Don't worry, no major leaks—but it's not exactly up to code."

"I know—I checked it out yesterday. I was trying to visualize what it would take to convert this place into a historically correct but functional boutique hotel."

"And?" Josh asked.

"We'd have to get very friendly with the building inspectors," I told him.

"Hmm. Bedrooms?"

"Again, Lisbeth and I took a look. And we did check out the help's quarters upstairs, but we didn't go poking into corners."

"The light is lousy up there. If you really want to see what's up there, you should come earlier in the day, with some big lights, and prepare to get filthy."

"No treasures? Like a trunk full of gold certificates?"

"To be honest, I really don't know. I'm not a treasure hunter, I'm a historian."

He hadn't been curious to see if Henry had left any documents up there? Personal or professional? An odd thought hit me. "Do you know if Cordy ever went up there?"

"I can't say for sure, because I'm not around all the time, and I can't see much from my rooms. The rare times I've been up there, I haven't noticed any signs of recent disturbance."

"Huh," I said intelligently. I was pretty sure Cordy wasn't interested in history, and she wouldn't have wanted to get her clothes dirty. I checked the time. It was after four now, and I still had an hour's drive home ahead of me, and it would be dark soon. "Well, I guess I've seen enough. It's a start."

"May I make one request?" Josh asked, almost sheepishly. "If you do decide to go ahead with this project, may I stay, at least until my contracted time is up?"

"I don't see a problem, although it may not be up to me. I don't think there's that much noisy work that needs to be done to the place, if it's planned right—and pitched right to potential guests. But I can't promise anything. Besides, don't you have a home to go to?"

"Not lately. I'm divorced, and my wife got the house. This was a handy fill-in while we sorted things out."

"Ah. Well, I'll let you get back to work, and I'll head home."

"When will you be back?"

"I don't know. But I promised the council a draft proposal by the end of the week. Can we walk out the front? I want to see the main view again."

"Sure." We descended the grand staircase, and Josh sorted through the keys until he found the one he wanted, a large brass one. He opened the massive door and pulled it back, but then he stopped in his tracks without crossing the sill, and I more or less bumped into him.

And then we were looking down at the body of Cordelia, and I was pretty sure she was dead. Fallen backwards on the stoop, draped over the massive granite slabs, her eyes staring at the sky. And a pool of blood under her head.

For a moment all I could see was flickering lights. I couldn't exactly feel my legs.

"Don't move," I heard Josh say, as if from a great distance. "You've turned kind of green." I realized he'd grabbed my arms and was more or less holding me up.

"I wasn't planning on it," I told him, swallowing my nausea and taking a deep breath. "Is she . . . ?"

"I'm pretty sure she is."

"How long?"

He let me go, and I turned to face him. "How long?" he asked, his tone incredulous. "Seriously? You think I know?"

My vision was finally clearing. "Well, no. I'm just wondering if we have alibis, or need them. Have you been here all day?"

"Yes. I was working."

"Did you see or hear Cordy's car drive in?"

"Car?" He looked around, bewildered, until he saw it parked off to the side. "No. I had my headphones on, and I was on my computer. What about you? I know when and where I caught you sneaking in, but you could have been there earlier."

"No way. I spent last night at my home in Baltimore, where I had dinner and did some Internet searching. I met Lisbeth just before eleven this morning, and then we spent an hour with the council, and then we had lunch together. So my morning is covered. The blood isn't dry yet, so she can't have been . . . gone for long. Unless you think I came to Asheboro at dawn, tracked Cordy down, killed her, and dragged her out here and dumped her before my meeting." I nodded toward the body. "From the look of her, it would have been messy, so you'd have to give me time to change clothes too before I addressed the town council."

"Did you have a motive?"

"Sure did. Most of the town probably knows about it. Cordy and I had a history. Okay, what about you? Where were you?"

He stared at me for a long moment. "Here. Working. If

anybody in authority cares to look, he would find evidence of our computer activity, right?"

I shrugged. "All I know is what I see on *Law & Order*." We both fell silent, until I finally said, "This is ridiculous. I didn't kill the woman, and I don't think you did. But someone did—she didn't just fall, hit her head, and bleed to death. I guess we should call the police. Who's in charge in Asheboro?"

"For the town, it's the local police chief Jack Wilson. For a homicide, it's the county police, over in Pikesville. But I think we have to go through the procedures. I'm the official care-taker, so I guess it's my responsibility to make the call to the local cops, and if they decide it's a homicide, they would call in the county."

"And you know this why?"

"The bank manager gave me a list of contact numbers when I signed on. It's posted on my fridge. I'll call now."

While Josh made the necessary call, I sat gingerly on one of the spindly side chairs against the wall in the hallway, fear-ful of contaminating a crime scene or disturbing evidence (and maybe breaking the fragile chair). At least I couldn't see Cordy's body from there. So Cordy was dead—that much was obvious. And I could think of a long list of people who might have wanted her dead, but that was from years ago. What had she gotten herself into since?

When Josh returned, we sat in stony silence, waiting for the police. There really wasn't much to say, and my mind was blank. I'd never seen a dead body before, certainly not some-one I had known—and hated with all of my teenage heart. But I knew nothing about her death. A tiny part of me was mad because I hadn't had the chance to confront her over her plans for the mansion—and win. Well, actually, I had kind of won, because she wasn't in the running anymore, but I wasn't going to point that out to the police. One old motive was plenty.

"Did you see a weapon?" I asked, more to break the silence than because I cared.

"Uh, no. But I wasn't looking for one. You?"

"Same here."

We went silent again. It was probably no more than fifteen minutes before the local police chief arrived, took one look at the body, and quickly pulled out his phone and called the county office. I wondered idly when there had last been a murder in Asheboro, and it was clear that the chief had little experience in that kind of investigation. An investigator from the county office arrived half an hour later, introduced himself, and ascertained my identity as well as Josh's. Since both of us looked thoroughly rattled and were not covered with blood, he told us we should expect to appear to give a full statement the next day at the county office in Pikesville. Then he said we could go home, which for Josh meant walking around to the other side of the building.

We moved away from the front. "Your car's still at the other end of the property. I can drive you to your car, if you want."

"That would be great, thanks. All I want now is to go home and try not to think."

It took only a few minutes to retrieve his car, two more to take me to where I'd left mine. When I climbed out I said, "I assume I'll be seeing you again. I want to talk to you more about the project."

He looked at me as though I'd lost my mind. "Really? You're thinking about that now?"

"It must be important, if somebody was willing to kill Cordelia to stop her from moving forward."

Josh was already shaking his head. "You don't seriously think that's why someone killed her, do you?"

"Do you have a better idea?" I replied tartly.

He didn't answer my question. "We'll talk later. Good night."

I climbed into my car and tried to remember how to turn it on, until the fog in my head cleared, and I started it and turned toward home. I managed to get there on autopilot, without thinking, and when I arrived I fell into bed.

7

I was awakened far too early by the ringing of my landline, and it took me a moment to collect my wits. Right: it was Monday, and Cordelia Walker was dead. Great way to start the week. I stumbled to the phone, and the caller ID said something about police. I answered, "Katherine Hamilton."

"Ms. Hamilton? This is Detective Reynolds of the Maryland State Police Criminal Division. I'd like to talk with you about the death of Cordelia Walker. You were present when the body was discovered?"

"Yes," I said. Keep it short.

"I understand you were acquainted with Ms. Walker?" the detective asked.

"Yes, in high school. I hadn't seen her since then."

"Why were you in Asheboro yesterday?"

Here we go. I took a deep breath. "I was invited by the town council to discuss ideas for the economic revitalization of the town." Wow, that was an impressive sentence I'd managed to string together with little sleep and no coffee.

"Why were you at the Barton house?"

"My primary professional experience lies in hospitality management. There was some discussion of utilizing the house as a hotel. I wanted to take a critical look at it. Was Cordelia murdered?"

"Yes." The detective did not elaborate, and an odd silence fell.

"What does this have to do with me?" I finally asked.

"You were in Asheboro this weekend, according to Lisbeth Scott."

"Yes. We're old friends. She thought the town council should talk with me. We got together for a quick tour of the town on Saturday, and she showed me the house. I came back yesterday to talk with the council, then went back to the Barton house after that. Joshua Wainwright walked through the house with me, and then we discovered . . . Cordelia on the front steps, and called the police. When did Cordelia die?"

"Ms. Walker was killed early in the morning on Sunday—yesterday. I'm merely verifying the time line. You were acquainted with her, and you made a several trips to Asheboro over the past few days. It's my responsibility to see if there is any connection between those two facts. Did you at any time see or meet with Ms. Walker?"

"No."

"As I believe you were told yesterday, you need to come in and make a formal statement."

I had nothing to hide. "When?"

"This morning, if possible. Is that convenient?"

His tone suggested that I should make it convenient. And there was no need for me to rush to my former job in the city. "Yes. Where?"

"At our headquarters in Pikesville. I understand that's not too far from your home."

"I'm sure I can find it. Ten o'clock?"

"Fine."

Damn, here I was driving again, and there was just me and the highway on the way to Pikesville. I tried to figure out what I was feeling—and thinking. No job, but I felt more sorry for George. He needed his job more than I needed mine. I was going to need a new job, but all options were on the table. I had enough money in the bank or would have with the severance pay, to take my time, survey the field, decide what I was really looking for. This Asheboro project had popped up at an ideal time, but I had to wonder how much Cordelia's death would complicate things. And now I had an appointment to talk with a police detective about Cordelia's murder. That would certainly be a new experience.

I arrived at the Pikesville State Police Headquarters before ten, and sat in my car for a moment, lining up my facts. I'd first talked with Lisbeth on Thursday, and then spent most of the day on Saturday with her, though I'd left Asheboro before dinner. I hadn't seen Cordy at any time. I'd driven straight home, although there was no way to prove that—I hadn't stopped to buy gas at some convenient gas station halfway between Asheboro and Baltimore, with a tidy date-stamped receipt. I suppose it was conceivable to a suspicious cop that I might have tracked Cordy down and killed her after I'd left Lisbeth. But I knew I hadn't harmed the woman, and as I'd already said, hadn't visited Asheboro in years. They might as well investigate Lisbeth—maybe she'd killed Cordy out of loyalty to me, after we'd parted. Or maybe since I'd last seen her she'd turned into a psycho killer. But if Cordy had died in the early hours of Sunday, the time line didn't work.

I gave a snort of laughter, climbed out of the car, and headed toward the building. Inside, I told the person at the desk that Detective Reynolds was expecting me, and she picked up the phone. I studied the interior: it was drab, neutral, and non-threatening, and gave nothing away. Which pretty much described the uniformed man who emerged from the back of the building and approached me. "Ms. Hamilton?"

"Yes, I'm Katherine Hamilton," I said cautiously. That seemed safe enough.

"Please, come with me." He turned and walked away, leaving me with no option but to follow him. He stopped halfway down a dimly lit hallway and opened a door, then stepped back to let me enter first.

"Have a seat," he said. I sat. "Thank you for coming in so quickly. As you can guess, we're still collecting information, but the sooner we can nail down some facts, the sooner we can find who killed your friend."

My mouth opened before my brain was in gear. "She was not my friend."

He looked at me. "Acquaintance?"

"I knew Cordelia in high school. We had some issues back then. I hadn't seen her since I graduated." Alive, at least, but I didn't add that.

"And that was fifteen years ago, right? I'm sorry, I seem to be doing this backwards, and there's always that dreaded paperwork." He pulled out a lined pad and a pen. "Could you give me your full name, please?"

"Katherine Eleanor Hamilton."

"Address?"

I recited my address. I knew he already had my phone number, thanks to Lisbeth.

"Employer?"

"The Oriole Suites Hotel in Baltimore. For about another week."

He looked up briefly. "Fired?"

Why did he assume that? "Let go. Corporate takeover."

"Ah. You've known Lisbeth Scott for how long?"

"Since high school. We were best friends then."

"Why were you in Asheboro yesterday?" He looked up and fixed me with a steely stare. Were his eyes gray or blue?

"That's a kind of complicated story," I said.

"I've got time." He sat back in his chair and waited for me to begin.

I wondered what I was in for. Should I have called a lawyer before talking to the detective? Sure, this nice solid-looking man had implied over the phone that he just wanted some basic facts from me, since my presence in town on the day Cordelia died as well as the day before was kind of an anomaly. I had popped up in town just in time for her murder.

What could I say about why I was in Asheboro over this weekend? I figured the town council would forgive me if I told Detective Reynolds why I had been invited to Asheboro. But when he found that that same council had taken up arms against fellow member Cordelia to stop her wily plans, and she ended up dead . . . Well, it did look a little suspicious. I amused myself by wondering just how much the good citizens of Asheboro would have offered me to off the woman.

"Ms. Hamilton?"

I gathered up my wool—figuratively speaking—and regarded him. "Detective Reynolds, do you know Asheboro at all?"

He shook his head. "I can't say that I do."

"Well, this story is going to sound rather odd, and what's worse, I'm not sure what I'm going to say puts me in a very good light with regard to Cordy. Let's just say you won't find a shortage of suspects. Before I get into it, can you tell me how she died?" I could make a pretty good guess.

"It may not be appropriate to share the details, although I'm sure the press will have this information soon. She was killed by a blow to the head with a blunt object—most likely a rounded rock—on the front steps of the building known as the Barton mansion outside the town."

"Obviously I know the place, since I was there yesterday. I grew up in Asheboro, and everybody knew about it. But that place was one of the reasons the town council invited me to Asheboro this week. To put it bluntly, the town needs help. They sank a lot of money into buying the mansion but they don't have enough to fix the place up, and now the town buildings need repairs as well. They wanted to know if I could recommend any new avenues for raising funds and bringing tourists to the town."

"And have you?"

"Detective, I've spent very little time in the town since I first learned about the problem from Lisbeth last week. That's not exactly enough time to create a rescue mission for an entire town. I proposed a rather ambitious idea to them at an informal council meeting yesterday, but I need a lot more information, and I need to look at examples in other areas that have been successful." And I needed to think hard about whether I wanted to be involved at all.

"Hmm. Did Cordelia Walker have a role in this?"

Tread lightly, Kate! "She was a member of the town council. She also ran a bed and breakfast in the town. I've been told that she had proposed turning the mansion into a much bigger and better version of that and possibly running it herself."

"Is that a bad idea?"

"I don't know yet, but I do know the council was resisting that plan. But as I understand it, Cordy was used to getting her way. She said if the council didn't get off the pot, so to speak, she had some other ideas, like corporate investors lined up who would step in and transform the place."

"And I'll ask again: is that a bad idea?"

"Done right, not necessarily. However, the plan Cordelia presented, which involved outside investors, relied on gutting the place on the inside and modernizing it. There are those in the town who did not like that idea. They'd rather see the place restored to its original glory—and believe me, it is glorious—then use that to attract tourists."

"Ah. So there was conflict between Cordelia and the council?"

"I think it's fair to say that. Would anyone on the council be willing to kill her to save a piece of the town's history? I don't know, having spent no more than an hour or two with the members of the council. I'd say it's possible but unlikely."

The detective nodded. "Based upon my discussions with a few people in Asheboro, I've gotten the impression that Cordelia Walker was not exactly popular with all of the townspeople."

Another crossroads. Well, in for a penny, in for a pound. "Let me be frank. Cordelia Walker was a bitch and a bully, back when I first knew her. She was the queen bee, the leader of the pack among the popular girls when we were both in high school. She ran everything, and she had her own clique of followers. From what little I heard about her yesterday, I gather that hadn't really changed. She went away to college, but then she came back—I'd guess she decided she'd rather be a big fish in a small pond than one of many minnows in the big wide world. She opened the B&B, but I doubt she had the right personality to make visitors feel welcome." That at least came from my area of expertise, not personal hostility.

"Ah, yes." The detective consulted his notes. "Were you aware that she was, until recently, married to a Ryan Hoffman?"

I felt like I'd been hit in the gut. "Oh, crap." Lisbeth hadn't mentioned that—she probably thought she was protecting me. Or conning me to get me to show up in Asheboro. When the detective looked startled, I hurried to explain. "Sorry, but everything so far just seems to dig me in deeper and deeper. Ryan Hoffman and I thought we were in love, our senior year in high school. Cordy didn't like me, and I think even then she wanted him—he was smart and funny and good looking. So she and her little band of bitches cooked up a way to break us up and make me look like a fool."

"And that would be?"

I had to tell him, or somebody else would. "The Barton mansion used to be a place for high school kids to get together and hang out—not for drugs, but usually for sex. We all knew how to get into the house the back way, and all the furniture was there. Including beds. So Ryan and I decided to . . ." I fumbled for words, because nothing felt right. Get it on? Consummate our love?

Luckily the detective got the message. "I think I can fill in the blank. So what happened?"

"Ryan and I went out there one night, and things were heating up quite nicely, when Cordy and her pack burst in with cameras flashing. Then they spread the evidence all over the school in the next few days. I kept my head down and my grades up for the rest of the year, and got out of town as fast as I could."

"Ah, so that's your motive? The mean girl embarrassed you more than a decade ago?"

"I suppose you could see it as a motive, but I hope I've moved past the embarrassment." *Not!* "And you're telling me she ended up marrying Ryan?"

"So it would appear. I take it you two didn't remain a couple for much longer after the . . . incident?"

"Not once Cordy got her claws into him. She usually got her way in the end."

"Not this time." He leaned back and studied me, and I wondered if I detected a hint of a smile. Finally he said, "So you're saying you fled Asheboro in what you perceived as disgrace years ago. You returned for the first time this past weekend by invitation. You learned that the town was broke and the council hoped you could fix it. And your high school nemesis ends up dead shortly after your arrival. Does that about sum things up? Oh, and I forgot to include that the dead woman married your first crush. Adding insult to injury."

This was a smart man. "Yup, I think that covers it—although I didn't know that she and Ryan had gotten married until you just told me. What now? You going to arrest me?"

"I think I might be laughed out of the department if I tried to arrest you on such circumstantial grounds."

"Well, that's good to hear." I was beginning to feel a lot more optimistic. "Who else are you looking at?"

"Ms. Hamilton, you must know I can't tell you that."

"Do you have a first name?"

He looked startled at the unexpected question. "What? Oh, well, yes, of course. Brady."

"Well, Brady, I'm Kate. Now that you've heard my most mortifying secrets, I think first names are appropriate."

"Buttering me up will not get you off a list of suspects. Let me ask you this, Kate: Are you going to work with the town on this project, or are you going to wash your hands of the whole thing?"

I took about four seconds to think about it. I was out of a job, but I had enough money to keep me going. I needed a distraction to keep me busy while I hunted for a new job. I was possibly a murder suspect, but since I knew I hadn't done it, the killer had to be somebody else in Asheboro, and if I stayed around Asheboro I could learn more about the town's current dynamics—and who else had been provoked by Cordy into a murderous rage. And that's what it had to be—a big rock was a weapon of opportunity and suggested that Cordy's death hadn't been planned, but that she'd pushed somebody's buttons once too often. And last but not least, the Barton mansion was magnificent, and if I could get the town to go along with my vision of the downtown portion, we might be able to inject some new life into struggling Asheboro. It was a win-win-win-win situation.

"If the town is still interested in my idea, I think I'm going to see if I can make it work. I like a challenge."

Did Brady Reynolds actually look pleased? "If I may suggest

something—strictly off the record—it would be valuable in my investigation to have someone on the inside, in a manner of speaking. Someone who knows the town, but is not of it, if you know what I mean."

"Someone like me," I said bluntly. "Does this mean I'm not a suspect and you trust me? And you want me to spy for you?"

Now he looked exasperated. "Nothing like spying. And I would not ask you to betray any friendships you have in the town, or to jeopardize your professional activities, if you choose to help the town council. But I'd like to think you can be a more objective observer than people who are closer to this crime."

I could count my Asheboro friendships on one finger, and I didn't think Lisbeth had killed Cordy. As for the professional side, I had no idea what the revitalization job would entail, if I decided to take it, or how long it would take, or how much it would cost. Once I dug into the details, I might decide it was hopeless—even I couldn't work miracles. But the time it would take me to assess all those factors was probably more than enough to allow the state police to solve this murder. Plus I'd be in an ideal position to ask questions that would otherwise be considered nosy. Like how successful Cordy's B&B was. How she'd tracked down outside investors—and whether she had called in personal favors. Or might these investors be interested in a modified project. And was there anything she knew that she hadn't shared with the town? Cordy looked out for Cordy, not Asheboro.

"Detective, I think we can work something out. I do have some fond memories of Asheboro, despite what happened. I'd hate to see it go down the drain because I walked away from it, now that I know about its problems. While I didn't like Cordelia Walker, I didn't wish her dead, if only for the town's sake. And, as it happens, I have some time off to really explore the options for the town. So, yes, I'd be willing to work with you."

"Excellent. What are your plans for the rest of the day?"

He certainly was in a hurry. "I think I'll go back to Asheboro," I said.

"Keep your ears open. If you notice something that seems out of place, let me know." He fished a business card out of his wallet. "Use the direct line, on the bottom there."

"Fine. I'll let you know if I hear anything interesting."

"Thank you, Kate. I appreciate your help, and I look forward to hearing from you."

"Right." I stood up, then wavered, wondering if he was going to escort me out. Nope. Apparently he trusted me to find the front door, so I left.

Outside I sat in my car and tried to figure out what had happened since breakfast and what I was supposed to do next. Cordelia was dead. I might have been a suspect for about a minute, but now apparently I was not. I had no job. And the state police wanted me to snoop in Asheboro, kind of. Interesting day so far, and it wasn't even lunchtime.

What I really wanted to do was go back and find more information about the Barton house. For that I should talk to Josh Wainwright. The detective hadn't said he was a suspect, so that should not be an issue. I really needed to have a heart-to-heart with Lisbeth, who hadn't bothered to tell me that Ryan had married Cordelia—although the marriage apparently hadn't lasted, and who was to blame for that? But I'd have to wait until her kids got home from school for that.

I reversed out of the police parking lot and headed back toward Asheboro. I had my plan: talk to Josh first, if I could find him, and then Lisbeth. That left the rest of the drive free for me to fantasize about the Barton mansion. I had to confess: it was turning me into a Victorian junkie. The Victorians with money to spend reveled in acquiring and displaying stuff. Their rooms had moldings upon moldings on the ceilings and walls, and the wallpaper was ornate and elegant. The real wood floors often had elaborate inlaid patterns. Once the space was decorated, the owners started adding pictures to the walls, sometimes in two or three tiers, one above the other. The floors would be covered with richly colored (real) Oriental carpets. The windows would be draped with at least two layers of curtains, underneath real lace (of course) and over that usually velvet (with swags and tassels and fringe). The fireplace would be surrounded by ornately carved mantles in marble or wood, and patterned tiles to protect the floor in front. In short, every inch of space received attention and decoration. If you were worried about housekeeping it would be a nightmare to keep clean—all that coal dust!—but the rich owners didn't trouble themselves about it—they had staff for that.

The final product was gorgeous—a feast for the eyes and senses. If you wanted to be politically correct, you could say the homes were offensively opulent, built with deliberate thumb-your-nose ostentation. But part of me was glad that now and then we could enjoy what unlimited funds could achieve. Henry's house did not disappoint.

I found myself wondering again what Henry's wife, Mary, had been like. Had she been sickly? How had she died? Had she had a hand in shaping the house, and had she lived long enough to enjoy it? I wanted to know more, even if it was only for my own satisfaction. If I took this project on, I'd be the one who had to find the financing. But I truly believed it would be worth it.

8

I'd outlined the problems to Josh already, and I hadn't minimized or exaggerated them. He had a different perspective on the broad problem, but the information he had collected on Henry could be useful. The town had asked for a proposal by the end of the week. Would Cordy's death have given us all a reprieve, in terms of time, even though her proposal had been conveniently wiped out by her death? Did anyone in town know who her mystery investors were? What kind of promises had she made to them? And were they going to show up in Asheboro with some kind of documents in hand and demand satisfaction? Heck, did they even know she was dead? Did they believe she had had the council on her side with her ambitious plans? I wasn't going to poke that hornet's nest right now. If those people chose to come looking for her, we'd deal with that later.

What did I need to do to put together this proposal? The Barton house was impressive, and in pretty good condition. Not a top priority for worry. I needed to walk through the town again and pay attention to details; to determine what changes had taken place over the past hundred years and whether they were reversible. I needed to talk with the current shopkeepers and building owners, to get a sense of their reaction to my still vague plan. Sure, I could let the council deal with them, but I wanted to see their faces, hear their concerns and objections. If they weren't on board with the plan, it wouldn't work.

I needed to look at funding sources. I knew the town itself was tapped out. I had to check with the bank to see what was left of the original endowment for maintaining the Barton property and see how much of that could be repurposed. I needed to investigate external funding sources—state and federal grants or foundations that supported historic preservation. I'd dipped my toe in those waters for the hotel in Baltimore, when we had wanted to preserve its original façade, but no way could I call myself an expert. Nor could I hire a municipal financial consultant, because the town council had no money. It would be necessary to find a way to finance this entire project, which wasn't going to be easy. Maybe not even possible. I doubted that Asheboro could raise enough taxes to cover the costs, and that wouldn't make the good citizens of the town very happy. I'd have to put "find money" at the top of the priority list.

Where did Cordelia's death fit in all this? Was it personal or was it related to her plans for the Barton house? Hard to guess right now. Those of us who had been victimized by her as meek students in high school had never compared notes about how Cordy had treated us, and we'd certainly never banded together to try to stop her. I did wonder if she'd changed as she'd gotten older, or if she still ruled her little world the same way. I suspected the latter.

And now the state police wanted me to snoop? Kate Hamilton, undercover police spy. In my old hometown. To help find the killer of a woman I once thought had ruined my life. Could I just go back to last week, when life was simpler?

I needed to talk to Lisbeth first. I owed it to her to tell her what had happened since we'd seen each other yesterday, but if I was honest I had to admit that I was not going to do this for her benefit but for mine. Right now I needed a friend—and she owed me an explanation about why she hadn't bothered to mention that my one-time high school love had somehow married the b-word who had split us up. Which kind of answered the question: that had been her goal all along. So before I could talk myself out of it, I pulled into a gas station on the edge of Asheboro, pulled out my cell phone, and hit her number.

She answered after five rings, and once again I could hear kid-type noises in the background. "Kate! I was hoping I'd hear from you. What's up?"

"Do you have time to talk? Because this is going to take more than a few minutes."

"Of course," her answer came quickly. "But I may have to keep an eye on the kids and make sure they do their homework. What's going on?" From the decline in background noise I deduced she had moved to a different room—one with a door that closed. I was already practicing my sleuthing.

"I think this would go better face to face. Can I come over?"

"You're in Asheboro? Sure, come right ahead."

It took only five minutes to reach her house. When she opened the door she gathered me into a hug. "I heard about Cordelia. You were there?"

"Josh and I practically tripped over her on the front step. Then we had to talk to the local police, and they handed us over to the state police, and I met with a detective this morning in Pikesville."

"Do they know who killed her?"

"Not yet, and I think there may be a lot of suspects. That's one of the things I wanted to talk about. But not the only one. I got laid off on Friday," I began. Lisbeth made appropriate dismayed noises, and we gnawed on that together for a while. Then I segued into my conversation with Detective Brady Reynolds of the county police. Lisbeth hung in there until I was wrung out. "So that's been my past few days, apart from the time we spent together. What do you think?" I wrapped it up. I realized belatedly we'd been talking for well over an hour.

"I think my life is boring," she said, laughing. "What are you going to do? Or is it too soon to ask?"

"For once in my life I really don't know. I do want to spend some time in Asheboro, to see if what I envision for its revival is even remotely possible."

"You're not just using that as a distraction? Because if you get the council's hopes up and then walk away if something better comes along, nobody will ever forgive you."

I hoped Lisbeth didn't believe I was capable to that kind of callous betrayal. "I don't think that's what I'm doing, but thanks for the reality check. No, I think I'd like to do something positive for the town. Now that Cordy's gone, I won't have to spend my time watching my back. Is it terrible of me to say that?"

"I know what you mean. She was not a nice person, and that's as far as I can go with kids in the house. I can fill you in."

"Actually I'd appreciate that. I'd really like to know how many other enemies Cordy had made in town."

"How much time do you have? It's not a short list. Cordy was completely tone-deaf when it came to human relationships, and she thought the world revolved around her. I'm surprised she survived as long as she did." Lisbeth hesitated. "Are you going to talk to Ryan?"

Finally she'd given me the opening I'd been waiting for. "How come you didn't happen to mention he and Cordy had gotten married?"

Lisbeth looked embarrassed. "Oh. Well, I didn't want to bring up the past, and I didn't want to upset you. Besides, I was pretty sure it wouldn't last, when they got together. And it turned out I was right."

"Why didn't it work out?"

"For a start, because Ryan was kind of a trophy husband, you know? Smart, good-looking, successful. And apparently easy to manipulate. She set her sights on him, probably just to see if she could land him. I don't think they even made it to their fifth anniversary. No kids."

"I'm not carrying a torch for him. We were kids back then. He didn't exactly stand up for me at the time, you know, and I never heard from him after I left town. But he doesn't live around here anymore, does he?"

"No, but I understand he's actually the owner of the B&B Cordy was trying to run—probably part of the divorce settlement—so I assume he's going to have to come back to take care of business. For all I know he's still the executor of her will—I can't think of anyone else she would have asked."

"Good point. Well, I won't go hunting for him, but if we happen to cross paths, I'm not going to run away. You don't think he killed her, do you? Was she running up his credit cards? Bleeding him for money? Anything like that?"

"Not that I know of, but I'm not really part of the 'ladies who lunch and gossip' crowd. I'm sure you could find out. After all, the B&B is part of the town, so you have to work out what you think could be done with it now. Will there be a need for a small operation like that, under your grand scheme?"

"I haven't thought that far. I'm guessing a memorial for Cordelia is not an option?"

"Not hardly. Oh, Kate, I'm so glad you called, and that we've gotten past the whole Ryan and Cordy mess. We'll all understand if you can't fix all our problems, but it's so good that you're willing to try."

With Cordy lying in the morgue, I wasn't so sure the mess was over yet. "And I'm not Cordy, so I don't plan to trash the town's history."

"Exactly. Listen, are you going to commute? I know you don't live too far away, but it could get old going back and forth, and we don't have much to offer in the way of accommodations."

A little idea blossomed in the back of my mind. "I could camp out at the B&B?" That idea was both appealing and repulsive at the same time.

Lisbeth reflected for a moment. "Maybe, and that would put you right in the thick of things."

"Mainly I'm just looking for an inexpensive, convenient place to stay," I told her. "Who should I ask?"

"I don't know, but I can find out," Lisbeth said firmly. "I'll see who's in charge of the place now—I don't think Cordy was exactly hands-on about the day-to-day running of it—and I'll let you know tomorrow if I can. Will you go home tonight?"

"I think so, if I'm planning to spend more time here. I need more clothes and my computer. Thanks, Lisbeth. I don't say it often enough, but thanks for being there, and thanks for listening."

"That's what friends are for. Let me walk you out, and we can talk tomorrow."

"Sounds good to me. Goodnight, Lisbeth."

Talking to Lisbeth had felt good. I didn't have any friends in Baltimore that I could talk to in the same way. Lisbeth had been right—it made sense to be in Asheboro, at least for the next week, so I could assess the commercial possibilities and talk to people. Maybe before Cordy's death I wouldn't have considered it, but it would be a lot easier now. Which was sad in itself, because I'd have to admit I'd been driven out of my hometown for the past fifteen years by that one mean-spirited woman. And I'd let her do it.

No more. I was going to reclaim Asheboro as my own. Maybe not permanently, but I could leave my mark on it, in a good way. Maybe to offset what Cordy had done. Maybe the problem was too great to solve now, but I would give it my best effort.

So now what? Go home and pack a bag. Clear out the pitiful contents of the fridge. Take out the trash, in case I wasn't back for a few days. Make sure I took my laptop and assorted chargers—and my all-important list of professional contacts (not all of which I'd confided to my computer), because I was pretty sure I was going to need them.

And then come back to Asheboro and see if I could fix it.

9

I was surprised that I slept really well that night. Not the sleep of emotional exhaustion, even though my life had been up-ended in a matter of days, but I slept with the sense that I was preparing myself for battle—and was looking forward to that battle. Had I really grown so stale in a job I thought I liked?

I was on the road before nine, and arrived in Asheboro by ten. I'd phoned Lisbeth before I left, to confirm that her children would be safely delivered to school by then and her husband would be out of the house. I didn't want to disrupt her established routine, but I needed to get myself set up somewhere, somehow. I couldn't exactly go to the town council and say "help!"—that would definitely send the wrong message if I wanted to persuade them that I knew what I was doing.

Lisbeth greeted me at the door and led me back to the kitchen, where a fresh pot of hot coffee awaited me. "My one vice," she admitted. "I really need a cup of good coffee in the morning, so I treat myself to the primo blends."

"Believe, me, I understand." I accepted the mug she handed me, and then sat down at the kitchen table, after pushing a stack of kids' drawings and papers aside. "You have anything new to report, Lieutenant?"

"Ooh, I get a rank and title? Yes, sir, Captain, sir. Or ma'am, I should say. The good news is, I've cleared it for you to stay at the B&B, free of charge, for as long as you need it. The bad news is, you have to have lunch with Ryan to get the keys. He's always owned it but rented it to Cordy for, like, a dollar a year. Kind of in lieu of additional alimony."

"I can handle that. Or if I can't, I should leave now. Did Cordy have a staff? I can't see her scrubbing the toilets, even if it was her own place."

"She used to have a couple of cleaners, more or less full-time—they took care of breakfast too. Then she started using local high school kids, probably to save money, and she graciously took over the breakfast part. So I'm not really sure what you'll find, but you'll be the only guest."

"For now. If I start beating the bushes for investors, I'll need a place to put them up, and the Barton house won't be ready for a while."

"Good point. You hungry? I've got muffins. Real ones, not store-bought."

"Sounds good—I need to keep up my strength. You make them?"

"No, we actually have a bakery in town that's pretty good."

I took a bite of a raspberry muffin and before I finished chewing I said, "Well, then, we'll just have to give them a reason to stick around, won't we? Yum." I swallowed then said, "You have a list of the local businesses? The ones in town, I mean, not the chains or the ones outside the center."

"I think there's a list on the town website, but I don't know if anyone has updated it lately."

"It's a place to start. I'm going to put together a wish list—the kinds of stores and such that I'd like to see in a Victorian village, which kind of eliminates anything high tech or even modern, and see where the existing stores fit. But at the same time I don't want to drive out anyone with a successful business—we need all the help we can get. It may be a juggling act for a while. Can I have another muffin?"

"Of course. Now I know where your weak spot is."

"Yup. Ply me with sweet carbs and I'm yours. Have you talked to anyone else since yesterday?"

"Like you think I have time? No, but I've thought about the whole project. Right now I think it's important to get people here excited about the idea, before we get to the nuts and bolts of which store and what style and how much it will cost. You planning to ask the store owners to pony up at least some of the money?"

"I haven't thought that far, and I know it could be a hardship for at least some of them. Who's running the bank these days?"

"Arthur Fairchild—you met him on Sunday. He took over from his father."

"Oh, right. Then I should talk to him sooner rather than later. He may not have the money in the bank to lend, or may not be willing to lend it even if he does, but he should have some ideas about where we could go looking. It never hurts to have a banker on your side, particularly a local one."

"Where do you want to start? I've asked Phil to pick up the kids after school so you have me for the day."

"Great. I'd like to be able to get into the B&B, but I guess that's got to wait until after lunch."

"You want me there for lunch?"

"I have a feeling it would be easier if it was just Ryan and me. What does he do these days?"

"Lawyer."

"Ooh. Local or city? Any particular specialization?"

"Contract law. He's with a midsize firm but not in Baltimore, and that's all I know. The backstory is, he went off to college, as did Cordy, but she roped him in the year after they both graduated. Before he went off to law school. After a few years he saw the light and moved on. She went around with steam coming out of her ears for a while after that, and I think part of the settlement was the house and some seed money to get the B&B outfitted. He hasn't had much reason to come back here since they split up."

"He married again?"

"Nope. Once bitten, twice shy? Unless he's been pining for you for the last decade."

"If he was, I don't know about it. He's never made an effort to get in touch with me. Maybe he's ashamed of what happened—not that we got caught doing what a lot of kids were doing in those days, but because Cordy blew the story all out of proportion, made him look like a big stud while I was a lame loser. I assume he figured that out at some point."

"Let's hope so, the jerk."

"Ah, don't be too hard on him," I said. I was now old enough to be gracious. "He was young, and the hormones were running high. And Cordy was an accomplished manipulator, even back then."

"Indeed she was. So back to Asheboro. We've got our one main street, which already has the library and town hall—I assume you plan to keep those?—and maybe fifteen or twenty shop fronts beyond that. What would a Victorian town have?"

"There are plenty of old town directories available online these days—we could pull up a few and look at what shops there were, and what their ads looked like."

"Ooh, great idea. What about eating places? Would there be a bar?"

"Shoot, I don't know. Was Maryland dry in 1900? Could a store sell liquor by the bottle, or only by the glass? I remember once taking a flight that went through Kentucky, I think it was, and when I wanted a drink during the layover, I was informed that an unescorted woman could not sit at the bar but had to sit at a table."

"You're kidding," Lisbeth said.

"No, I'm not. Places are weird about liquor licenses. Too bad there's not a real hotel in town, with a sit-down restaurant, but it's too late to fix that. Maybe a tearoom? People are going to want to eat and drink somewhere, and I don't want to see soda machines lined up along the street. When did cars first appear in Asheboro?"

"You think I know?" Lisbeth giggled. "I'm not even sure how to find out. Our old friend Henry Barton had the most money of anyone in town, and he lived a ways out—maybe he bought one. There might be an article in the paper about that."

"Oh, right, that reminds me. I need to check out what the local library has in the way of resources. Josh said it's a pretty fair local history collection, all things considered. So there should be newspapers, although probably not scanned. Local histories. Maybe genealogies. There's a lot I don't know about how Henry ended up here. Who was his wife? Was she a local girl? Or did she arrive with him?"

"Sorry, can't help you there."

"I didn't think you could—I'm just thinking out loud. But I bet we can find out a lot of that online too. Wow, I'm beginning to wish I had a whole staff helping out. We need to find out about small-town commerce, the genealogy of Henry Barton and his wife, what the place looked like in 1900—the library might be helpful there. And practical things, like, was there a doctor in town? Did he literally hang up a shingle on Main Street? Veterinarian? Pharmacy? Where was the earliest school? How many churches were there? Was there an influx of ex-soldiers after the Civil War? Even freed slaves? We're going to have to have some sort of diversity here if we hope for any public funding. I'd rather not have former slaves played by re-enactors. The children of freed slaves, maybe? I'm embarrassed about how little I know about that era and what actually happened in this town."

"Hey, I've lived here all my adult life, and I don't know much more. When do you want all this information?"

"Yesterday. Well, it kind of depends on the council, and whether they're willing to push back the date of when they want my proposal. Their next meeting is less than a week away. But in any case, if I can identify potential funding sources, then we need to have a pretty professional-looking pitch assembled and ready in only a few days. One with some solid historical information, pictures—whatever is available. Nobody's going to hand over six or seven figures just because we smile nicely at them and ask."

Lisbeth smiled. "I'm tired already, just listening to you.

Look, the council has been wrestling with this—and I do mean wrestling, because Cordy was pulling in one direction and they were pulling in the opposite direction—and now this project will either fade away, along with the town, or it will shift into a higher gear. What do *you* think is a reasonable time line?"

"I don't know if I can give them a rough proposal by the end of the week, as they asked—one more week would be helpful. Based on what I've seen, most of the work to restore both the Barton house and the town shops, at least outside, won't be too difficult to accomplish because not much has been changed in them. I'd tell them that we wouldn't be able to go public with even part of this for at least six months, which takes us into the fall. But there will be a catch-22 of a sort: we need the money up front to do the work, but nobody's going to give us money, or certainly not all of it, until they've seen that it's a good investment and that we can follow through."

Lisbeth looked deflated. "And here I was just beginning to get excited about all this."

"Hey, I don't mean to burst your bubble. I'm just laying out the things we need to consider. And in fact, we can't promise success to the council, because we won't know if it works until we're open for business. Chicken and egg problem." Were there any other stale clichés I could trot out? Cart before the horse? Aha, got one. "But Rome wasn't built in a day, and we have to start somewhere. Do we have time to go to the library, or should we save that for after lunch?"

"Why don't we stop in at the library and I can introduce you? Audrey closes from twelve to one like clockwork, but you aren't quite ready to start doing research, are you?"

"No, this is just a fact-finding mission. That sounds like a good idea. And then I can trot over for lunch with my former dreamboat."

Lisbeth cocked an eyebrow. "Dreamboat? Seriously? How old are you?"

"You should know. I was always kind of out of the mainstream. Do I know the librarian?"

"Audrey Perlaw. You might know her, because we overlapped in high school. But she was pretty much invisible."

"I can't seem to call up an image of her. Never mind—maybe I'll recognize her when I see her. What do I need to know about Audrey?"

"Raised here in Asheboro. Went to college, worked somewhere else for a while. Never married, then came back to Asheboro to take care of her aging parents—really sad. Her mother had early-onset Alzheimer's, and as soon as she passed on, Audrey's father was badly injured in a car accident and then declined gradually for quite a while before passing away. But Audrey's still here, although if it had been me I'd have gone as far away as I could once my parents were gone. Anyway, Audrey knows everything there is to know about the library and its collections."

"You are very good at these thumbnail sketches of people, you know. Will she help?"

"If you ask nicely and promise not to mess up her very tidy library. She must care about the town if she's stayed this long."

"All right, then." I stood up. "Let's go pay a call on Audrey, and then I'll go to lunch, and we can regroup afterwards, if that's okay with you."

"Fine. I've got some errands to run. Want me to drop you off for lunch?"

"Where am I going?"

Lisbeth smiled. "I told you, there's only one decent place to eat around here, and you've already seen it."

"I'll put it on my list of things to fix."

10

10

I'd spent a lot of time in the library when I lived in Asheboro. It could be hard to snag a ride to the library because so few of my peers actually went there, preferring to hang out at one of the fast-food places on the edge of town. That suited me fine—and went a long way toward explaining why I got A's in my classes (which did not make me any less unpopular). I was a walking cliché, which was probably why I fell so hard for Ryan when he began to show interest in me. He'd seemed like a nice enough guy—until Cordy had threw a monkey wrench into our relationship, and it had imploded. No, that was too melodramatic. It had wilted and shriveled up and died a quiet death, except for a snigger or two from one of Cordy's blondes in a school hallway now and then.

Kids, especially teenagers, could be cruel, but that cut both ways. There wouldn't be bullies if people would stand up to them.

At midday on a Tuesday, half an hour before the lunchtime closing, there were maybe three people in the library, in addition to the librarian. I was beginning to remember her now from school, where she had been a couple of years ahead of me. Tallish, skinny rather than slender, hair obviously colored at home. Her clothes back then were selected to blend into the woodwork. In fact, if any of us had thought about her at all, we would have pinned the label "Librarian" on her long before she'd graduated. Now, of course, a librarian's job included a wider range of skills than just shelving and checking books out: there were computer responsibilities, tracking of the collections, offering the occasional course, and so on. It was the collections I was interested in, and now I remembered that the local history collection had its own room, in sight of the librarian's desk, in case anyone was thinking of swiping a 1922 phone directory. I wondered if the recent surge in interest in genealogy had been a boon, or if all that happened online now, bypassing original documents. Still, it seemed to me that small rural libraries were never going to have the money to scan all their collections, unless one particular individual in the town took an interest and found the funding to do it, so they still held unique information.

Lisbeth made a beeline for the desk, a smile plastered on her face. "Audrey!" she said, with a carefully calibrated pitch. "I was hoping you'd be here. Do you remember Kate Hamilton? We were all at the high school together, although you were a couple of years ahead of us."

Audrey put on her professional smile. "Can't say that I do, Lisbeth. Welcome back—Kate, was it? Mostly I kept my eyes on my feet back then and just tried to get through each day. You still live here? Moving back?"

Oops. I had forgotten to put together an excuse. It was too early in the process to tip my hand about the town council's ambitious plan. "No, I left for college and really haven't been back much. I live in Baltimore now. My parents stayed here awhile longer, but they moved to Florida a few years ago. Actually they asked me to look up a few things for them, mostly out of sentiment. They moved to Asheboro right after they got married, and I came along a few years later. So I should be looking at old newspapers, town directories, things like that, right? High school yearbooks, maybe?"

"Yes, we've got a lot of those. Still on paper, though. For the time you're talking about, they'd probably still be in the history room, over there." She waved toward the back of the building. "For really early stuff—there's not a whole lot of that—it's still on site here, but it's archived in the basement. Climate controlled, of course. But I'd have to know what you're looking for—we don't let the public just go wandering around down there. What made your folks choose Asheboro?"

"I'm not really sure. My dad was an engineer at a plant north of Baltimore, but I don't think they could afford city house prices, and this seemed like a pleasant community, with convenient highway access. Or maybe they had a friend or two who already lived here. I can ask them, next time we talk." Why had I never done that before? Why are children so clueless, assuming their parents existed in the world solely to take care of their children, with no prior history of their own? We'd had no near family here, so why *had* we ended up in Asheboro? That was a question for another day.

"You staying around here?"

"I'm hoping she'll stay with me," Lisbeth spoke up quickly. "We used to be best friends, but we don't get near enough time to just chat, you know?"

I noticed that Lisbeth hadn't mentioned the B&B plan. She was turning out to be a good co-conspirator. Although I wasn't sure why I was hiding anything from Audrey—we needed her help.

"Yes." Audrey didn't elaborate. "Kate, why don't you let me put together a list of our resources about the town, with date ranges, and then you can decide what you want me to pull out for you? You know nothing can leave the building, but I think you can work in the Local History Room without being disturbed."

"That sounds perfect." I tried to look cheery and enthusiastic. "How long would you need to get that list together?"

"How's tomorrow morning?"

"Great. You open at nine?" When Audrey nodded, I added, "I'll be on your front step waiting. I appreciate your help, and I'm sure my parents will too."

Lisbeth pointedly looked at her watch. "Kate, we have that appointment, remember? We'd better get going if we don't want to be late."

"Oh, right, of course. I'll see you in the morning then, Audrey."

Once we'd escaped to the library's front steps, I said. "Wow, I didn't think this through, did I?"

"I thought your story about the memory book was simply charming," Lisbeth said.

I looked at her to see if she was kidding. "It was the best I could do on short notice. But to tell the truth, I never did know why we ended up here rather than somewhere else."

"No family ties here?"

"Not that I ever heard about. No cousins dropping in. The in-laws all lived a safe distance away and only showed up for alternating holidays. Maybe that was the point. Do you get along with your in-laws?"

"I do—they're great people. Of course, I may be the exception to the rule."

"You're lucky. But I should have planned ahead. I hope Audrey won't be angry when—if?—she finds out I'm poking around for the town council, although I'm not supposed to be spreading that fact around. At least the library is from the right period, so that's safe."

"I'm sure Audrey will understand. I'd better hustle you over to the hotel for your hot date."

"Give it up, will you? It's a meeting, period. Hey, will I recognize Ryan when I see him? He hasn't gained fifty pounds or gone bald, has he?"

"No. He looks mature and distinguished, and he buys expensive suits. Business must be good."

"I thought you never saw him around here?"

"Rarely. It's like sighting a white tiger in the rain forest or something like that. Maybe he was checking up on his investment. I'm pretty sure he wasn't yearning for his ex. He was AWOL a lot even when they were married. Cordy always put out the story that he was just so busy, first making partner, then being partner, that he kept a small apartment for himself for those late nights he just couldn't get home. And she, brave soul, had to take up the B&B just to keep herself busy."

"A B&B as a substitute for a husband? I can't say I've tried it, but I don't think that's the way it works. So what's your take? The marriage fell apart and she slunk home to Asheboro without telling anyone? It had to come out sometime? She couldn't exactly kill Ryan off in a convenient war far, far away."

"Alas, no, although I think she would have liked to. Then she got herself involved in local politics, and nobody had the nerve to tell her it was a bad idea and somehow she ended up voted into office, most likely because nobody else wanted to run. Luckily she missed more meetings than she attended."

"You aren't actually on the council, are you?"

"No—I don't really have the time. Maybe someday. But I help out when I can."

"Like calling me. Don't worry—I won't hold it against you. Obviously the town needs some professional help, and I'm both an outsider with relevant experience and an insider with a history in Asheboro. Perfect match."

"I'll remind you of that later," Lisbeth said.

"Do I look all right?" I asked, as we drove toward the hotel.

"You look fine. You nervous?"

"No. Well, maybe. It'll be fine once we break the ice. You talked to him? What did he say?"

"I told him you were here and why—it didn't seem right not to mention that, since his ex-wife's death is tangled up with it—and asked if you could stay at the B&B while you checked out the scene. He was fine with it."

"He's not staying there, is he?"

"No, he's at the hotel tonight. I think the B&B isn't grand enough for him. But he probably thought he should stay close while the Cordy mess is sorted out."

I wasn't sure how I felt about having him hanging around town. "So at least I won't have to worry about running into him at the B&B."

"Nope, you're in the clear. You sure you don't want to stay with us?"

"Maybe when the business side of this is over. Right now I need someplace closer to the center of town, and where I have some peace and quiet to work and get in touch with other people who might be useful. This isn't going to happen overnight. If it happens at all."

"That's okay, I get it. Our house can get rather chaotic. Here we are." She pulled into a parking space near the door of the hotel. "Ryan will probably volunteer to take you to the B&B and let you in. But if you want a ride, just call me and I'll pick you up, okay?"

"Will do. Thanks for setting this up, Lisbeth. I appreciate it."

"Let's see how you feel about it after lunch. Good luck!"

I watched her pull away and turned reluctantly toward the hotel, pulling my jacket down and smoothing my hair. Why was I nervous? I had handled multimillion-dollar budgets. I had welcomed CEOs and local politicians. Was I really worried about meeting a guy who I'd crushed on years earlier and had seldom thought of since? Well, now and then, maybe when one fledgling romance or another had crashed before it really got off the ground. But I might as well get it over with. I strode into the dining room attempting to radiate confidence, and stopped in the doorway to scan the crowd for my First Love. There he was, in the corner, at a table for two. Damn, he looked good. It wasn't fair. But, as I reminded myself, if he'd been dumb enough to fall for Cordy and actually marry her, his mental capacities must be lacking—something I hadn't noticed all those years ago. I made my way through the mostly empty tables, waving off the assistance of the hostess, until I arrived in front of him.

He was busy texting on his cell phone. He didn't even look up. If it turned out he was tweeting, that would be a deal breaker.

"Ryan?" I said, after about thirty seconds.

Finally he looked up, then shoved his chair back and stood up. "Kate! Oh, sorry, I didn't see you. Work stuff, you know." We wobbled through that awkward moment—hug? kiss cheeks? shake hands? We settled on a half hug with plenty of air between us. "Please, sit down. You look great!"

"So do you," I said, in all honesty. He'd grown into himself. "I hear you're a lawyer now."

"I am. Went to law school right after college. Look, I'm sorry we lost touch. Actually, I'm sorry about quite a few things."

Might as well get it over with. "Like marrying Cordelia?"

He smiled ruefully. "Yes, that's on the list. Are you in a hurry, or do we have time to talk?"

"As long as you feed me lunch, I'm good. You don't mind if I stay at the bed and breakfast?"

"Heck, no. Maybe you can hold an exorcism."

"That bad?"

"It is. Was. You ready to order? Would you like wine or something?"

"Coffee's fine." I wanted to keep a clear head, especially since I wasn't sure what I wanted from him, or what he might want from me. I also had to decide whether to discuss the town council's idea, then figured I might as well since his ex-wife had been part of that council, and the B&B she had been running was smack in the middle of town—and that still belonged to Ryan.

11

We ordered lunch, and when the waitress had vanished, he said, "So, Kate, what have you been doing for the last fifteen years?"

I gave him the short version: college, degree in business management with emphasis on the hospitality industry, the first couple of jobs, and the past five years at the Baltimore hotel. I didn't add that that job had just evaporated.

When I wrapped it up, he said, "You haven't been back here much, have you?"

"Not since my parents left. I didn't have a lot of happy memories of the place. Well, except for Lisbeth. She's always been the one bright spot."

"Let me say now that I regret any role I might have played in keeping you away. I apologize for how I treated you our senior year—or how I let Cordelia treat you. Please allow me to blame it on teenage hormones and the stupidity of youth. I hope I've outgrown both. Truce?"

"Ryan, I gave up worrying about that years ago. Cordelia was a piece of work. How did you come to marry her?"

"Condensed version? We both left for college, at different schools. During our last year she got back in touch with me and we started seeing each other. I don't think she was ever happy in college—too big a pool for her to be noticed. When I got into law school she decided I was going places and latched on to me like—what's a good analogy? A remora eel? The one that attaches itself to a shark and feeds off it."

I had to laugh. "Now, there's a lovely image. How long did that last?"

Ryan smiled down at his still-empty plate. "We got married after my first year of law school. I think we had a couple of good years, a couple of so-so years, and one year from hell, and then she came back to Asheboro and declared she wanted to have her own business."

"The bed and breakfast?"

"That's what she decided on. I bankrolled it and bought the building for it, but she said she wanted to run it. She lost interest pretty quickly—too much work, not enough admiration. I'm not sure why she hung on to the place, but I'd guess she couldn't think of anywhere else to go. And she didn't find another willing sucker in Asheboro who would take her away from all this."

The waitress appeared with our meals, and we fell silent as she distributed plates in front of us. Then I said, "You knew she was on the town council?"

"I did, although I wondered how she managed to get enough votes."

"I had the same thought. My guess is that there were still enough people in town who'd been bullied by her and didn't want to face that again." I paused for a moment. "Did she tell you what's been going on with the town recently?"

"No, we didn't talk. I paid the mortgage on the place, and she took care of operating expenses. No contact required. Why do you ask?"

"This is still confidential. You're a lawyer, so you should understand that. Plus you still own a property right off Main Street. So here goes. The town is basically broke, since they bought the old Barton place outright."

"Really? Our Barton place?" He added air quotes to the last question.

"That very one. It appears that Cordy had a yen to move up in the little Asheboro world. She persuaded the town to buy the place by dangling visions of a luxury hotel and high-end guests at the place. Run by her, of course."

"She was never short on ego. No, she hadn't told me anything about it. Still in the planning stages?"

"The very distant planning stages. Buying the property, even at a bargain rate, took about all the money the town had. It's a familiar story—small town, little or no industry, too far out to be a bedroom community, declining tax base, et cetera, et cetera. And then the storm hit, and the town realized they didn't have any money to fix anything."

"What's it going to take to restore the old place?"

"That's a funny thing—not much. The former owner, Henry Barton, loved the place and wanted to see it survive. When he died, over a century ago, he left an endowment to sustain the place physically while the bank was finding a buyer. Only they never did. Luckily there was enough money to maintain the property well. It really is a beautiful place."

"So where's the problem?"

"I gather that Cordy got tired of waiting for the town to act, and she was shopping around for outside investors. She claimed she had some lined up, but they had a very different vision for the place—kind of executive modern, rather than prime Victorian. The town was not happy with the idea."

To his credit, Ryan sat back and digested what I had just told him. "And then Cordy was found dead. At the Barton house."

I wondered if the police had shared any more details with him. "Yes, the day after Lisbeth asked me, on behalf of the town, to find some way to preserve the house and to bring some money back to Asheboro."

"So you were here before she died."

"I was, but not at the time she was killed, it seems. Lisbeth filled me in a bit on the background with the council. I gather they dug their heels in and refused to cave to Cordy. That's why I was there—to meet with the council and look at other options. We met on Sunday, but Cordy wasn't invited."

Ryan shook his head. "I had no idea . . . Are you a suspect?"

"You mean, do the police know about our, uh, relationship and how it ended and think it's a good motive for murder after all this time? I gave them the story, but more to the point, if they look carefully I can show that I was in Baltimore using my computer at the time of her death. I'm not sure whether any of the council members are under suspicion. Or if there's anyone else Cordy harassed at some point, who might have decided that this was the last straw."

"What a sad thing, to be so hated in your own town. But I'll be the first to admit she asked for it. I don't think she was ever happy about anything, and she took it out on other people."

"You are very charitable, Ryan. But you certainly knew her

better than I ever did. You said you're the owner of the B&B property?"

"Yes. Why?"

"Buy me dessert and I'll explain." We ordered, and then I launched into part two of the discussion. "I told you I saw the Barton place, and it is gorgeous. I can certainly see it as a high-end hotel, but it would be more interesting as a themed hotel—a step back in time to the Victorian era, with all the best it had to offer. That's the easy part. But I don't see how that alone can sustain the town, no matter how many rich guests it brings in—it's simply not large enough. I'm not sure even Cordy's corporate model would work, although I'd guess she was more interested in running the place than in making money for the town."

"I think that's a fair assessment. So? You have a plan of your own?"

"I'm working on one, but please keep this under wraps. This week I walked around the town center. I haven't been back much, so I could look at it with fresh eyes. It's shabby-looking, and any changes in the shops have been for the worse. It's a pretty typical story for a lot of small towns since malls took over retail—and now the malls are dying in the face of Internet competition. That's business. Then there's the recent storm damage. But in an odd way, that might be a plus. When I looked closely at Asheboro, with all the missing shingles and siding, I realized that the fabric of the place really hasn't changed since Henry Barton's day. The majority of the changes have been cosmetic and superficial. So I got to thinking, What if instead of repairing the shops in town, we stripped off those so-called improvements and converted the town center into a Victorian village? The Barton house would be the anchor, but people could stroll along Main Street and picture themselves in another century."

"Interesting concept. You'd try to divert some of the battle-field traffic?"

"Exactly. And make it a destination and offer something different. Now, before you start arguing, I know it will cost money, and I know that it will take some sweet-talking to convince the shop owners to buy into the idea. But right now they haven't got much to look forward to, so I think they'd be willing at least to listen. Am I completely out in left field?"

"Actually, no, I don't think so. But there would be a lot of work as well as some money involved. How would you plan to integrate the Barton house, which is, what, a few miles outside of town, with this bustling Victorian village?"

"I haven't worked out many of the details yet. Horse-drawn trams? Carriages for hire? And as for Henry Barton—do you have any idea what they made in that factory on the edge of town?"

"I can't say that I do. It was closed long before our time."

"I want to do some research on Henry—where'd he come from? Why was he here? Apparently he'd fought for the North in the Civil War and settled here after that and built his house. He married but had no children and outlived his wife. And he had *lots* of money—from his family? Or from that mysterious factory? And, yes, I've already stopped in at the library, and Audrey is going to put together some resources for me."

"Did you tell her about the town's idea?"

"No. I'm not ready for that. I'm not an employee or an elected official of the town, just an unpaid consultant so far. There's no proposal on the table yet. If anything about this idea trickles out, the town will get flack from all directions, pro and con. Conservationists will want to preserve the status quo. Developers will want more, sooner, and oh, by the way, wouldn't you like to add a strip mall, cheap? And housing for a few thousand people? Historians will no doubt have widely varying ideas of what happened here—if anything. Do you know about the Barton house resident custodian–slash–historian?"

"Uh, what?" Ryan asked, looking confused.

"The Barton trust made provisions for someone to live rent-free on the property—over the stable, not in the house— to keep an eye on things, watch for leaks or vandals or whatever. Somehow that funding has survived to this day. The current custodian is a history professor who's researching and writing about post–Civil War industrialization."

"Did he know Cordy?" Ryan asked.

"I gather they crossed paths a time or two. They did not see eye to eye."

"Does that make him a suspect?"

"Heck, I don't know. It's not like he knew her well. Would he have killed her because he disagreed with her taste in interior design?"

"Seems unlikely. Look, is there anything I can do to help?"

"Nice of you to offer. What kind of law do you practice?"

"Mostly corporate litigation. No violent crime."

"Anything for nonprofits?"

"Now and then. Why?"

"If this goes forward, we might want to set up a nonprofit corporation in parallel with the town. We may want to solicit support from philanthropic donors, who would want to see us have nonprofit status."

"Lady, you don't mess around. You came up with this idea what, three days ago? And since then there's been a murder that might or might not be connected, and you're already talking about creating a nonprofit corporation. How much have you told the town council?"

"Just a broad concept, so far. I haven't seen them since Cordy died. But I guess I'm getting excited about the idea. It's bigger than anything I've ever tried."

"Well, I'm happy to help."

We finished dessert quickly, and Ryan asked, "You ready to go check out the B&B?"

"Sure. You driving?"

"Yes, of course. I haven't been inside the place myself for a while, and I want to make sure everything is all right in case I decide to sell. Or maybe your hypothetical corporation can buy it to use as a headquarters."

"Or maybe you and your rich buddies can gift it to the hypothetical corporation," I shot back with a grin. "Nice tax deduction, right?"

"I'll take it under advisement."

12

I'll admit I was curious to see what Cordy's bed-and-breakfast establishment looked like. I'd driven past it, and from the outside it appeared to be a modest late-Victorian building painted in San Francisco Painted Lady colors—not quite typical of this part of Maryland, but pretty in its own way—and in better repair than most of the central Asheboro buildings. There was a tasteful sign planted in the midst of the small lawn in front. Ryan pulled up and parked.

"This is it," he said.

"Good location. How much parking?"

"Five spaces directly behind the house. Otherwise street parking."

"I'm surprised Cordy didn't try to wangle the council to provide more street spaces for her."

"You think she didn't try?" He grinned.

I was not exactly surprised. "How long did she have this place?"

"About five years."

"And how many of those years did she make a profit?"

"No comment."

"Great investment, Ryan."

"If it kept Cordy out of my face, it was worth every penny. Ready to go in?"

"Sure. Did she have any bookings that needed to be cancelled?"

"Nope. I think once the novelty had worn off, she got bored. She was kind of chained to the place. She couldn't go out to lunch with the girls as much as she would have liked and stir up trouble. She didn't put much effort into it over the last year or two, and the bookings fell off."

"How sad," I said. "She never really changed, did she?"

"I'd hoped . . ." Ryan stopped.

"That marrying you would make things better?" *Or change her?*

"I guess. I did love her, you know. At least at the beginning."

"Don't blame yourself, Ryan. She was who she was, and I don't think anybody could have changed that. Should we go in?"

"Sure. Oh, before I forget, here's a set of keys for you." He handed me a key ring with several keys on it.

"Which does what?" I asked. "Is there an alarm system?"

"Exterior alarm, but that operates from keypads. I'll give you the code number. You disarm the system then you use the key to open the door. The keys are for the doors—front and back—and your room. I've put you in the best room."

"Gee, thanks. Has the place been cleaned lately?"

"Only Cordy would know. I can tell you that she hated housework."

I wasn't surprised. The manicure took top priority. "Can I use the kitchen while I'm here?"

"Sure. Even if you burn the place down, the place is insured for guests, and you're a guest. How long do you think you'll be needing a room?"

"Somewhere between one and a few hundred nights. Seriously, right now I'm operating day to day. If I find some positive things, I'll stick around for a few days. If it looks hopeless, I'll tell the council and then go home. Is that a problem? Or are you planning to sell it ASAP?"

"No to that last question. I wouldn't have pulled the rug out from Cordy, unless she was really trashing the place. Truthfully I didn't think she'd stick it out much longer. But I'm nowhere near to putting in on the market. I may wait to see if your grand scheme works out."

"I wouldn't hold your breath, but we'll see. Did she leave a will?"

"Yes—we had them drawn up years ago, and we modified them when we split. As you know, the building is in my name. Cordy had very little to leave."

I'd always thought her parents were reasonably well off— but maybe that was what she wanted us all to think. "What are the burial plans?"

"Cordy's parents were buried here, just outside of town, and there's room for her cremains in that plot. I don't suppose anybody will object."

I was reminded that I didn't know where Henry Barton was buried—I should check. If it was local, that could be woven into his story. If it was somewhere else? Well, that might give me a clue to his origins. Surely there would have been an obituary in the local paper—I could check in the morning.

Ryan disabled the front door alarm as I watched, and let me in using his own key. The interior was cool and dark. From a brief glance, it was like a Barton house in miniature—central hallway and stairs, doors leading off to rooms on both sides. "How many bedrooms?"

"Four," Ryan said. "Two share a bath, and the others are *en suite.*"

"Kitchen at the back?" When Ryan nodded, I went on. "Neighbors?"

"It's a mixed neighborhood, a combination of residential and home office—a dentist, an accountant. That kind of thing. Nothing obviously commercial."

"Can I use whatever food I find?"

"Sure. And I'd bet Cordy laid in some good wine, but I don't know where she kept it."

"Are the police finished with this place?"

"They never even got started. Cordy was killed where she was found, they told me. End of story. There was no sign of anything disturbed here, so no reason to search the place."

That sounded surprisingly sloppy for Detective Reynolds. "You went through the building?"

"Only briefly. As I said, the police didn't seem interested, and I wasn't either."

"Any documents or souvenirs you want to take with you?"

"I already have copies of the legal documents, like the lease, and I took along the preliminary proposals from her mystery corporate partners. I gave copies to the police. As for jewelry or mementoes . . . well, I don't particularly want anything to remember her by. If you stumble on something valuable, let me know, but as far as I'm concerned it's finders-keepers."

"Noted. Well, that's all I need for now. You're staying at the hotel?"

"Yes, until the final arrangements are made. I could

commute, I supposed, but it would be wasting time. Dinner?" he asked.

I didn't waste a lot of time thinking about it. "Not tonight. I want to get my bearings, and I have a lot to think about. Maybe later in the week if I decide to stick around. Give me your cell number so I can reach you."

He looked a bit crestfallen, but he fished out a business card and scribbled his cell phone number on the back, along with the digits of the door code. "I'll let you know if there'll be a service."

"I'd appreciate that." Much as I'd disliked Cordy, at least a memorial service would give me some final closure, and I was curious to see who else would show up. Still, Ryan's hesitation suggested that maybe there wouldn't be a service—out of fear that no one would attend? "I'll let you know if I make any decisions. Thanks for lunch, Ryan. It's been good to see you."

He wavered a moment, then went back down the hall and out the front. I wondered if he'd cherished some hope of rekindling what we'd had, but even if he did, now was not the time. My car was still parked at Lisbeth's house, so I needed to call her first.

She answered quickly, as if she'd been waiting by the phone. "Hey, Katie. Where are you?"

"At the bed and breakfast. Ryan dropped me off, and he just left. Listen, if you can come get me, we can take a look around this place, and then you can take me back so I can collect my car."

"Ooh, I get to snoop? Cordy was living there, right?"

"Uh, I gather. Why, you want to paw through her underwear?"

"Ew, no—that's creepy. But I'll admit I'm curious. Listen,

why don't you have dinner with us, and then you can drive back?"

"Okay, sounds good. You haven't heard anything from the council, have you?"

"Nope. I think they're waiting in deference to the late Cordelia. Or they're afraid to hear what you might tell them, like there's no hope."

"Don't give up yet. See you in a few."

After we'd hung up, I wandered back to the kitchen. It wasn't intended to be a public space, but it was passably neat. I opened the fridge: as I expected, it was mostly breakfast fixings—milk, butter, eggs, bread, and the like. The freezer held several bags of frozen muffins. So much for home-baked, not that I'd expected it from Cordy. I poked around in the cupboards, where I found some attractive mid-price matching china and cups, as well as glasses. Including wineglasses. I wondered where Cordy would have hidden the good stuff.

I strolled out through the dining room and across the hall. The main parlor had a handsome fireplace, apparently functional, flanked by bookshelves holding real books, mainly mysteries and romances. Things that patrons had left? Or did Cordy have a taste for light fiction? I didn't care. If I had a book, a comfortable chair, a fireplace, and a glass of good wine, I'd be a happy camper for as long as I stayed.

I wandered up the stairs. Ryan said he'd tidied up the "best" room, which I assumed was in the front, over the parlor. It was. The room was plain but clean, although the bed had been stripped and not remade. I wondered where the linen closet might be hiding, but I would look later. The adjoining bath had its original fixtures—and clean towels. Back in the bedroom I tested the lights and made a mental note to get some light bulbs that were brighter than 25 watts. I peeked in the closet: empty, except for some bent hangers, an extra pillow and a couple of dust bunnies in the corners. I sensed that Cordy's heart really hadn't been into making this a welcoming place. What had she been thinking? Had she really believed she was a "people person" and could charm guests? That must have gotten old fast, but where else could she go?

I heard a knocking downstairs and I went to open the front door for Lisbeth. "Come on in," I said. "Have you ever been inside before?"

"I think Cordy once held a party for the council members here—grudgingly. That's about it. Find anything good?"

"I've only been here ten minutes, but the whole place feels generic, if you know what I mean. Kind of the bare minimum standard. Ryan hinted there might be a secret stash of wine, if you want to go looking for it."

"A treasure hunt! Have you checked out Cordy's room?"

"No, I only got as far as the room where Ryan said I should sleep, and the bathroom. So she lived here too?"

"I gather she didn't have a choice, financially."

"Ryan said the police weren't interested in this place, and he's taken all that he wants. Shall we go explore?"

"Let's!"

Cordy's room proved to be a small one at the back of the house. Unlike the rest of the place, this one was kind of messy, except for the clothes, which were hung neatly in the closet, on a standing rack—and in any other possible place. I spied some designer labels. Lisbeth and I surveyed the room. I knew that I felt uncomfortable, prowling around the personal possessions of someone we knew, who had been murdered, even if we did have all the permissions we could want.

"This is creepy," I half-whispered.

"I know what you mean," Lisbeth replied, in a similar tone. More loudly she said, "Are we looking for anything in particular?"

"I don't really know. Ryan said he found the preliminary documents for that corporate deal she was hinting about."

"So it was real? I figured maybe she was making that up just to pressure the council."

"Apparently there was something in the works. And it makes sense, from her perspective. This place doesn't quite fit with her own self-image. Anyway, what kind of item would spur anyone to kill her? And where would she leave it?"

"Nude photos?" Lisbeth suggested. "Maybe she was blackmailing someone. Or several someones."

I had to smile at the idea. "On one hand, I can see her enjoying that kind of power over other people. But on the other hand, I can't see her sleeping around for money. She thought she was better than that."

"Hmm. Maybe she was a drug addict and her dealer killed her?"

Lisbeth's day-to-day life might be dull, but it appeared that she had a lively imagination. "Easy enough to check the bathroom and drawers for her—what do they call it? a kit?—but I don't think so. She would want to keep her wits about her."

"Listen to you—you've been reading too many old mysteries lately. But I get your drift. Your turn. Come up with an idea."

"Maybe she was harboring a secret passion for someone who wasn't interested, and she wouldn't let go and her lover had to kill her?" I suggested.

"Possible. But I can't see Cordy being that needy. And

she'd be more likely to be a blackmailer. You know, seduce some poor guy and threaten to tell his wife unless he pays up. She probably needed the money. But the guy—or maybe one of many—could have snapped and killed her?"

"Let's keep that on the list. What if she was blackmailing someone and his wife found out and whacked her? If she was one of Cordy's earlier victims, that would be a twofer."

"Doesn't shorten the list much," Lisbeth commented. "Cordy bullied half the girls in Asheboro. So we'd need to identify one of the many, who's married to a guy who Cordy was able to seduce."

I sighed. "I suppose it's possible. But we're getting ahead of ourselves, you know. We'd have to find the incriminating pictures first. I wonder how she took them. I doubt she'd have an accomplice with a camera."

"True. You see a computer here?"

"No. But maybe Ryan took it with him—I can ask him. It might have belonged to the business. There's not much else of value here, but if she was blackmailing someone, he'd want to find the evidence."

"If it exists," Lisbeth pointed out. "This is just one theory. Got any more?"

"She seduced one of the corporate partners she was wooing?"

"Fits her self-image better. You could ask Ryan who was listed on those documents."

I checked the time: three o'clock. "You said your husband was dealing with the kids?"

"He's picking them up from their afterschool sports things in a bit. Why?"

"Well, if we can find the liquor cabinet, we have time for

one respectable glass of something before we head for your house, right?"

"One glass only—that's legal, right?"

"So I've heard, although I haven't tested it. Besides, you must be friends with the police department."

"Yes, but I'd like to keep it that way. Let's look anyway."

13

We found Cordy's secret stash of wines, and they were indeed fine. The bottles had been carefully concealed behind a wooden wall panel in the parlor. Had Cordy found it ready and waiting when she moved in, or had she created it for her own use? Didn't really matter now. The wines, nestled in racks that were obviously more recent than the house itself, bore labels that even I recognized.

"Glasses in the kitchen," I told Lisbeth. "I'll get a couple. And a corkscrew."

"I'll while away my time in the front parlor," Lisbeth said, then giggled.

I found two glasses appropriate to the vintage we had selected and returned quickly, bearing a corkscrew. "Sorry, no snacks to be had. Ryan said there hadn't been many guests of late." I proceeded to demonstrate my expertise in opening good wine, thanks to plenty of practice at the hotel, and the cork slid out gracefully.

"Shall we test it?" I asked.

"You just want to show off. Go right ahead—I might need to know how, once the kids graduate from college."

I did the expected sniff, taste, make silly slurping noises, and pronounced the wine fit to drink. "Shall I pour?"

"Please," Lisbeth replied.

We settled ourselves in the two richly upholstered chairs that flanked the unlit fireplace and sipped appreciatively. "This is really nice," Lisbeth said.

"You're absolutely right. This is a treat."

"So," Lisbeth said, swirling her glass before taking another sip, "what was it like seeing Ryan after all these years?"

I searched for an honest answer. "Not exactly memorable. I was surprised he hadn't remarried, after Cordy, but we didn't talk about a lot of personal stuff, either at the restaurant or here, and I didn't want to ask. I gather he saw through Cordy fairly quickly once they were married, but I think he hoped she would change. We know how well that worked out. I'm pretty sure he was the one who left, which must have really pissed off Cordy. This place was Cordy's compensation, at least in part. Ryan didn't exactly look back, after he left."

"So no flickering embers of lost romance?"

"Sorry to disappoint you, but no. He's a good-looking, successful man, and he's single, but there weren't any sparks. And this is just a guess, but I don't think he felt strongly enough about Cordy now to do her in. He was glad to wash his hands of her."

"Okay, just checking. Are you sorry?" Lisbeth asked, her gaze on her wineglass.

I took another sip of my own wine, relishing the way it glided down my throat. "No. If it didn't work out then, there's no reason why it would now. He might be a good resource as a lawyer, though. I told him about what the council was talking about and why I was here. And I told him it wasn't public knowledge yet, so he won't spread it around."

"Good idea, on both counts. I didn't mean to be nosy—my daily life is a bit lacking in grand romance."

"And you love it just the way it is. That's fine. I love my job, or did, at least. There's no man on the horizon, but I'm open to the idea, when it seems right. But I'm not hitting the bars or checking out online dating sites."

"Hey, you don't have to explain yourself to me. I'm glad you're here, and I trust your judgment about what can be done to salvage Asheboro. If anything. I am *not* playing matchmaker, not that there are a lot of options around here."

"Enough said," I declared. "So, what else can we hope to learn from Cordy's home here? Oh, by the way, I asked Ryan to let me know if there would be a memorial service—it might be interesting to see who shows up."

"Good point," Lisbeth said. "As for this place? I don't see that she spent a whole lot of money or energy on it. In a way I feel sorry for her. She left town with high hopes, then came back with her tail between her legs. She married the hometown boy—handsome, a lawyer—and that turned out to be a disappointment, although she probably wouldn't ever admit that might have been her fault. She decided she wanted to run a business of her own and cajoled Ryan into buying her this place—"

"Which he still owns, by the way—"

"Ah. Maybe she could have made a go of it, but I'd guess she got bored fairly quickly, and she didn't like catering to other people. Then she decided to dabble in local politics, and promptly made a bunch of enemies around town. She tried to do an end-run around the council about the Barton house, and that didn't sit well with them."

I interrupted. "We're assuming that she wanted to run the place herself, which no doubt she would see as a step up."

Lisbeth nodded then went on. "And then someone bashed her over the head with a rock and killed her. End of story."

"Except there's still a killer out there," I reminded her.

"And a boatload of suspects." Lisbeth drained her glass. "I'm driving, so I guess I'd better stop now."

"Don't worry, you can take the bottle home with you and enjoy it after the kids are in bed. There's more where that came from."

"Lucky you! Anything else we need to cover, before we jump into the mob scene at my house? You have a game plan?"

"Not really. We still don't know enough about the history of Asheboro, which is why I'm headed to the library tomorrow morning. Even if the records are in apple-pie order, there may not be anything in them on which to build a compelling story that will bring in plenty of tourists. I mean, there was never an important battle here. It was never a major center for anything. The train line that came through the region in eighteen-hundred-whatever skipped it entirely. The best we could hope for is the world's largest rutabaga, since I think the world's largest ball of string is taken."

Lisbeth nodded her agreement. "So what we've got here is a pleasant little town in the middle of nowhere, that's dying a natural death."

"I'll do my best to come up with something, Lisbeth, but I can't make any promises."

"I understand, and I appreciate your coming here and

trying. So, ready for dinner? Not gourmet—I thawed a casserole this morning. I think the main ingredient is last Thanksgiving's turkey."

"Let's do this. You take the bottle," I said, shoving the cork back into the top. "I've got to figure out how the door works, and that will take both hands. It's got keys and a keypad, but I haven't tried it yet."

I left a light burning in the back parlor and turned on the porch light, and then I managed to get the door opened and closed without setting off any alarms. Once Lisbeth and I were pointed in the right direction, she said softly, "Will you be okay all alone in the house?"

"What, you think Cordy's going to come back and haunt me? Taunt me is more likely. Can't you hear her? 'What makes you think you can save this town, huh? You ran away as fast as your flat feet could carry you. You believe you can charm donors and charitable organizations? Heck, I stole your boyfriend out from under your nose and then I married him. Let me tell you, he was no bargain, but you couldn't even hold on to him. Loser!'"

"Oh, Katie, is that really the way you feel?"

"No, not anymore. Once, maybe. But I've got the perfect answer now for her: 'I'm alive and you're not.'"

"Good one. Although it's barely possible that she killed herself, you know."

"By bashing herself over the head with a large rock? That I'd like to see."

Our laughter and chatter took us to Lisbeth's house, and once inside I had to greet the kids—remarkably well mannered, I thought—and make small talk with Lisbeth's very pleasant husband and eat the substantial casserole. I turned down dessert. "I'd really better get going before I fall asleep. I'll be at the library in the morning, and I'll let you know if I find anything good. By the way, should I tell Audrey what's going on? I'd hate it if she found out from someone else and was annoyed at me—I need her help."

"What the heck, go ahead and tell her. It'll make her feel important, which she is to the town. You can blame the council for making you keep quiet about it."

Lisbeth walked me to the door and hugged me impulsively. "I know we haven't solved a darned thing, but it's good to have you here. Happy hunting tomorrow."

I drove back to the B&B carefully, even though I'd laid off the wine. I wanted to see the town after dark. Lisbeth's house lay in a near suburb, and the houses grew larger, as did their lots, as I approached the town center. Which didn't take long. It had never been a large town, or even a medium-size one. Just another ordinary American town. You could have dropped it in any number of different states and it would have been just the same.

I pulled into the otherwise empty driveway and parked. I retrieved the keys from of my bag and approached the door. For all my bravado, I found myself thinking of too many TV crime shows: this was the moment when some guy in a ski mask would leap out of the bushes and try to kill me. Since I was the heroine of this dark fantasy, I would of course overpower him, and after tying him up with the garden hose, I would have discovered in his pocket the single clue that would explain everything. Then I would call the local police and triumphantly explain to them that I had solved the case for them. Laughing,

I disarmed the alarm, unlocked the door, and let myself in—
but I made sure to lock the door and reset the alarm, and I
left the porch light on.

Inside I wandered aimlessly from room to room, looking
for . . . what? A clue? Cordy hadn't died here. She'd barely
lived here, and she'd left very little imprint of her own personality. What would a bullying, manipulative personality look
like if it was a house? I amused myself trying to imagine it as
I retrieved a fresh bottle of wine from the secret closet and
took it to the kitchen to open. Every item in relentless order,
and afraid to even twitch lest it be thrown out for insubordi-
nation? An interior that was uniformly bland, the better to
showcase its colorful owner? Or an interior that was riotously
colorful, as if the owner dared the surroundings to outshine her?

Ridiculous, I knew. I took my glass of wine and went back
to the parlor and sat. Maybe I should try to conjure up Cordy's
spirit, and then she would tell me who had killed her and we'd
all live happily ever after. No, Cordy wasn't the type to share
anything. She'd want to figure out a way to tell the police
herself so she could get the credit. Except she was dead, which
would make that difficult. Wherever she was now, I bet she'd
hate it if I solved this mess.

As I sat in the near darkness, my mind drifted aimlessly
from topic to topic. Henry Barton was the key to it all, I was
convinced. What had drawn him back to Asheboro? The
people? The views? The natural resources? (Were there any?
I'd have to check.) The fact that it was some place that was *not*
where he came from? Had he been fleeing from something,
or looking for something new? A clean slate? And where the
heck had all his money come from?

I finished my single glass of wine and stood up. I still had to find sheets and make the bed, and figure out how the plumbing worked (please let there be hot water!), and make some sort of list for what to look for at the library in the morning. All in all, a busy day today, and more to come. Good thing I didn't have that pesky day job anymore, I thought to myself as I trudged up the stairs with my small suitcase.

14

Nobody murdered me while I slept. Nor did Cordy haunt my dreams, even though I was under what had been her roof. A decent start to the day, I figured.

I hauled myself out of bed, trying to smooth the mismatched linens I'd found the night before. I took a quick shower and went down the stairs to hunt for breakfast. If there weren't provisions for making coffee somewhere in the kitchen, I'd have to kill Cordy all over again.

There was coffee and a large French press. I brewed myself a pot, nuked a frozen muffin, and sat myself down at the kitchen table to make a list. Should I start with Henry or with the town itself? Henry was no doubt the catalyst, but it would be more difficult to piece together a picture of what the town had looked like in 1900, and that was what I should be looking for at the library.

Americans have a kind of fixed image of small-town Main Street. It signals home, a simpler, gentler time, when more people walked places, and all the stores were in a central location and easy to reach on foot. What would be essential in a small town? Food, of course, but food wouldn't be available in a huge supermarket, with one-stop shopping, More likely food vendors would be scattered along the street, with a butcher shop—did they also handle chickens and eggs?—and a grocery store that sold canned goods, cleaning products, and the like. Then there were clothes. Many women would still have made their own, but they had to get the fabric and notions somewhere, so that was another store. Or they could have had a dressmaker in town. Things that could not be easily made, like hats, might be sold at a dedicated store or a so-called general store, along with gloves and shoes and—gasp—unmentionables. No handy mail order in those days, although I should check when the Sears Catalog first became popular. A supply and feed store, although that might have been on the fringes of town—where farmers would buy tools and feed and harnesses. A doctor's office, although maybe Asheboro hadn't been large enough to warrant a full-time doctor. A pharmacy, of course.

Was there a social hierarchy for the town? Was one end of the town classier than the other? What about side streets? And where had the factory fit into the whole picture? Somebody must have a history of that—what I had taken to calling the Barton Widget Works, for want of a better title. I really needed to find the real name, and what it produced. It was a big building, so it must have employed quite a few people in its day.

I made another heading for Henry Barton and his house. Henry had arrived, fresh from the war, with a new wife (or acquired said wife shortly afterward), and settled in Asheboro. He set up some kind of factory in the tumultuous postwar years, and by 1885 or 1890 he had a handsome factory in town producing lots of widgets and earning him buckets of money, and he could afford to fancy up his house and furnish it at the peak of current style. A decade or two later he had died and been forgotten. Poor Henry. I needed censuses, directories, local histories—oops, look at the time!

I needed to get my town clothes on and get my butt to the library or I'd be late, and I didn't want to insult Audrey Perlaw on my first day there.

I made it to the library with five minutes to spare. Audrey was waiting inside and unlocked the door for me, then locked it behind me. We stared at each other for a long minute, and she didn't look happy. Finally she said, "I remember you now." And stopped.

And I immediately felt guilty about my mild deception. "Look, there's something I've got to tell you. Can we sit somewhere?"

"This way." She turned on her heel and marched toward what must be her office, a cubicle behind the checkout desk. She sat behind the desk and gestured toward a chair opposite. "Why are you really here?" she asked.

"I'm sorry I, uh, misled you about why I was here. If you remember me, you know my parents did in fact live here, and they moved to Florida a few years ago. I'm here because the town council invited me to talk with them."

"That Barton place, right?"

I should have realized that she would know what was going on, even if it wasn't public knowledge. "Yes, at least in part. You live here, and you must know a lot of people, including the council members, or maybe their kids. So you must have a pretty good idea of the financial state of the town."

"In a word, lousy. So?" She wasn't giving an inch, and I'd have to fight for her trust.

"I was told that the town bought the Barton property with

its last dime, more or less. With voter approval, as you must know, although I'm pretty sure most of the voters here haven't pored over the town budget. The council had high hopes that it could be turned into a moneymaker of some sort, a high-end hotel or maybe a conference center."

"Why'd they think of you?"

"In no particular order, I'm from here, I have a degree in the hospitality industry, and I've been managing a boutique hotel in Baltimore for the past five-plus years." Had she thawed a degree or two? I wasn't sure. I plunged ahead. "Lisbeth Scott mentioned this to the council, so they called me in as a kind of hired gun, or a fixer. To see if their idea made sense, and if it did, did the numbers work. The first I heard of any of this was last week, so I told them I needed to do some research, get a feel for the place, particularly the Barton house, before I could begin to give them an opinion."

"Fair enough," Audrey said. "And?"

"I went home for the night, and by the next day Cordelia was dead."

"You have any idea *why* she died?" Audrey's expression remained carefully neutral.

"You mean, who killed her?"

"That too."

I considered how to phrase my response to avoid looking like a whiny teenager—again. "In high school—when I still lived here—she made a lot of people's lives unpleasant, including mine. If she continued that sort of behavior as an adult, I'd guess she had a lot of enemies here by now. I can't begin to guess how many were angry enough to kill her. I'd like to believe that her plans for the Barton house were the last straw for someone—they didn't want Cordy to trash the place and then get a job out of it. One that she probably believed would let her look down her nose at the rest of the town."

Audrey nodded once. "So you think it was someone who loves this town and its history *and* who hated Cordelia."

"Something like that. Do you disagree?"

"Not necessarily. Although there might have been better ways to remove her from the project than killing her. Have you met Josh Wainwright yet?"

"I have. He must know the house well by now."

"He will have told you he's an academic historian but his main interest is not period architecture. He's interested in Henry Barton's role in the industrialization of the South."

"He mentioned that." Which was one thing I really needed to explore, and for that I needed Audrey's help. "Has he used your resources here at the library?"

"He has. He's told me that we have a stronger collection in some ways than even Johns Hopkins," she said proudly. "I'm not sure what kind of research you may have done in the past. Many people labor under the misconception that everything has been digitized and uploaded for computer access. But for small towns and local history, the library has custody of most of the documents. Or maybe a historical society, if there is one—which there isn't here. Where do your interests lie? Whether the building can be converted to a hotel, and how many rooms and baths you can squeeze in?"

She certainly was slow to warm up. "Audrey, I hope I'm not as crass as that. And there are plenty of people the council could hire who could move walls around and update the plumbing and make it perfectly respectable. The problem is, people would have no reason to come here, or at least not in large numbers, just because there's a quaint hotel here. It's not enough of a draw. And I would have told the council that. But after I had walked around the town a bit, I started thinking about what I saw, and I think I've come up with a different approach with a bigger scope."

Was that a flicker of real interest I saw in her eyes? "And that would be?"

Here goes nothing. "What if we make the Barton estate the centerpiece of a larger ensemble? From what I've seen on my walks, the changes made to the town since 1900 are largely superficial. We could make it look authentically Victorian quickly and without spending a lot of money. But what I would envision would be dignified and historically correct, not tacky and commercial. Think of places like Old Sturbridge Village or Plimoth Plantation in Massachusetts, Williamsburg in Virginia."

Audrey nodded again, unsmiling. "All of those required a lot of time and money to create that deceptively simple appearance."

"I know, but I was only suggesting them as models, and all of those are substantially larger. And those sites had to adhere to specific historic events. If we could take Asheboro back to an ordinary town, serving ordinary people, we wouldn't face some of those constraints. It would be informative but not oppressively so. Yes, we'll need ordinary modern businesses for local residents, but they're mostly concentrated outside the town center. And we'd need to get the people who have shops and businesses in the heart of town to participate as a group—it has to be consistent throughout. What do you think?"

Audrey didn't answer immediately but gave it some thought. I kept my mouth shut, waiting. Her first comment surprised me. "I notice you said 'we' throughout. Do you see yourself as an ongoing party in this—well, I suppose one could call it a reverse-development? Or would you drop a glossy plan on the council members' laps and wave farewell?"

A surprisingly good question. "To be honest, I haven't thought that far ahead. There are no guarantees that I can convince the council that it's a good idea, and I certainly haven't had time to draw up plans and cost out the improvements and talk to all the people who would be directly affected. I'm just throwing the idea out there."

"You didn't exactly answer my question. It's your vision. Would you stay on and be part of it?"

"I . . . think I might." *Wow, where had that come from?* But I realized that I was more excited about the pie-in-the-sky plans I had thrown together in my mind than I had been about much of anything for a long time. It was a challenge. It could be fun. Hard work, of course, but I was confident I could do it. Not alone, of course—there would be a need for people with a wide range of expertise, in fundraising, finance, history, authentic restoration, and more. And they'd have to agree to work for a pittance, or maybe pro bono.

Audrey was still watching me, but I thought I detected a faint smile. "If you think I'm crazy," I said, "now's the time to tell me, before I get in too deep. You know this town: could it work?"

"I don't really know, Kate. But we need something here to jump-start us. We've lost too many good people, who had to leave for purely practical reasons like a job. New people are not replacing them, and why should they? We don't have a lot to offer. Trying to return Asheboro to its Victorian state wouldn't necessarily be easy, but it could make a significant difference. So, if this goes forward, I'd like to help."

I felt a surge of triumph: I'd won her over. "Thank you! You're the one who's sitting on all the history here, and I'd need you. But we're still a long way from that. I have to sell the council on the idea, if I think it's a viable project, and for that I need at least a rough estimate of costs and a mock-up of how it could look. Things like that."

"When would you want this to happen?"

"I think we could open the Barton house by September. The rest, maybe by next summer." There, I'd said it. It sounded insane. "Kind of a phased opening. But I want to catch the fall season this year. Sort of a taste of things to come."

Audrey almost laughed. "Maybe you're crazier than I thought."

"Will you still help?"

"With the planning phase, at least. After that, let's wait and see. And the town won't blow away before next spring."

"Fair enough. So, did you find anything helpful for me to look at, now that you've heard the whole story?"

"Well, I might need to rethink a few things, but I've set out sort of a buffet for you—old town directories, a few copies of the newspaper, some local histories actually written by local people. Will those help?"

"Definitely. I need to familiarize myself with what life was like around 1900. Would you have any genealogy stuff? Family histories that never made it to print? Anything on Henry Barton? I suppose it's too much to hope for that he left a detailed journal."

"It certainly is. By all accounts he was a good man, but not particularly literate."

"You've been in the house?"

"Yes, I was given a tour some time ago. I was concerned

that if there were still books on the shelves, that they would be vulnerable to damage by mold or damp. I was pleased to see they were surviving well. The caretakers hired over the years have done an excellent job of stabilizing the place, which was their mandate."

"Do *you* know what Henry made in the factory?"

"I can't say that I do. I was always a bit timid when I was younger, but I knew people who sneaked in to see if there was anything in there, and I won't swear that their intentions were entirely honest. But the valuables in the interior had been pretty well cleared out, except for the furniture and fixtures, or maybe what they found was too big to carry away in a pocket. The factory was certainly well built, or else it would be a heap of rubble by now. I suppose we should count it as a blessing that no eager developer decided to take on the property. But probably it wouldn't have been worth it."

"I'm sure I can find something constructive to do with it, as part of the whole. Do you know who has the keys to the factory building?"

"I'd assume the town council, or the town's solicitor, or the bank manager. You can probably track down to whom Henry left the factory—I don't know if it was linked to the house. That you would find among the county or state documents rather than here."

"I'll check out the property records." I looked through the glass at the top of the office door to see a few hardy souls clustering at the front door. "It looks like you have customers, Audrey. I'll start going through the documents you've assembled and you can go on about your business. And I really do appreciate your help."

"That's what I'm here for, Kate," Audrey said primly, and escorted me out of the office.

I made straight for the Local History Room at the back of the building, where a stack of materials was waiting for me.

15

Three hours later I had barely made a dent in the stack of materials that Audrey had collected for me. The fact that most Victorians used extremely small fonts for anything printed (I had often wondered how anyone in those days could hope to read anything at all) didn't help, and the handwriting varied widely in those few documents that were not printed. This was not going to be a quick survey. I could tell myself that I didn't need to read everything—only enough to get a sense of the character of the era on this first pass. But I couldn't wade through the research forever; the town council wanted to hear from me sooner rather than later. I needed to know myself just what I was thinking. Was this project going to consume the next six months of my life, or should I let the town down gently, pack up my bags, and go find another long-term job? I was still on the fence but I could certainly spare a few more days.

I stood up and stretched, and realized I was hungry. There was next to nothing to eat back at Cordy's place, so I needed to do some basic food shopping, even if it was for only a short time. That meant going to the supermarket, which was too far to walk. I'd have to walk back to the B&B, retrieve my car, and go to the market. If I was lucky I could pick up a sandwich or something there, and then maybe head out to the Barton place to—what? Commune with the dead? I hadn't seen the basement yet and barely glanced at the attic, although they would most likely never become public spaces, no matter what happened with the house. But I liked to be thorough. And if I saw evidence of a crumbling foundation and six inches of standing water in the basement, that would add a lot of zeroes to the cost estimate. Ditto the attic: if I could see birds flying between the roof shingles, that cash register would go *ka-ching* a few more times. Not that I doubted that the caretakers had done their job—but I had to see for myself.

So, plan: walk to B&B, get car, find food, go to Barton house. Done. If I could find keys to the place. Which Josh should have, but where would I find him? Or Arthur at the bank. I should have asked somebody to give me a set, just for the week.

That simple plan worked for about five minutes. I rounded the corner from Main Street to the B&B and saw a state police car parked in front. Detective Reynolds was standing in front of the building. What now?

"Can I help you with something?" I asked when I was close enough to be heard.

The detective turned in my direction, and after a few moments he recognized me. "Ms. Hamilton? What are you doing here?"

"I'm staying here for a few days, with the owner's permission. What are *you* doing here?"

"I thought this place belonged to Cordelia Walker. I am

informed that the police did not feel it necessary to search this place for any evidence of the possible killer, so I am remedying that. How can you be staying here?"

"The building is owned by Cordy's ex-husband, Ryan Hoffman, and he said I could use it while I'm here. He told me the police hadn't even asked to look at it, and there was no crime scene tape. You may certainly look all you like, if my permission counts."

"Now that you've tramped through it. What parts of the building have you visited?"

"Most of it. I'm staying in the big bedroom in the front, but I checked out the other rooms—women staying alone in an unfamiliar place do that, you know. I've also used the kitchen, and I'm sure you'll see the evidence of that." Since I hadn't bothered to wash the dishes before I dashed off to the library.

"Did Mr. Hoffman accompany you here?"

"Yes. He showed me around the place, plus how to manage the alarm panels at the doors, and gave me the keys. Why are you asking?"

"Just trying to ascertain who has been in the building since the murder."

"Are you looking for anything in particular?"

Detective Reynolds appeared to consider his options. He wasn't under any obligation to tell me anything, but he had asked for my help, after all. He decided to speak. "We were curious about Mrs. Hoffman's financial situation. Also any information she might have left about her preliminary negotiations with potential investors."

"She used the library on the first floor as her home office. But Ryan told me he took whatever legal or business documents he found, since no one had told him he shouldn't. He said he'd turned copies of them over to your people." Did I need to mention the wine?

As I watched his face, I wondered if members of his staff were going to get a lecture about investigation procedures and coordination. Still, it was unlikely that there would be another murder here any time soon, so Detective Reynolds might just decide to save his energy. "When you first entered that room, did it appear that anything had been disturbed?"

"It seemed neat enough to me, but I don't know how Cordy usually kept it. And Ryan had already been there. If someone was looking for something, he or she tidied up well."

"Did you find anything of interest?"

"No. I didn't even see a computer or laptop. Cordy must have had one, to keep track of reservations, do accounting, that kind of thing. Ryan might have taken that away as well— I haven't asked him. Have you met him by now?"

"Yes, briefly. He has an alibi for the time of the murder, but from what little conversation we had, I got the impression that Cordelia Walker was a thorn in his side."

"He as much as said so to me too. So what is it you want from here?"

"Nothing specific. Just following through."

"Will you be taking fingerprints? Because my friend Lisbeth Scott was here with me last evening. We opened a bottle of wine. There's a secret compartment for wine in that wall there." I waved vaguely toward the parlor. "Good stuff, too. And probably expensive."

"You're suggesting that Cordelia was a drinker?"

"No, not necessarily. But the stuff was well hidden, where guests were unlikely to find it. And if she was hard up for money, what I saw seems a bit above her bracket. A gift, maybe? Ryan said I was welcome to drink what I found."

Detective Reynolds's mouth twitched.

"Still no idea who killed the woman?" I asked, mainly to divert his attention from the wine.

"Given the height, direction, and depth of the fatal blow, I think it's safe to say it wasn't a child. Or a short person."

"What if she was sitting down?" I pressed.

"On the front step of the building?"

"Maybe she was rummaging through her purse trying to find the keys." I sighed. "All right, maybe if it was a big purse with a dark interior and a lot of stuff in it. And if she wasn't in a hurry. What do your crime scene analysts say? Was she sitting down? Were there microscopic flecks of granite or marble on her butt?"

Detective Reynolds gave me an almost-smile. "You do ask the oddest questions. As she was found, she did not topple over from a sitting position. She fell face forward, with her head away from the house. As you well know."

"So somebody sneaked up behind her from inside the house?"

"So it would appear. Do you happen to have a convenient list of who had access to the building?"

"What if it was someone who accompanied her to the building? Apart from that, I'd guess that at least one council member would have keys and could get in at will." I paused to think. "Tell me this: why a rock? That's a pretty unsophisticated weapon. If someone had gone to the house with the intention of killing her, wouldn't they have brought their own weapon, rather than picking up something lying in front of the house? Did you find any footprints?"

The detective ignored my first question. "You've seen the approach. There's a brick pathway leading from the drive in front. It does not take footprints. You know, you seem to be enjoying this."

"I am, I guess." Was it wrong of me to feel that way? Especially because the detective knew I'd been the one to find the body. "Nobody seems to miss her."

"A rather harsh judgment," he commented.

"You didn't know the woman. So now what? Do I need to let your team alone while they hunt for clues? Do I have to point out which items are mine? What I've touched? I can give you fingerprints if you need them for comparison."

"If you have some errands to run, we shouldn't take long, and you can come back after we're done."

"Right now I need lunch. Do you eat, Detective? Can I get you something? Because there's not much in the house, whether or not it's evidence."

"Maybe another time. You go ahead. We should be out of here by three at the latest."

"Fine."

I left. Reynolds didn't want to share, or maybe he had nothing to share. I had no idea what he hoped to find in the house. He might do better to talk to Ryan, who'd been through the place before I had. But I wasn't about to tell a police detective how to do his job.

So, change in plan: lunch, then Barton house, then grocery shopping. I decided I could handle fast food and pointed the car toward the road leading out of town, where I found a Wendy's. I wasn't desperate enough to use the drive-through window, so I went inside, ordered something resembling a hamburger, and settled myself at a table. I consumed the whole mess in ten minutes and took to the road again—and remembered the gate at the Barton house would still be locked. Clearly I had too much on my mind.

I pulled over and called Josh's cell phone, and luckily he answered. "Where are you?" I asked.

"Working. At my place. Why?"

"I want to get into the house, and I can't even get through the gate. Oh, have the state police been by?"

"Why are you asking?"

"Because they showed up at the B&B a little while ago. Apparently they dismissed the B&B a bit too quickly, and now they're hunting for something. They didn't share what."

"Well, if they come out here, I'll let them in. Although they've already checked out this place."

"Maybe they have a piece of information that points in a new direction."

"Or maybe they're getting desperate. Whatever. Come on over—I'll meet you at the front gate."

I was there in five minutes. When he saw me he unlocked the gate and let me pull my car in, then locked it behind me again. "Isn't that kind of like locking the door after the horse has left the barn?"

"Maybe. But I'm responsible for this place, and I'd rather be safe than sorry. What is it you're looking for today?"

"I'm still trying to get a feel for the place. You gave me the basic tour the other day, but I haven't seen the basement or most of the attic."

"Why would you want to?"

"Because I like to see everything with my own eyes. Because Henry is still a mystery to me. Maybe there's a gold mine in the basement, or maybe Henry buried twenty bodies down there. Think of what treasures you might be missing! Original documents that nobody's read for a century! And they're all yours."

"All right, I get it. You want to start with the basement or the attic?"

"I think it will take less time to go through the basement, and I don't expect to find much down there. But I want to check. You don't have to come with me."

"And risk you doing serious damage to the boiler? Or yourself?"

I noted that he'd put the boiler ahead of me. "Fine, you can come along."

"All right. Follow me back to the house and we'll park in front."

16

"You aren't exactly dressed for wandering around the basement, you know," Josh said.

"I wasn't planning to dig up the floor. I'll manage. Where's the entrance?"

"There are two—one outside, for big stuff, and one tucked under the main staircase."

"How big is it?"

"It extends under the full house, so it's big. You having second thoughts?"

"No, I'm just trying to wrap my head around it. Furnace?"

"Coal originally, then the bank replaced it with an oil furnace awhile ago."

"How was the heat distributed?"

"Passively. Grates in the floor on the first floor, and then the heat was supposed to migrate up to the second floor. Of course, there are small fireplaces in the bedrooms to take the chill off. The maids were supposed to lay those and light them. And dump the thunder mugs. And bring up hot water for the morning wash."

"Well, they had a job, right? And food and a bed? Tell me, O Industrial Historian, was that a better or worse job than the girls had in factories about the same time?"

"Good question. Things were changing fast then. There was definitely a migration to the cities. Look, let's quit stalling and just get down there. I've got a chapter to finish."

"Lead the way."

I followed him through the hallway and to a door set discreetly in the wall beneath the grand staircase. "Is it locked?"

"No. There's nothing down there worth stealing."

"Was there ever?"

"There was a cold cellar for root vegetables and plenty of space for tools. Apart from that, I have no idea why they wanted so much open space down there."

The stairs were old and well worn; they dipped in the middle, the wood worn away by years of the hired help trudging up and down.

We reached the bottom of the stairs. I stopped and turned around slowly. Fieldstone foundation, between four and five feet high. Brick above that—could use some repointing. The floor joists—good heavens, they had to measure at least ten inches by three inches, something nobody ever saw anymore—were low, and I could barely stand upright. The furnace was a hulking behemoth, sprouting ducts in all directions. The ducts disappeared into the flooring above.

I was beginning to think that if I spent enough time looking—really looking—at how things had been put together back when the house had been built, I would come to understand how the people had lived in the house, both upstairs and downstairs. There was a logic to it that was no longer obvious now, but it made sense if you stopped to think about it. And took your time.

There was something odd about the space, the more I studied it. No, not the space, but the perimeter, the footings for the building. "Hey, Josh?"

He'd been pottering around at the far end of the room, poking at piles of what appeared to be junk that had been abandoned in the corners. "What is it?"

"There was already a house here before Henry built this place."

"What? Why do you think that?"

"Come back and stand where I'm standing." He came up beside me and looked quizzically at me. "See the changes in the stonework around the bottom? Not the brickwork—that's consistent. But the stones and the way they're set varies, and there's a pattern to it."

He still didn't look convinced. "Which is?"

"I'm going to guess that there was a smaller house here before. Maybe a farmhouse. Henry was thrifty and reused as much of the foundation as he could. He had to use bigger stones for the new parts because he was building a bigger building. Do you see it?"

"Damn, I think I do. You're saying you think maybe Henry bought a simple farmhouse when he first settled here, and when he made his money, he built over and around it?"

"It's possible, isn't it?"

"I guess so. I haven't looked at property records."

"Audrey said I should check out the country records, which include deeds," I said slowly. "We can find out who lived here before Henry, and when Henry bought the place. Figuring out exactly when he started the bigger building will be more guesswork—I don't know when they started issuing building permits locally, but we can go by materials and styles, which I'm guessing date to around 1880. Maybe even newspaper articles—there might be some society news there, if they ever entertained. I wish I knew something about his wife. I don't suppose you've looked up anything about her?"

"No, not really," Josh said. "She's kind of a shadowy figure in all of this, but she's not exactly relevant to what I'm looking at, unless she brought one heck of a big dowry with her. You want to take Mary on, along with Henry's genealogy?"

"I plan to—I already alerted Audrey. I'm hoping there may be a story in it. You know, war veteran settles here, makes good, builds his dream house for his lovely bride. His life is touched with tragedy when the children they both so wanted never happened, so he built an orphans' home or something. You get my drift."

"Yeah, sounds like something out of a bad romance novel."

"Romance sells. If we want to attract people, we have to humanize this place. Was the mystery wife an invalid? A madwoman he kept in the attic? Did she pick out all the furnishings and decorate the place, or did he do it to please her, out of love? Things like this matter."

I glanced at Josh to see if he was still laughing at me, but he looked oddly curious. "You're really into this," he said, not unkindly.

"Yes, I guess I am. It's like creating, or re-creating, other lives, other times. Don't you find yourself doing something like that, when you talk about the changes that the factories brought in the nineteenth century? How much people's lives

changed? How the whole demographic of the country shifted?
And what was the impact on the national psychology? The
country was redefining itself under everybody's eyes."

"I guess I hadn't looked at it like that," he said in a sub-
dued tone. "I'm a person who likes facts, order. My research
is on how we became an industrialized nation after the war.
But I will concede that that misses a lot of the human element."

I smiled. "Am I actually converting you to my point of
view? Look, here's an example where our viewpoints overlap.
Look at the height of the ceilings in this place, the large single-
pane windows. How incredibly wasteful a place like this was
to heat! But there was what must have seemed like endless fuel
available, so nobody worried. Until the fuel got harder to find,
and technology wasn't keeping up, and it got more and more
expensive. And then they started putting up storm windows
and making furnaces more efficient. Not to mention lowering
the ceilings. You could say it was a period of conspicuous consumption, when the rich flaunted their riches, and then they
couldn't do it anymore."

"So now you're seeing this place as a model of conspicuous consumption? Who's your target audience?"

"Now you're making fun of me. But I'm trying to tell you
what I mean about weaving a story around the place. There's
the possible internal story—two people who loved each other,
who faced their own troubles together—Henry's war experi-
ences, their childlessness. Then there's the external story—the
rise of the factories and the changes that came with them.
Did Henry see what was happening, and did it make him sad
or proud? He must have taken pride in this place, but did that
make him feel guilty, that he had so much more than most

people? And all his money couldn't bring his wife back, and the children that never happened. I wonder if he had a dog . . ."

Okay, I had wandered off on a tangent, but I was really beginning to feel for poor Henry. Then Josh began to laugh. "You are really something else."

"You're laughing at me," I said stiffly. I refrained from hitting him.

"Yes, but in a good way. You know, you're beginning to convince me that this is all possible. You'll probably wow the town council."

"Thank you—I think. Now all I have to do is find the money to make it happen."

"Seen enough of the basement?" he asked.

"For now, I guess. I wonder if Henry ever even spent time down here, or just sent the servants down to see to things like stoking the furnace. I wish there was a way to get to know the man!"

"Well, unless you're into spiritualism, you'll have to settle for genealogy and local histories. It sounds to me like you'd better do a quick survey of all the things you mentioned, so you can pitch it to the town. You can get into the in-depth stuff once they're on board."

I felt a bit deflated, but I knew he was right. I had to focus on the high points for now. "But can we look at the attic? Just a quick pass through it?"

"If you'll let me set a time limit and allow me to drag you away when time's up."

"Oh, all right. It'll be dark soon enough anyway."

We'd reached the main hallway when there was a pounding on the front door. I looked at Josh, and he shrugged. "I'm not expecting anyone."

Once again I realized how isolated the place was, and I was glad that Josh was there. "Better go see who it is." I made no move to go to the door, so Josh had to. Hey, it was part of his job, wasn't it? He pulled the door open to reveal . . . Ryan? "Ryan, what the heck are you doing here?" I demanded.

"Not my idea," he said, sounding surly. "A state police detective called and told me to meet him here."

"How'd you get through the gate?" Josh asked sternly.

"Cordy's keys." He held up a loaded key ring.

"Hold on," I interrupted. "Do you two know each other?"

"No," Josh answered first. "But apparently you do. You want to fill me in, Kate?"

Ryan wasn't going to stand for that. "I'm Ryan Hoffman, Cordelia's ex-husband. I found her keys at the B&B she was running in town. I suppose I should return them to you?"

"Yes. I'm the official resident caretaker, although my day job is history professor. I'm on sabbatical. Joshua Wainwright."

The guys shook hands more or less politely. I wondered why the state police wanted to talk to Ryan now, and why here. "Josh, you said the police didn't call you today."

"Uh, no, but my cell is out in my apartment out back, so I wouldn't have heard it. They know about this watchman arrangement, and they already interviewed me, but I don't know if I'm supposed to be here to talk to them now."

"Well, they definitely don't know that I'm here." I did hope they'd let me stay, in any case. "Ryan, did they say why they wanted to meet you here?"

He shook his head. "Just suggested that I be here. I have to assume it had something to do with Cordelia and her connection to the place." He turned to Josh. "I know Kate here had a long history with Cordelia, but how about you, Josh?"

"I think I first met her when I talked to the town council about taking this temporary position a few months back. Then she started dropping in, and sometimes she brought other people. She didn't bother to introduce me to them, but I assumed they were potential buyers or investors."

I wondered briefly if Josh had been put off by Cordy treating him like the hired help. That must have been the period when Cordy was trying to pressure the council into doing what she wanted. Maybe talking down to the caretaker was supposed to demonstrate her power? "Did any of them come more than once?" I asked.

"I can't tell you. I wasn't always here. And she had the keys to get in."

Simultaneously we heard the sound of another car approaching by the long front driveway. "Damn. Did you lock the gate behind you, Ryan?"

"I thought I did."

Josh sighed. "Well, either you messed up, or there may be more copies of the keys out there. If it's the police arriving now, I wonder where they got their set, if you have Cordy's set?"

"And I have Lisbeth's set," I volunteered. "Which she got from the bank manager."

"So half the town could have come and gone here whenever they wanted. That's going to make this investigation even more fun," Josh said, sounding frustrated. "I should have demanded a list from the beginning."

The car stopped, a door slammed, and after a strong knock, Josh opened the door to Detective Reynolds. He scanned the group, noting my presence with a raised eyebrow, and nodding to the two men, whom apparently he'd already met.

"Mr. Hoffman, thank you for agreeing to meet with me. Mr. Wainwright, I'm glad I found you here, and you're welcome to join in the conversation. Ms. Hamilton, what are you doing here?"

"I came to check out the parts of the house I hadn't seen before. For this possible hush-hush town project that I've told all three of you about. We just came up from the basement, and we haven't gotten to the attic yet."

"I see. Is there someplace we can all sit?"

"The dining room," Josh said, and led the way, followed by Ryan, the detective, and me.

17

We made an odd group, seated around the table. I wasn't sure who was supposed to be in charge, beyond the fact that I certainly wasn't—I was merely an observer. Detective Reynolds seemed unperturbed by any undercurrents among us, and he was the one who had asked to meet with Ryan—and ended up with two extras. Ryan had assumed his lawyer demeanor and looked solemn. Josh looked wary and out of his depth. Me, I tried to look invisible.

The detective took his time before speaking, and I wondered if the delay was to rattle us. He couldn't rattle me because I didn't know anything so I couldn't possibly be hiding anything. Finally Detective Reynolds cleared his throat. "You may be wondering why I asked Mr. Hoffman to meet me here."

Well, duh, I thought. Josh didn't comment.

"The investigation of Cordelia's murder is under the jurisdiction of the state police. I was somewhat disappointed by the degree of thoroughness in the original inspection, so I am reviewing whatever has been collected to date. I know

Mr. Hoffman here was formerly married to the victim and is the owner of the physical property where she was operating a small business. This suggests an ongoing connection between them."

"But . . . wait . . . I didn't—" Ryan sputtered.

The detective held up a hand. "I'm not accusing you of anything. I'm only pointing out that certain aspects were not considered in the first round of investigation. And I think we—I'm speaking for the police—need to reexamine this Barton property more closely. It would appear that Cordelia had a strong interest in this place, for her own reasons. It was here that she was killed. One should consider whether there is a connection between those two facts," the detective said. "Now, Mr. Wainwright, based on phone records, it appears that you and Cordelia exchanged quite a few phone calls. Business or pleasure?"

Josh looked at Detective Reynolds for a moment, then burst out laughing. "Are you seriously asking if Cordelia and I were involved personally?"

"Yes, that's exactly what I'm asking. Were you?"

"Most definitely not. I could give you reasons why, but if I say something negative about the woman you could twist it to make it look like I had a reason to kill her."

"I've confirmed your alibi, Mr. Wainwright, and I'm not questioning it. You can speak freely." Detective Reynolds glanced briefly at Ryan. "I hope that if you take offense at anything Mr. Wainwright might say about your former wife, you'll restrain yourself from commenting."

Ryan looked incredulously at the detective then he also laughed. "I doubt he can say anything I haven't already thought about her. We'd been apart longer than we'd been together. Fire away, Josh."

"All right," Josh said. "I told you people when you first interviewed me, but I'll say it again. Since I'm not part of the town of Asheboro, obviously I don't know the whole backstory, but I understand that the town was looking into making this house into a small elegant hotel. Cordy saw an opportunity to move up the food chain and made a bid to run it. The idea was greeted with what might be called muted enthusiasm. And there things sat for a while. Then, when things weren't moving fast enough to please her, she called in a backup team, some corporate group or a bunch of rich investors, and told them to put together a proposal for use of the place, which they did. The town council hated it. And talks kind of stalled. Keep in mind that this is mostly hearsay and gossip that I've picked up since I've been looking out for this place."

I knew that Detective Reynolds had heard the same story from me, but he didn't mention that. I kept silent—again.

"And where did you enter this equation, Mr. Wainwright?" the detective asked.

"I'd already signed on as caretaker before all this came up. As I said, I'm an outsider, and I won't be around long. In any case, Cordelia made a play for me—kind of threw herself at me. And she expected me to melt. I didn't."

"Was this a one-time effort or an extended campaign?" I asked. Detective Reynolds sent me a warning look.

"Somewhere in-between," Josh answered. "She didn't give up easily, and she seemed convinced that her feminine wiles would wear me down eventually. But for all I know she could have been trying to seduce half the town. Sorry, Ryan."

And then an idea hit me between the eyes. "You know, Josh, maybe she was making up to you because she knew she might need you."

He turned to me. "Why on earth would she need me? Apart from any, uh, romantic reasons?"

I quickly laid out my reasoning. "She had had access to this place for a while now—she had her own keys. Maybe there's something here that she found, something that she thought might be valuable or useful or something. But she couldn't just pull it out and say, 'Gee whiz, look what I found!' I think she'd have to have someone with more expertise vet it, to add credibility. Like a respected history professor."

"And that would be me?" Josh said. "Well, even if she did find something, she didn't bring it to me. And see what you've done? Now you're going to have the police thinking something absurd, like she found something incredibly rare and desirable, and when she showed it to me I went crazy with lust for it—not for her, mind you—and killed her to get my hands on it." He turned back to Detective Reynolds. "Do you like that scenario, detective?"

Brady Reynolds had a half smile on his face. "Well, it's an angle I hadn't considered. Would she be selling it for personal gain, or did she want to use it to promote this place? Or maybe we should be looking at it from the other side. Maybe she planted something important here and was planning to pretend to find it, for the same end. And she'd still need you for your stamp of approval."

"That won't fly if she had to buy something appropriate to do it," Ryan interrupted. "She had no money and no collateral to get any. And I can't recall any terribly valuable heirlooms from her family either. If she was trying to leverage an artifact of some sort, it would have to have come from this building."

"I knew I had come to the right place," Detective Reynolds

said calmly. "You've already given me several useful ideas. Anything else?"

After a pause, I said slowly, "Detective Reynolds, much as I respect the abilities of your police force, can you see your people sifting through this place looking for some historic artifact that might be worth big money? Jewels, silver, all that kind of stuff, fine, but they're already in the bank vault, I understand. But documents or books? I'm not sure what they'd recognize. In any case, assuming this priceless whatever existed, then either nobody's found it, or Cordelia or someone with a key did find it, or Cordelia let someone else in, and they found it and then he killed her to keep it for himself."

The detective steepled his hands. "Why do I think there's a suggestion coming?"

"Because you're a smart detective," I answered promptly. "Let Josh and me do the looking—deputize us or authorize us or whatever. You know we both have alibis for the murder. Josh would most likely recognize this valuable thing, whatever it is. Or at least he would know who to call to verify it."

"And why do you need to be there?"

"Two sets of eyes are better than one? No, seriously: I'm being selfish. I would love to find something of value, whether it's monetary or historic or sentimental, so I can use it to promote this place. It's not for me. In a sense it's for the town. Look, if you don't trust either of us, assign one of your men to keep an eye on us. Film the whole process. Whatever it takes."

"Interesting proposal. You have any idea what you're looking for?"

"Not a clue," I admitted cheerfully. "George Washington's

cookie recipes. Nude pictures of Ulysses S. Grant in bed with a lady of the evening. Who knows?"

Detective Reynolds turned back to Josh. "Mr. Wainwright, what do you think of this scheme?"

Josh was looking a little shell-shocked. "I think it has possibilities. To tell the truth, Cordelia was in and out quite a bit—more than her responsibility to the town might warrant, so it could well have been for other reasons. I didn't follow her around like a puppy dog to see where she went or what she looked at—that wasn't part of my job description. I've been through the house, of course, because that's what I agreed to do, but haven't examined the attic in any detail, because it's cold and dark up there—I was waiting for spring. So I can't tell you whether or not Cordelia was up there, once or many times. I will be happy to explore the contents of the attic now, with your permission."

The detective sighed. "As far as I can tell, it can't hurt, although recruiting civilians is somewhat unorthodox. We certainly know she wasn't killed up there. Mr. Hoffman, did your ex-wife have any expertise in antiques or fine art or old documents?"

Ryan shook his head. "Only in her dreams. She never had any formal training in anything like that, and her taste was conventional at best. She wasn't an antiques person. In fact, she had a particular dislike of all things Victorian, and she was really annoyed that she couldn't change the décor of the bed and breakfast. Unfortunately for her, tourists like Victorian interiors."

"Detective," I said tentatively, "she's the one who ended up dead, which means somebody killed her. But if our nice theory about some great find is true, it could that she had a partner, who seized whatever it was she or they had found and took it away. Who wanted all the proceeds or the glory for himself? They could have arranged to meet here, so there might be no record of a phone call at the right time. And then he—or she—double-crossed her. Since none of us knows what we're looking for, that person could easily dispose of it somewhere else. Isn't that explanation possible?"

This whole scene was absurd. Here we were, four outsiders, trying to figure out who might have been the killer, in a town none of us knew very well in the present. But, I realized, it might not have been someone from Asheboro. It could have been an art expert from somewhere else, whom she'd called in, and nobody would have known him. Or her. That might make sense, since Asheboro seemed a little short on art experts, but there were some major cities not far away that were overflowing with them.

We could speculate all day, but to me it made more sense to look around more closely to see if there were any signs of a search. "So, do we have permission to look around?"

The detective sighed. "I don't see why not. It could be said to fall under Mr. Wainwright's purview as the official caretaker, so implicitly you also have the town's permission. Mr. Wainwright?"

"Works for me," Josh said promptly. "As I said, I've been planning to dig around in the attic anyway, to see if there are any historic documents, and now I have a great excuse. Since I haven't seen any signs that anything large has been removed from the house during my tenure here, I'm going to assume that whatever it is, it's smaller than a breadbox. Cordelia was not a particularly sturdy woman, although she could have had a stronger partner. In my estimation, the attic is the best place to start. I'll try to get some floodlights so we can see to work. Are you okay with all that, Kate?"

"Sure," I agreed. "But can we start tomorrow? This sounds like a grubby-clothes job."

"No problem."

Detective Reynolds cleared his throat. "In my official capacity, I need to tell you not to mention what you're planning to anyone in town. There are altogether too many people who we haven't been able to eliminate from our list of suspects."

"Got it," I said. Josh nodded in agreement, as did Ryan. I had to wonder what single item, or collection of items, would be worth killing for, and if Cordy's killer was involved somehow, whether he—or she—might come back to finish the search, as long as our plans remained secret.

The meeting seemed to be over. Everyone stood up. "Josh," I said, "you want me to meet you here in the morning? Say, nine o'clock?"

"Fine," he said.

"Why don't you and I have dinner together tonight, Kate?" Ryan volunteered. "We still have a lot of catching up to do. Is there any place around here that does decent takeout? Because it's hard to talk freely in a restaurant, and I don't expect you to cook at the B&B."

"I'm sure we can find something," I said absently. "Detective, are we free to go now?"

"Yes, you are. Please keep me apprised of anything you find. And if you find anything, keep it safe."

"Of course. And thank you for letting us help." I had a feeling he was bending more than one rule in doing it.

18

The detective left first, then Josh said, "I have to lock up so I'm going to ask you to clear out." Ryan and I followed Josh meekly out the front door. He said goodbye, leaving the two of us standing awkwardly on the front stoop.

"So, dinner?" Ryan asked.

"Sure. Pizza all right? I don't think we've got a lot to choose from in town."

"It's not the same pizza place we used to hang out at, is it?"

"Oh, no. But they made terrible pizza, at least in hindsight. This one couldn't be worse. Did I mention that Lisbeth and I found Cordy's secret wine trove?"

"You did not. Anything good?"

"I'm no expert, but there were bottles in there that I've drooled over but could never bring myself to actually splurge for."

"Interesting. Cordy was never really a connoisseur. I wonder if she had them to impress someone? Her corporate allies? Or her mystery partner?"

"Possibly. The cache was well hidden, not where anyone would just stumble over it and snag a bottle. Can we drink one? It might do wonders for bad pizza."

"I'm executor of her estate, so I officially approve your request for one bottle of wine. Although if it's really good stuff, I should probably make a note for the inventory, at least for inheritance tax purposes."

"Whatever. Pickup or delivery?"

"What? Oh, does this pizza place deliver?"

"I have no idea. Remember, I haven't been around much for more than fifteen years, until this week. Let's go to the B&B and call. If they do deliver, I'll show you where to find the wine."

"Sounds like a plan," Ryan agreed amiably. "I'll meet you there, since we've got the two cars."

"Great."

He waited for me to locate my car keys then we made our way to the front gate and headed back to the center of Asheboro. As I drove, I reviewed the impromptu plan I had come up with at the Barton house. That there might be something of value in the house somewhere seemed perfectly plausible to me, although I had no idea what it could be. Judging by the décor of the house, Henry Barton had plenty of money to spend, at least after 1880 or so, and he had chosen the best of the best at the time. Although, I amended, what I'd seen of the foundation in the basement suggested that the place had begun as a much simpler house when he bought it, which in turn suggested that when Henry had become wealthy, he had expanded it to reflect his new status. I'd have to check property records. And any society news in the local papers, I added to myself. Or maybe finding a site for his factory had dictated where he would settle. I made another mental note to see what history there was about the factory. I really needed another session at the library. Maybe Audrey could point me in the right direction.

I parked behind the B&B. Ryan's car was already there—did he know a shortcut, or was he a faster driver than I was? Probably the latter—I was still reacquainting myself with the area so I took it slowly. He still had a key so he had let himself in, and he was already on the phone ordering something or other. I really didn't care what we ate, although I had to make a mental note to myself: if this pipe-dream of a town makeover actually happened, we'd need to attract at least a couple of better places to eat.

I tossed my jacket on the coat rack in the hall. Cordy must have hated the thing, because it was about as Victorian as it could get: large mirror, marble-topped seat, spaces for umbrellas and walking sticks, hooks for hats and coats, and gingerbread everywhere that wasn't already occupied. I loved it. Ryan emerged from the kitchen, slipping his cell phone into a pocket. "Fifteen minutes. So, where's the wine?"

"I'll show you." I led him to the back parlor and knelt by the wainscoting, then showed him how the panel opened. "There you go." I stood up and stepped back.

He knelt and peered at the space. "That's good work—it really is invisible if you don't know it's there. How'd you ever find it?"

"Actually it was Lisbeth and me, working together. Plus persistence. We just assumed she'd hide the good stuff, so we started looking for hiding places."

"Yes, Cordy probably offered a glass of wine to her guests, but I doubt she would have shared something this good. Not that she was into fine wines herself, except maybe for their snob appeal."

"Maybe it was for her partner in crime?" I suggested, as I went into the kitchen to get wineglasses and a corkscrew.

Ryan followed, carrying a bottle. "You buying that theory? That she was working with somebody else, who may have double-crossed her?"

"I don't really know what I think. I hadn't seen Cordy since high school. Everyone in town who knew her has been—how shall I put it?—very careful in referring to her. Like they aren't sure whose side I'm on."

"They're the ones who called you in, right? Are they paying you?"

"It was Lisbeth who drafted me—I think she's the only one who knows what I've been doing for the past few years at the hotel. As for the money, no. They're kind of desperate, and they're hoping I'll come up with a proposal out of the goodness of my heart, or for old times' sake. Or because I have a history with Cordy and they figured I might want a chance to wreak my revenge. Of course, if we come up with a plan for the town that would work, I'll expect them to pay me. But I've barely scratched the surface, and having my chief competitor and old nemesis found dead in the middle of it all, literally and figuratively, isn't making things any easier."

Ryan had opened the wine with a skill that suggested a lot of practice, and he filled two glasses. He handed me one, and picked up the other and raised it. "What shall we toast to?"

"To burying the past and bringing it back to life," I said, after a moment's consideration.

"I like that. Here's to your success."

We clinked glasses and I took a sip. Nice. Velvety on my

tongue, with a hint of . . . oh, who was I kidding? I might not know a lot about wine, but I knew that this one tasted very good. And I should pace myself, especially on an empty stomach.

We sat across from each other at the kitchen table. "So, you lived here in Asheboro when you and Cordy were married?"

"Yes. I had my law degree by then and passed the bar, but I opted to work for a midsize firm outside of Baltimore rather that setting up here in Asheboro."

"You're still there?" I felt a small pang: he had been in the same city as me for years, but he had never looked me up. Water under the bridge.

"Yes. It was the right choice, especially in light of what happened—when Cordy and I split up."

"You know there are a lot of questions I'd like to ask about that, but I have no right to."

"Are you sure about that? Cordy pulled a really nasty trick on you back in high school so you might say I'd be repaying a debt by being honest with you."

"What she did to me—to us—was hard to forgive, and she wouldn't have let me forget it if I tried. Did you know what she was planning back then?" I hadn't had the heart to ask back when it happened.

"No. Honestly. It was cruel, and I wouldn't have gone along with it. I was as surprised as you were."

And as embarrassed? Unlikely. "So knowing what she was capable of, how on earth did you two end up together?"

Ryan studied the ornate ceiling moldings, avoiding my eyes. "Pity? Stupidity? She could be very persuasive, you know. But you didn't see her when she first moved back here. She thought she'd go to college and be the queen bee there, but she figured out pretty fast that she was one of a whole lot of pretty blondes, and some of them were a lot smarter than she was. She was stuck in the middle of the pack, and she didn't like it."

"So she figured she'd come back and reclaim her throne?"

"Maybe. But she was disappointed that it didn't happen. She hadn't realized that there was a whole crop of pretty girls that had come up after she left."

The doorbell rang, and Ryan got up to answer it. He returned a minute later with a pizza box that smelled like heaven. I must have been hungrier than I thought. I got up to fetch paper plates and napkins, and we settled again in our former seats. We both devoted the next minute or two to inhaling pizza. Ryan poured another glass of wine for each of us while we chewed.

After the first piece had disappeared, I picked up the thread of the conversation. "So how'd she get back together with you?"

Ryan sighed. "Looking back, I think she went through the roster of available men in town and she set her sights on me, although I only realized that later."

"And you went along with it?"

"Well, I wasn't seeing anyone else at the time, and she was still pretty and blonde."

"So you proposed eventually?"

"I did, God help me. Uh, it was when she told me she was pregnant."

"Was she?"

"No—it was her final ploy to snag me. Not a good start to a marriage. It didn't get any better. If I had to sum her up, I'd say she was basically an unhappy person. Nothing was ever good enough for her. Nobody recognized how talented and smart she was. She had no friends, once her high school posse had moved on with their lives. And I didn't seem to be able to give her what she wanted or needed."

Ryan's assessment was fair—and kind. It made it a little easier to feel sorry for Cordy, but not much. Had she died because of one of her manipulative games? She would probably have been horrified to know that the murder weapon was a common rock—if she'd been planning the event, she would have chosen something more fitting, like a silver chalice. I smiled at the idiocy of my own thoughts.

"What?" Ryan asked.

"I was trying to imagine Cordy planning her own murder. She would not have liked that rock as a weapon. Very low class."

"I see what you mean." He smiled too, but only briefly. "Kate, have you ever been married?"

I shook my head. "Not even close."

"Was it because of, well, us, and what Cordy did?"

"No, Ryan. I moved on. What you and I had then, well, it was sweet. Puppy love. But we probably would have broken up as soon as we'd graduated anyway. It was the sheer venom of what Cordy did that upset me the most. She really enjoyed making other people suffer. I can see why she would have felt frustrated at college if nobody took her seriously, or even paid attention to her."

"Are you seeing anyone now?"

I cocked my head at him. Why was he asking? "No. Please don't ask if I think you and I should try again. I think 'You and Me: the Rerun' is a bad idea." And if he was thinking I was dessert, he was way off base.

He shrugged. "So, what now?"

"About the murder? Frankly this is not my area of expertise.

I think Josh and I should check the attic to see if there's anything of interest—or if it looks like Cordy or someone else has been rummaging around. If there was something valuable, it could be long gone now, and we'll never know what it was. I suppose as executor you could check Cordy's financial records and see if there are any unexplained deposits."

"You mean, like bribes or payoffs, or maybe the results of the sale of something important? Huh. Worth a try, I guess. She could have been tempted—she was always short of money."

"What about staff at the B&B?" I asked.

"I think I told you, there weren't many. She hated housework, but she knew she had to maintain certain standards for guests, no doubt grumbling all the way. She hired part-timers, short-termers, and I'm sure she loved bossing them around. Your pal Lisbeth would be more likely to know who they were that I would."

"She would have declared their salary as a business expense, wouldn't she?"

"Oh, right. I'll look for her tax returns. Anyway, I doubt it will be a long list. Why do you think it matters?"

"It probably doesn't, but you don't know what people around the house might hear or see or find, and maybe even talk about, so it can't hurt to ask. And after that I'm pretty much out of ideas."

Ryan paused for a moment, then said, "You think you can pull off this Save the Town campaign?"

"I really don't know. There are a lot of 'ifs,' and this murder won't make it any easier."

"I'm sure you'll try your best." Ryan stood up. "Sorry, I'm

getting sleepy, and I've still got a drive ahead of me, back to the hotel. Walk me out?"

"Sure." I followed him to the B&B's front door, unlocked it, and pulled it open. But he wasn't quite ready to leave yet: he reached out and pulled me close and kissed me. I felt a twinge of sadness—no sparks at all. And when I didn't respond—at least, not the way he had hoped—he stepped back and smiled.

"Sorry. I just wanted to be sure. We can be friends, right?"

"Of course. I'll let you know if Josh and I find anything."

"And you can celebrate with the rest of Cordy's Secret Cellar. Good night, Kate."

I watched as he walked down the front walk to his car. Then I shut the door—and double locked it.

I threw out the paper plates Ryan and I had used, rinsed out our wineglasses, and trudged up the stairs, wondering what I was going to wear in the morning to sift through an attic that hadn't been disturbed for more than a century.

19

I hadn't thought to bring along anything to read, and apparently Cordy didn't cater to a literary crowd: I'd noted earlier that the books in the library were mostly light vacation reading. I could have boned up on Civil War history on my laptop, but I figured that would put me to sleep fast. I selected a tattered paperback romance from one of the library shelves, and that knocked me out about fifteen minutes after I'd crawled into bed.

Of course I woke up early, since I'd fallen asleep so early. I had a few hours until I was supposed to meet Josh, and nothing I needed to do. It felt odd, not having to check in with the hotel to make sure everything was running smoothly and no crises had erupted overnight. There were slim pickings for breakfast, but I managed to make coffee and snagged another couple of the rather dry muffins from the freezer and ate them. That took all of fifteen minutes. After I'd finished the muffins, I refilled my coffee mug and wandered around the ground floor of the B&B. I should ask Ryan whether Cordy (using his money) had bought it complete with furnishings, or whether she'd gritted her teeth and furnished the place with Victoriana to please guests.

I had trouble picturing Cordy as the gracious hostess of a small guest house of any sort. What made that kind of place work was someone who would welcome visitors and make sure they had a comfortable and pleasant stay. That meant looking after them—assuring that the room was clean, that supplies were restocked regularly, that there was breakfast, and snacks and coffee and tea were available throughout the day. But it took more than that. Innkeepers had to make guests feel valued. Guests also needed to feel that the manager had gone the extra mile to make sure that they knew the best places to eat locally, where the local monuments were, and how to reach them with a minimum of fuss. Basically it meant putting the needs of others ahead of your own—and I couldn't visualize Cordy doing that. No wonder she'd gone looking for something bigger and better—a setting that featured *her*. I doubted that she would have found it if the Barton house had become a luxury hotel: she'd still have been a glorified servant.

I wandered into her office–slash–library. The room seemed oddly sterile, and somehow I doubted that Cordy had spent much time in it. Lisbeth and I had snooped only until we'd found the wine stash in the parlor, but there could well be other hiding places in this house. This hypothetical valuable mystery item would definitely have to be smaller than a breadbox, if it was concealed in any potential hiding places in the library. If it was here, it had been carefully hidden.

Where would Cordy hide something, if she had found something she thought was important? The desk would be too obvious. There were books on the shelves, but I didn't see Cordy thinking of a book as the best place to hide anything. A safe? Would she have kept a place for visitors' valuables and cash receipts she hadn't had time to take to the bank? Possible. I scanned the perimeter of the room but didn't see anyplace large enough for a safe, old or modern. There was an elegant oriental rug covering most of the floor, so I dismissed the idea that something was hidden under it—Cordy would have protected her manicure rather than drag a dusty old rug around.

But what I did see, in the clear light of morning, was a crack around one of the wainscoting panels that ran along the wall under the bookshelves. The crack was a bit larger than the rest of its mates. It looked a whole lot like the panel that hid the wine cache in the parlor. Could the original owners have built in not one but two hidey-holes? Only one way to find out. I crossed the room and felt gently around the edge of the panel, and in one corner I pressed it and the panel sprang open.

Unlike its counterpart in the other room, this one had no wine rack. What it did have was a single large manila envelope lying on its floor. I sat back on my haunches and thought about it. It was clean, so it hadn't been sitting there for a hundred years. Would there be fingerprints on it? Cordy's or someone else's? If I touched it at all, would I be contaminating evidence?

But of course I was itching to know what was in it. Maybe if I could find a pair of rubber or latex gloves, and something flat and narrow to open it and at least peer inside? My other choices were, option one, to call Detective Reynolds and tell him about it, although it was hard to say that it was a top priority. What were the odds that Cordy had sat down at her desk and scribbled a note saying, "If I am found dead, it will be So-and-So who killed me," and then stuffed it in an envelope and hidden it behind a panel in a place that nobody knew existed? Small. Reynolds would just tell me to leave it where it was and he'd send someone over when he had the time. Option two, I could ask Ryan, since technically it was his house, and Cordy's possessions were now his. But would he drop everything and come racing over? Unlikely. It was altogether possible that it was nothing more than pictures of Cordy's family and a regrettable one of her with glasses and braces, or maybe the envelope wasn't Cordy's at all.

I decided to find gloves and take a peek. Luckily there were clean latex gloves on a shelf in the pantry next to the kitchen.

When I returned to the office, suitably gloved and having added a pair of kitchen tongs so I could pick up the mysterious envelope without handling it, I reached in with the tongs, carefully grasped the envelope, and withdrew it from its hiding place into the light. So far, so good. Definitely a modern envelope, and nothing exotic about it. Hardly full: I could feel the outline of what seemed to be one letter or document, and it crackled when I pressed it gently. Old paper?

I carried it over to the desk and sat down in the chair, placing the envelope on the surface in front of me. It wasn't sealed, so I reached in with my gloved hand and pulled out the contents. I turned out to be two smallish pages of old paper, folded in half, with no envelope. Even before I opened them, I could tell it was a handwritten letter. I unfolded the pages and laid them carefully on the desk in front of me, weighting the edges gingerly with a couple of books. And then I focused on what it said.

The handwriting was large and clear, so it didn't take long to read the letter. And reread it. When I was finished I laid down the letter again, and sat back in the desk chair to think.

I believed what I had just read was a letter sent to Henry Barton not long after the end of the Civil War. It appeared that Henry had been searching for one of his brothers, who hadn't returned from the war, and no family member had heard from that brother since, and naturally feared the worst. He was asking for help. The letter was short and to the point: the writer had little to report but would keep Henry apprised of her progress and would be delighted to report upon the status of her investigations on behalf of her cousin Henry.

The letter was signed "Clara Barton."

I was at best a casual historian, and usually interested in only what concerned my work. But even I had heard of Clara Barton, founder of the American Red Cross and an extraordinary nurse who had ventured into battlefields as a single woman and performed nursing feats I couldn't begin to imagine, under the worst possible conditions. It had never occurred to me to connect Henry Barton with the much more famous Clara Barton, yet she had called him "cousin."

There was only the one letter in the large envelope. Was this the only one—a polite brush-off—or were there more somewhere else? Had Clara Barton followed up? Where? This letter seemed to be in good condition, so if we were lucky and there were others, they should be equally well preserved. Could this be the tip of the iceberg of the hypothetical discovery that had gotten Cordy killed? It was kind of a stretch, but here was the letter, and there couldn't have been many people who knew about the spot where it had been hidden.

Where would Cordy have found this, and why would she have removed it and hidden it? I would have guessed that if she'd found it, she would have trumpeted her discovery to the press and the world. *Kate, stop and think about this.* If she had found the letter—and its siblings, if there were any—at the Barton house, she would have had no legal claim to them. But since no one knew they existed, she could have stolen them and pretended to find them somewhere else—like in the house where I now sat. Right time frame, and Henry Barton hadn't started out rich. Maybe this had been a boarding house right after the war. Or Cordy could have taken word of her prize find to the corporate investors she was courting and said, Look what I've got, this could be a big draw for your new conference center, maybe you could interest the medical community in staying here. Or she could have approached the town committee and told them that she had found something important, but she wasn't going to reveal it until she got the green light to move ahead on her own version of the project. Or, heck, she could have just taken them and sold them on the open market. I had no idea what Clara's letters might be worth if sold openly, or if their value would be increased if there was an actual collection, not just a single letter.

Too much I didn't know. But I did know, selfishly, that such a collection could be a real attraction for history and Civil War buffs who came to visit Asheboro. They were worth more than just money to me—and to the town.

I glanced at my watch and realized I'd better hustle if I was going to meet Josh on time, but at least now I could tell him I thought I knew what we should be looking for. I debated briefly about taking the letter with me, but it was old and fragile, and I didn't trust myself to transport it safely. If Josh really wanted to see it, he could come back with me later in the day. I replaced it carefully it the envelope in which I'd found it, put the envelope in the secret compartment, and pushed it shut firmly, then stepped back to make sure it was concealed once again.

Then I darted upstairs to put on the only pair of jeans I'd brought, a faded sweatshirt, and my running shoes. I checked my bag to make sure all the keys I had were where they should be. Then I added a camera, just in case we found something important. I looked at all the doors downstairs to be sure they were locked, then took off in my car.

Josh was waiting on the front steps when I pulled in. "Am I late?" I asked, when I opened the car door.

"No. I was just enjoying the spring weather."

"Have you stopped locking the front gates?"

"Over the last few days, there's been a lot of coming and going—you, the police, Cordy, a killer. It hardly seems worth it. It's more a psychological barrier than a practical one."

"So you don't get cruising kids out here anymore?"

"Not that I've noticed. Now they tend to head for the city if they want to get rowdy." He stood up. "Ready to dig in?"

"Yes, but I've got something to talk to you about."

Josh sighed. "Why does that always sound ominous?"

"This time it's good news. Maybe."

"Then let's go inside."

I followed him to the opulent dining room and we sat at the table as we had the day before. I took a deep breath and launched into my discovery. Josh didn't interrupt. When I ran out of steam he asked, "So you're guessing that this was Cordelia's big discovery? Clara Barton slept here?"

"I don't know where it fits in the realm of big discoveries, but would Cordy have thought it was important? Or anybody else around here with whom she shared that information?"

"I can't really say. I know Clara Barton was active for quite a while, but she was involved with humanitarian concerns, not industrialization, so she wouldn't have turned up in my own research. But I do know she was a very public figure, and I'm sure there's plenty of information on her available."

"And you don't know anyone in the business of buying and selling artifacts and memorabilia, I assume?"

"That would be correct. I could ask around. Look, if it's just the one letter you found, it might not be worth a whole lot on its own. If it's part of a larger collection, that could be a different story. Either way you'd have to have it authenticated. And the title might be murky. If it was found at the B&B, it could have belonged to Cordelia, and then it would go to Ryan, since he still owned the underlying property. If it came from this house, we'd have to assume it was addressed to Henry, and he left everything to the bank, which sold it to the town, so now the town owns it. As well as any others that might exist, if they're from the same cache."

"Sure, I get that. But it could be worth something to the town beyond its monetary value. Anyway, we're theorizing ahead of our facts. Today we go up to the attic and we look to see if there are footprints, or if any of the items look like they've been disturbed or if anything has been removed. And if we're really, really lucky, we'll find that Clara Barton sent more than one letter to her dear cousin Henry, and there will be a shoebox full of them tucked away somewhere. By the way, what would we do if we did find them?"

Josh looked troubled. "Normally I'd say leave it where we find it—if we find it—for the sake of provenance, but with all the turmoil lately that doesn't seem very safe. We could take it back to the B&B and hide it where you found the one letter."

"Yes, but the accomplice could already know about that," I pointed out.

"We could take it to Ryan. He must have a safe or something for client papers."

"Are we sure he's not involved with this somehow?" Was I sure?

Josh looked exasperated. "Do you have any better ideas?"

"Maybe stash it at Lisbeth's house? I trust her, and nobody would think to look there. We'd have to make sure to put it somewhere where her kids wouldn't get to it, though."

Josh stood up abruptly. "Why don't we just go see what's up there? If we don't find anything, it's moot. I'm sure we can find someplace to hide one piece of paper."

Josh was right: I was putting the cart before the horse. We didn't need a hiding place until we knew we had something to hide. I was kind of hoping we would find something.

20

I followed Josh to the second-floor door that led to the attic. Stacked outside of it were a couple of large lights on stands, plus a long heavy-duty extension cord. Josh was quick to say, "I haven't been up there since we talked last night—you were right about looking for any disturbances, including footprints, so I thought I'd wait for better light."

Good call on his part. "I've already told you that Lisbeth and I were up here before, but we didn't exactly search the place. As you say, it's cold and dark—I pity those poor servants who slept up here. But I still feel kind of silly, making this all cloak-and-daggerish. If I hadn't found that one letter, maybe I would have said, don't bother. I don't think we have anything we could take to Detective Reynolds—he'd just laugh at us."

"We don't have anything *yet*," Josh corrected me. "But we've got a whole attic to explore. This is original research at its best—nothing's been touched since it was shoved up here, as far as I know. It's like a slice of Victorian life, even if there's nothing more than stacks of old magazines. And we're about to open the treasure chest."

I had to smile. "You really are excited about this, aren't you?"

He smiled sheepishly. "Well, yeah. My own research can get kind of boring, and I've been doing a lot of reading lately. I haven't managed to write much beyond a general outline and some draft chapters. So rooting around in a place like this is the perfect antidote, and maybe it'll jump-start my thinking process. Does that make sense?"

"Actually, it does. And now you've got me drooling over the possibility that the wife's good dresses, complete with accessories, are lying peacefully in a handsome steamer trunk just waiting for me to bring them back to the light of day."

"That's the spirit!" Josh said.

"I wish I knew more about the family connections. Clara Barton referred to Henry as 'cousin', but what did that mean back in eighteen-sixty-something? Was it a courtesy term, or were they actually related? I've got lots of questions."

"Look, we can stand here all day and talk about the 'what ifs' we'd like to find, but we may as well get up there and start looking."

"Lead the way!"

"Here, you can carry one of the lights." He thrust one at me. I grabbed it and juggled it. "Are there plugs up there?"

"There was minimal wiring added around 1900 or just before, hence the one lonely light bulb up there. I've plugged in the extension cord on this floor—it should be long enough."

"I brought a camera," I volunteered. "So we can record the process. And any footprints we find."

"Great. Here we go!"

Josh trudged up the uncarpeted wooden stairs, wrangling the awkward light fixture with its tripod, and paused a couple

of steps short of the top of the stairs. I almost bumped into him.
"What?" I asked.

"I haven't been up here in a while—usually I just stick my
nose in to make sure there aren't any mice or squirrels or birds.
But from this angle, I can see footprints."

"Some of them are going to belong to Lisbeth and me, but
we did not follow the crates and trunks all the way to the end.
Maybe halfway. Not yours?"

"Nope, I haven't been up here, past where I am now. What
I see are smaller ones, like a woman's. One woman, alone. You
and Lisbeth seem to have shuffled around and made a mess."

I ignored his comment. "A few? Lots? Where do they go?"

"Slow down, Nancy Drew. Here, pass me your camera."

I fished it out of my pocket and handed it to him. It took
him three seconds to figure out how it worked, and he began
taking pictures from a low angle, turning slightly between
each shot. Then he climbed up the next two steps and did the
same thing.

Finally he said, "Okay, in answer to your questions, it looks
like you and your pal milled around at this end of the attic,
and checked out the rooms on the side. But if you go past that,
you find the sets of single tracks, presumably Cordy's. I'd say
she made two, maybe three trips—there's not a lot of prints,
and not much overlap among them. One trip was a scouting
mission—there's a line of tracks that run from one end of the
attic to the other, and back. The second time she was more
focused and went straight to one part—the prints are all jum-
bled there."

"So that's where we should start," I said firmly.

"Let me get the lights set up so we don't trip over them,"
Josh said.

I managed to control my eagerness while he first set up the light he was carrying, then came back and took mine from me and set that up too. There was a hanging bulb on a cord in the center of the attic, over the staircase, but it shed about as much light as a candle. Anybody looking for something would have had to bring a flashlight. In fact, that person would probably have known she would need a flashlight, because she had known how dark it would be up here. One more strike against Cordy.

"Okay, all set. Watch the cord," Josh warned.

I stepped cautiously up to the top of the stairs and surveyed the attic that ran from front to back of the house. There was a small, dirty window set low in the gable at each end, but no other outside light source. Along the one side, under the eaves, boxes and trunks and odds and ends of furniture were stacked, surprisingly neatly. A path had been left down the center. Naturally nothing was labeled: the owner—or his servants—was supposed to remember where they'd stored their possessions. I wondered if Henry had been a hoarder and whether there would be any evidence from the house before he had remodeled it so extensively. Something to think about later.

"So, where did Cordy start looking?" I asked. "Wait, we really haven't looked at *why* she started looking up here. I mean, she wasn't an attic kind of person, right?"

"As far as I know. What are you asking?"

"Well, I would have expected her to look for silver or jewelry or maybe art first."

"None of which are left in the house. The bank trustees weren't stupid—they made an inventory of the valuables and moved the good stuff to their vaults. Of course, for this stuff they most likely wouldn't have bothered with details, so they would have peeked in and written 'chest full of letters' in the inventory and left it at that. And not bothered to move it because it didn't seem important to them."

"Good to know. But Ryan said Cordy wouldn't know what to look for in books and documents—that's more specialized. And it's not pretty or sparkly."

"Your point is?"

"Someone must have told her to look in the attic to see if there was anything there that might be valuable, or historic, or both. And Cordy would have pouted and said, 'Why? I don't even know what to look for.'"

"Ah, I see what you mean. Somebody else would have sent her up here and said, 'Look for old papers or boxes or whatever.'"

"Exactly. So Cordy started with the easy stuff that she could reach. And it looks like she started with that big trunk in the back. You can see it's been pulled out of line so she could get the top open. Is the lock broken?" I asked.

"Not that I can see. Maybe it was unlocked, or maybe she found the keys somewhere in the house. Anyway, it's open now."

"And apparently she didn't look any farther so she must have found something!" I said triumphantly.

Josh seemed to consider that idea. "All right, say she opened it and did find a stash of Clara Barton's letters in the trunk. What did she do next?"

"She took one letter for proof, to show her partner. She left the rest right where they were—after all, they'd been safe here for over a century." I hoped I was right. It felt right, knowing what I did about Cordy's character. The bigger question was, who was pulling her strings? How did Cordy expect to benefit?

"You know, Kate, this is still speculation. We could just open the trunk and see what's in there," Josh said wryly.

"I'm channeling Carly Simon. You know, 'Anticipation'?"

"Just do it, will you?"

"What, no gloves?"

"I'm a historian, not a forensic investigator. Don't touch anything you don't have to." I rubbed my hands together, approached the trunk head on, and tugged at the lid. It rose easily, which was encouraging. It was one of those lined with richly patterned paper, and it had a tray lying across the top. And nestled in that tray were several stacks of letters, bound with blue satin ribbon. To my unskilled eye, the handwriting matched that of the one letter I'd seen. "Bingo."

Josh moved quickly to stand beside me. "Seriously? I thought we were just spinning a story. There really are letters?"

"Looks like it," I said, grinning like a fool. I estimated that the three stacks might total maybe twenty to thirty letters. It looked like Cordelia hadn't dug into them, merely pulled out the top one to take with her. And if there were in fact that many letters, it was likely that this was more than a polite brush-off—*sorry, couldn't find your relative, the war took a heavy toll*, et cetera. This was would indicate a more personal correspondence, which to me was good news. "Wow," I said reverently. "Makes you wonder what else is hidden up here."

"One thing at a time. We came up here to look for possible evidence of a motive for murder, and it looks like we've found it. We can save the rest for later."

"Some researcher is going to have a field day up here."

"Like me, you mean?" Josh grinned.

"Well, it's not me—I'm no scholar. Tell me, Josh, when you took this job, did anyone explain to you why nothing was touched here? Henry Barton died without heirs, right? But he did make careful provisions for the care and ultimate disposition of his property, at least in the near term. Except he never thought that no one would want it."

"Practically speaking what was up here was most likely simply personal correspondence, discarded books, maybe memorabilia," Josh said. "Nothing that would have been valuable in itself, I'd guess. Presumably he assumed that whoever moved in was welcome to it—let them worry about clearing the place out. He was old by then, and there was no one to help him. Or he didn't remember, or he didn't care."

"Poor Henry. The more I learn, the more I want to know more about the man. I've got to get back to the library and dig into his background, his genealogy."

"What do you want to do now?"

"You're deferring to me?"

"Your find, your call."

I thought for a moment. "The fact that we found the letter at the B&B and matched it to this trove here suggests strongly that it is somehow involved with Cordelia and may have led to her death. Even though she might only have been considering a little theft. So logically we should run right over to the state police headquarters and hand them to Detective Reynolds, with our explanation."

"But?" Josh said, smiling.

"I guess I'm afraid he wouldn't believe us and would send us on our way. Or he'd nod and smile and stuff them all in an envelope and shove it into the evidence box or locker or whatever and get around to actually examining them a whole lot later. I'd like to suggest one intermediate step: we get the letters authenticated. For all we know, they're a collection of recipes from Henry's aunt Bertha, and maybe she liked to sign her letters Clara Barton because she nursed him through measles when he was a child, and he saved them out of sentiment."

"A sensible idea, but it's still an open murder investigation, so we can't afford to send them off to some expert and wait for his opinion."

"Ah, but I have an idea. I know someone in Philadelphia who's the head of a museum there, and if she doesn't have someone on staff who specializes in authenticating this kind of document, she'll know someone who can. I know her well enough to say that it's urgent." Well, I did, sort of. I'd met her when I worked in Philadelphia and we'd hit it off and kept in touch since, getting together at conferences now and then. From what I knew of her, I had the impression she would care about the history of the letters. "I can call her."

Josh didn't look convinced, but neither did he object—or propose a better idea. "We have to set a time limit. If this pans out the way we think it might, Reynolds will skin us alive for sitting on the information."

"Well, it's still only a guess. I'll call her this afternoon." And pray that she wasn't on vacation in Hawaii or something. I took a deep breath. "So, back to our earlier discussion about where to hide them, now that we know that somebody else knows they're here? Or at least, in this house."

Josh rubbed his chin. "My first impulse is to leave them here, and I'll keep an extra-close eye on the place in case he or she comes back. But I don't know what keys this person might have, or how desperate he is, and I really don't relish the idea of wrestling with someone in the middle of the night. And most likely the same person knows you're involved and knows you're staying at Cordy's old place, so that's out. Which brings us back to your friend's place, which the person most likely *doesn't* know about. Have you been to her house since you got here?"

"Yes, including after Cordy died. I didn't notice anyone following me around, but I certainly wasn't watching for that. You really think I should keep my eye out for a tail?"

"Sounds ridiculous, doesn't it? Say these letters are what we think they are. Even on the open market or at auction they might bring in a hundred thousand tops, I'm guessing. To some people that would be a lot of money. And somebody may have killed Cordelia for them. So, short answer: yes, make sure you aren't followed. Tell your friend Lisbeth not to say a word to anyone about the letters, and to put them in a very safe and not-obvious space. And if we're lucky, your Philadelphia friend will hop in a car and race down here to see the letters tomorrow, and we can get them off our hands."

"That works for me. Are we done here? Because I'd rather talk to Lisbeth before her kids get home from school. And then call my friend in Philadelphia."

"Makes sense. So you should go now. But first we've got to wrap up these letters, and I don't think a plastic bag from the market is the best choice."

"Let's go back downstairs and look for something better."

21

I'd driven about halfway back to town before I started getting paranoid. Josh and I had found a wonderful cache of Clara Barton letters. That was good. But so far *only* Josh and I knew about it, well, apart from Cordy and her mystery accomplice, assuming there was one. How much did I know about Josh? He'd said he was fairly recently divorced, which explained why a not-young tenured professor was camping out in an apartment above the garage in a remote part of the state. Maybe. Sure, it would be a nice quiet place to work, and with the Internet he could do research anywhere. But how badly did he need money? Not that these letters were worth what, say, an undiscovered Shakespeare folio might bring, but he'd guessed somewhere in the six-figure range. Tempting. Well, not to me, but I was ridiculously honest. Most people weren't. Was Josh?

Josh had outlined the pitfalls of bringing anyone else into our little circle. Yes, the police might not see our find as important, and they might sideline it for who knows how long. I thought it would be safe to say that no one on the police force would try to sell the letters, although they might not handle them carefully. I didn't think that fingerprint powder would be good for antique paper.

And what about Ryan? He would have a different interest in the letters. I didn't know what his financial picture was—maybe *he* needed money. I also didn't know whether he'd been in on Cordy's plan, divorced or not. Maybe there had been more letters, from Clara or from other noteworthy figures, that Cordy had already fenced. Maybe she'd demanded a bigger share of the profits and he'd bashed her. No, I wasn't prepared to trust Ryan, especially after he'd tried making moves on me and I'd turned him down. Which, of course, might put me in his line of fire. But, wait—he didn't know I knew about the letters. That I knew of.

This was getting far too complicated. Then my anxiety ramped up another notch: Did I want to drag Lisbeth and her family into this? Did I have the right to even consider it? Sure, I could be careful handing over the goods—we could don big hats and dark glasses and make the handoff in a café three towns over. *Stop it, Kate—this is starting to sound like a bad 1960s spy movie.* And Josh now thought I was headed for Lisbeth's house. He'd told me to be careful. But if he was the bad guy, he'd head straight there. Crap.

What other options did I have? I could call Nell Pratt and hand them over to her—I hadn't mentioned her name to anyone. All I'd said was that I had a friend who might be able to help. But Nell might not be available, or might not be willing to drive down here and back, or she might just laugh at me and tell me I'd gone crazy. Scratch that idea, even though I had to get her down to Maryland to see the letters, in the event that nobody murdered me and stole them overnight.

Get a grip, Kate! I was creating problems where there might be none. I was sounding paranoid even to myself. And in this small town, I didn't know of anywhere to hide.

Come up with a plan. I could take the letters back to Baltimore and stash them in the very secure safe at the hotel I used to manage. A desperate person might search my home but wouldn't be able to get to the letters in the hotel. I could leave a message for Detective Reynolds: *Dear Detective, If I die mysteriously, there's an important clue in the safe at the Oriole Suites in Baltimore.* Right. Then *he* would think I'd lost my mind. So I backtracked. The only option that seemed to make sense was to call Nell Pratt and somehow convey the letters to her. She could take them back to her museum, where nobody would be likely to look for them. She could get them verified while those of us in Maryland tried to figure out all the rest, including the murder.

I had reached town, but instead of going to the B&B I pulled into a parking lot behind Main Street and retrieved my cell phone. I didn't have Nell's personal number, but it was easy enough to find her work number. I sweet-talked my way through her assistant, and after about five minutes I was talking with Nell Pratt.

"Kate!" she said enthusiastically. "To what do I owe the pleasure of this call?"

"It's complicated, but I need your help. Do you have time to talk?"

"Sure. What's going on?"

It took me twenty minutes to explain the weird chain of events that had led to my request. She listened and asked some pointed questions, and finally said, "Wow, you don't mess around, do you! You've been in that town for less than a week and you're in the middle of a murder investigation and a possible high-dollar theft of historic items. Not to mention juggling a handsome stranger and an ex-boyfriend. I wish my life was half as interesting."

"I seem to recall you've run into a few criminal speed bumps of your own. And a dash of romance."

"That's true on both counts. So—what is it you think I can do?"

"A couple of things, I guess. First, I need someone to tell me if these letters are the real thing. Second, I need to get them to some safe place that isn't in or near Asheboro, and I'm not even sure where that would be now, because I'm not sure who else is involved. I think I've got to get them out of my hands in order to do that, somewhere that no one will think to look."

"Have you considered that you may be at risk, even if you hand off the letters?"

"You mean, someone might come after me thinking I still have them? No, I hadn't thought about that. Thanks for a new dose of paranoia."

"You don't think you can go to the police?"

"I could, but I don't think they'd see why a bunch of old letters would be worth killing someone over. They'd just pat me on the head and tell me not to worry. That's why I thought of you. You understand their significance."

After a long pause, Nell said, "Where are you?"

"About an hour northwest of Baltimore."

"Which means more like three hours away for me, by car."

"Look, I'm willing to drive to Philadelphia, if that will help. I'd really like to get these letters out of Asheboro, if you know what I mean."

"If you're okay with the drive, fine. Actually I live in Chestnut Hill, and I've got plenty of bedrooms. I can meet you at the house at, say, five?"

"Great. Just give me the address and I'll figure it out."

"Done. And I'll check with my staff about the best person to authenticate your letters."

"I can't thank you enough, Nell. This whole thing has got me spooked. Maybe a drive will help clear my head, and when I get there you can tell me I'm being silly."

"If your gut tells you something's wrong, it's better to listen to it than ignore it. Maybe you'll feel stupid, but at least you'll be safe. See you later!"

I debated about stopping at the B&B to pick up some clean—or cleaner—clothes, but I decided I could pick some up along the way. Surely I could manage with a man's XL T-shirt as a nightgown for one night, while I washed the rest. And I wasn't a girly girl who needed my very own special shampoo or moisturizer. I could cope. I pulled out of the parking lot, filled my tank at a gas station on the way out of town, and hit the open road. I knew how to get to Philadelphia, and Chestnut Hill was just outside it. I could look up the details when I got closer.

I opted to go by way of Harrisburg to pick up the Pennsylvania Turnpike and stopped along the way for a quick lunch, the aforesaid T-shirt and a toothbrush, plus a map of the greater Philadelphia area. Then back to the open road. I found Chestnut Hill with little trouble but made a few wrong turns on local roads there before I found Nell's house. It was a handsome midsize Victorian with a spacious lawn around it. And a good-looking man I didn't recognize standing on the front steps.

He grinned at me when I climbed cautiously out of the car and stretched, keeping one eye on him. "Are you Kate? Nell told me to expect you. I'm James Morrison, her—hell, what is the popular term these days? Partner? Cohabitor? You can pick whichever you like. And I'm also a Special Agent with the FBI, so you should be safe."

I relaxed just a bit. "Good to meet you. Did Nell explain my problem?"

"Only in the barest terms. Come on in and bring the letters."

I retrieved the precious bundle from under the passenger seat where I'd hidden them and followed him into the house, and then toward the back into the kitchen.

"You want a drink?" he asked.

"Sure. But better make it wine, if you have it, or I won't be coherent for more than an hour."

"No problem. So, how do you know Nell?"

"I worked in Philadelphia a few years ago, and we kept crossing paths. Somehow we managed to keep in touch after I moved to Baltimore. She's the only person I know in the museum community, so I called her when all this . . . stuff started happening."

"You don't have any contacts in Baltimore?"

"Not really. I managed a small boutique hotel there. The closest I came to art or anything like it was choosing the paintings for the walls. I'm way out of my depth now, but I know Nell's Society has a lot of document collections and I figured somebody there should be able to help. Of course, I worked that part out before I got nervous about someone trying to get the letters back, and I didn't know who to trust."

James busied himself with opening a bottle of wine and

filling two glasses. Without looking at me, he said, "Someone died?"

"Yes. The town prima donna, my high school nemesis, self-proclaimed femme fatale, et cetera. She'd been running a small B&B in town—the town where we both grew up—but she had bigger plans. Look, maybe I'd better save the story until Nell gets here, so I don't have to tell it twice."

He handed me a glass of wine. "Makes sense. How did the woman die?"

"Somebody bashed her head in with a rock from the garden around the Barton manor house."

"Barton as in Clara?"

Funny that he went straight to that point. "Maybe. Probably. The house was built by one Henry Barton, but I don't know for sure if there's a connection between them and I haven't had time to find out. But that's where Cordelia died." I took a sip of the golden wine, and then another one. "Damn, this is good."

"You have any idea who killed her?"

"Nope. There are some in town who might say I have a motive, but I didn't—really." When he quirked an eyebrow at me, I waved my hand at him. "Long story, but not relevant now. The best idea I've come up with was that she was working with someone who double-crossed her, possibly in some theft from the Barton mansion. She could be a very annoying person." I took another sip of wine. "In fact, *nobody* in town liked her, so there are plenty of suspects." I drained my glass and held it out to him. "More, please."

He filled my glass without comment, for which I was grateful. That was when we both heard the sound of keys in the front door, and James went out to the hall to greet Nell. I wondered if he was going to warn her that I was delusional and half-drunk, but I was too tired and frazzled to care.

Nell came into the kitchen and immediately said, "So it takes a murder to get you back to Philadelphia?"

"Well, I've been busy. But now I don't have a job, so I've got plenty of time. As long as I'm not arrested for murder."

"Most of that sentence will need explaining. James, can I have a glass of whatever you're having?"

"Of course. Should I order food?"

"Please." She accepted a filled glass from him, sat down at the high island in the kitchen, kicked off her shoes, and said, "Okay, start at the beginning. Or no, wait. You brought the letters?"

"Yup. Are you going to kill me for them and bury me in the backyard?"

"They aren't worth *that* much, Kate. But Clara Barton was an amazing woman, in her day or in any era. I'd like to see them, and then we can put them somewhere safe."

I pulled out the package I had slid into my tote bag, but before I could open it, Nell said firmly. "No, not here. It's not clean. Let's wash our hands, then take them into the dining room and use the table there. Technically we should be wearing cotton gloves, but I think we can skip that this once."

"Yes, ma'am."

We dutifully washed and dried our hands, then went to the dining room and spread out the letters across the polished mahogany surface. Some had envelopes, but most did not. Nell scanned them as a group first. "Definitely all the same general period. The paper looks right. And from what I can see, they were all written to one person—a Henry Barton?"

"Yes. It was his house where they were found, in a trunk in

the attic. He bought the place sometime after the Civil War, built a factory in town, apparently made some good money, then remodeled the house. Now it belongs to the town, but they only acquired it recently, and nobody has been through it for years."

"Interesting. How much do you know about Henry Barton?"

"Not much, even though I grew up in the town. He was kind of a recluse, and he's been dead for over a century. I was planning to do some genealogy digging, but I haven't had the time."

"Why were you there at all?"

I filled her in on the details of how the town had ended up owning the building and all the rest—a story I was getting far too used to telling.

Nell nodded, but her eyes never left the letters. "Have you read any of these?"

"Only the first one that I found. It looks like Henry had asked Clara to help find his brother, who hadn't been heard from since the war."

"Are you familiar with the Search for Missing Soldiers? The organization in Washington organized by Clara Barton?"

"Never heard of it. What is it?"

"Something Clara Barton put together right after the war, with the support of Abraham Lincoln. Most people have never heard of it. But it was really something special, particularly in a time when women didn't usually hold jobs. She tracked down something like twenty-two thousand soldiers so she could tell their loved ones what happened to them, and she answered queries about a lot more. And although she was from

Massachusetts, she helped a lot of families from the South as well as the North."

"And all anybody ever talks about is the Red Cross part?"

"Exactly. And it looks like you have a capsule history of the search for one missing soldier."

"You think they're authentic?"

Nell nodded firmly. "I do. And I know who'd love to see them. Once we figure out who killed your not-friend."

22

I crashed pretty quickly after supper. I felt bad about that for maybe three minutes, since Nell was being so kind to put me up for the night unexpectedly, but it had been a long and exhausting day. The wine might have helped a bit too.

I woke up early the next morning. It was good to have an ally like Nell, one who had zero connection to Asheboro or any of the people in it. Plus she knew enough about history in the region, and documents, and authentication to be worth her weight in gold.

I had not counted on James the FBI agent. I hoped that now that he knew what was going on, he didn't have some sort of legal responsibility to do something about it. This whole mess was complicated enough without bringing in another agency, which probably wouldn't make anybody happy.

I rolled over and stared at the ceiling, admiring the moldings. The Victorians sometimes skimped on the fancy details on the second floor, saving all their efforts and money for the more public spaces, but not here. It was consistent throughout the house. What now? I'd left town in a hurry, without notifying anyone, including Detective Reynolds. But he'd already cleared me, right? He'd never said "don't leave town." Lisbeth might be worried if she couldn't track me down, but she had my cell number. The first step for today was to hand off the documents to Nell or the colleague of her choice. They'd be safe, and they'd be authenticated. I didn't have to tell anyone where the letters were. Second . . . and there I stalled. Cordy's murder was still an open case, unless something wonderful had happened since I left town less than twenty-four hours earlier and it was all wrapped up with bows on it. I wanted to ask James if he had an opinion, but at the same time I didn't want to get him more involved than he already was. Plus as far as I knew, he had no jurisdiction in the matter. Unless investigating the theft or sale of stolen items of historical value was included in his job description?

But surely we could figure this out on our own. Asheboro was a small town, one of those where everybody knew everybody else. I hadn't been kidding when I said that nobody in town liked Cordy, but that didn't mean that a lot of people hated her enough to kill her, or would even know how to do it if they wanted to. Still, a rock was a pretty unsophisticated weapon—good for a spur-of-the-moment crime, an unthinking act of passion or anger. And this wasn't something any person would carry around in his pocket, just in case the opportunity presented itself. It had been sitting there, handy, and someone had chosen to use it. Who in town would react that strongly? Man or woman? Had Cordy been seeing anyone lately? Would he admit to it if she had been, under the current circumstances?

I was getting nowhere, unless depressing myself counted. I was relieved when I heard a quiet rapping on the door. "Kate? You awake?"

"Come on in, Nell," I told her. That giant T-shirt concealed all there was to conceal.

Nell slipped into the room. "Just wanted to let you know that there's coffee and food, if you want it. We didn't have much time to talk last night, so I didn't know whether you were a morning or an evening person."

"Both, as needed—you may have noticed that hotels never really sleep, especially if you're catering to rich and demanding clients. Left to my own devices, I'm more of a morning person. Coffee sounds great."

"Well, then, get yourself sorted out and come downstairs when you're ready."

"I will. Uh, Nell? I didn't know about James—I mean, that you were in a relationship with an FBI agent. He doesn't have to jump in and take over, does he?"

Nell shook her head. "He's not that kind of guy. If you ask for help, he'll give it freely, but he won't insist on running the show. And he won't tell anybody else about it."

"That's good to know. If he doesn't mind, I'd welcome any suggestions he has. I am completely out of my depth."

"Been there, done that. See you downstairs."

Getting dressed didn't take long since I had few choices. I washed my face and brushed my hair and declared that it was as good as it was going to get. Then I meandered downstairs to yet more lovely moldings, inlaid floors, brass sconces—I was getting jealous.

James and Nell were seated at the island in the kitchen, and the coffeepot was sitting between them. "Good morning,"

I said. (I had never claimed to be a brilliant conversationalist first thing in the morning.)

James's mouth was full of toast, but he raised his mug at me.

"Toast? Eggs?" Nell asked.

"Toast is fine."

Nell got up and started retrieving bread and butter and jam and honey and whatever else looked good to her. Over her shoulder she said, "James and I were talking last night, after you went upstairs."

"What did you come up with?"

"Well, what I was hearing from you was that you wanted to keep the letters safe, first and foremost, which of course I applaud. There's one person I'd really like you to talk with. She doesn't work for me, but she did an internship at the Society a couple of years ago. She's working on a graduate degree at Penn on working women in the later nineteenth century, so of course she knows a lot about Clara Barton. I can connect you two if you want."

"Sounds great. And apart from confirming the letters really are from Clara, maybe she can put them in context, on where Clara was in her own career, and what the dating of the letters would be. You see, Henry Barton is still a mystery to me, and maybe your friend can point me in the right direction."

"You're more than welcome to use whatever resources the Society has."

"Thank you, and I may want to take you up on that at some point. Right now I feel that I need to be in Asheboro to help sort out Cordy's death. But assuming that can be accomplished fairly quickly, there's another project I'd really like your input on. Could you come down to the town for a day, maybe? I'm staying at what used to be Cordy's bed and breakfast, so I can put you up for the night."

"I'll have to check my calendar, but I think I could manage that. Are you going to give me any hints?"

"Sure. I want to suggest to the council that they turn the central part of town back to its Victorian form, and market it as an authentic Victorian village. The good—or bad—thing is, it wouldn't take much work, since nobody's done any major building since 1900. Most of the original store façades are just covered by later paint or siding, which would be easy to remove and wouldn't cost much."

"Interesting," Nell said thoughtfully. "I'd love to kick ideas around. I take it nobody's got a lot of money to pour into this?"

"Nope. They blew it all on buying the Barton house. They can't raise taxes because there's no tax base left—people are moving away from the town to where the jobs are."

"Would that house be part of this project?"

"I hope so. It's kind of the centerpiece of this project, even though it's not exactly in the middle of town. But I think Henry jump-started the town. He moved there after the Civil War and built a factory, and that kept the town going for a long time. But he died, and the factory went into a decline, and whatever glory days there were faded away."

"Let me guess—you're hoping that connecting Clara Barton's story with Henry could give your project a boost?" Nell said, smiling.

"I won't deny it's crossed my mind, but we only found the letters yesterday, so I'm not sure how that would fit. But my gut tells me it could be useful."

"I'll admit I'm intrigued. James, you've been awfully quiet. Are you thinking or just digesting?"

James smiled at Nell. "This really is your turf more than mine. I have no place in the murder investigation, and it's not clear whether there's a theft involved in the letters, since you said you found them where they appeared to have been for a century."

"True. I did find the first letter in a different location, and one could argue it was stolen, but I reunited it with the rest. I don't think anybody's going to accuse me of stealing the lot of them—technically I think they belong to the town, and they more or less gave me the run of the place, but maybe Nell or her friend should give me a receipt, just in case. But one concern we did have was that maybe Cordelia and her invisible accomplice had been stealing documents from the attic for a while. After all, nobody really knew what was up there, so they couldn't tell if anything was missing. And—Nell, you can correct me if I'm wrong—as long as a person is discreet about selling these kinds of items, and not just dumping them all on eBay—nobody is likely to notice. Is that accurate?"

"Close enough," Nell agreed. "It happens. But let's stick to the one batch we know about. I haven't read through them all, but they look to be a more or less complete series, from Henry's first contact with Clara to when she finally and regretfully declares there is no more she can do—or she finds the missing brother. Do you happen to know?" When I shook my head, she said, "You know, you might do well to look up wills for the family."

"Great idea, Nell, but I don't know the brother's name, I don't know for sure what state he was born in or what his parents' names were. Henry had no heirs, so the story stops with him. But I'll get right on it."

"It was just a suggestion," Nell told me, buttering her toast.

"I'm sorry," I said, immediately contrite. "I really am looking forward to getting to know Henry better. I feel guilty that I lived in Asheboro for years and never knew anything about the man." I turned back to James, who was absorbed in reading the paper. "So, James, if I do find evidence that anything was stolen, do I get in touch with you?"

"Sure. But get that murder cleared up first."

"That's my plan. Nell, what do you want to do next?"

"How long have you got?"

"Well, I kind of left town without telling anyone, so I should get back sooner rather than later before someone starts worrying about me." And who would that be? Lisbeth? Josh? "Although if either of you has a hot lead, I could be persuaded to stay."

"Let me call Carroll and see when she's available." Nell stood up, grabbed her phone from a table, and walked toward the front of the house.

I poured myself more coffee and asked James, "Am I your typical houseguest?"

"I think you're our *first* houseguest—we haven't lived in this house for long. But your story is certainly interesting."

"I can't believe that all I did was say yes to an old friend, when she asked me to talk to the town council. And that was barely a week ago! And you know what? I feel kind of pissed off that I will never be able to resolve my conflict with Cordy. I haven't given you all the details, but let's just say that she made my senior year in high school very unpleasant, and I fled to college and never looked back. But as an adult, I would like to have had the chance to move past that." I had to wonder if somebody had had a worse time than I had with Cordy, back in high school, although it was hard to imagine.

"Maybe that's why you want to see her murder solved," James said. "It would give you some kind of closure."

I hadn't looked at it that way. "Maybe," I agreed. "Anyway, since my job evaporated, I can reexamine my life and decide where I want to be next."

"You seem very excited about this Victorian village concept."

"Do you know, I am. It just sprang into my head, but I can see it so clearly. And this Clara Barton angle plays so neatly into it. And I'd like to know more about the factory and what Henry was making, And . . ."

Nell walked back in. "Carroll can meet us for lunch today, if that works for you."

"Great. How much did you tell her?"

"Not a lot—I'll let her draw her own conclusions."

"Good. And will you take the letters so they'll be safe?"

"Of course. I really don't think your detective would make much of them, and I shudder to think what kind of damage his crew would do if they looked for fingerprints."

"Then I'd better call my friend Lisbeth and let her know I'll be back in Asheboro in time for dinner."

Like Nell before me, I located my cell phone and wandered toward the front of the house to call Lisbeth. She answered on the fifth ring, sounding breathless.

"Kate? You're not dead? I tried your phone and the B&B line, and you weren't answering."

"I'm sorry! I'm in Philadelphia, which W. C. Fields might have something to say about. I'm fine, and I'll explain when I get back. Has something happened?"

"No, not really. Nobody's solved the murder yet, if that's what you're asking."

"I came up here to follow up on a new angle on that. I hope I didn't alarm you but I wanted to keep it kind of hush-hush until I knew more."

"You don't have to apologize to me—I'm just glad you're all right. When will you be back? Or should I say, *will* you be back?"

"What, you think that pesky murder turned me off? Don't worry about it. I hope to be back there in time for dinner."

"Are you angling for an invitation?"

"Are you offering one?"

"Of course, as long as you can deal with the kids."

"I'll manage. See you six-ish, if all goes well."

"Will you be able to talk about this lead you're following?"

"I really don't know."

23

"A re you driving?" I asked Nell. "Because I usually get lost in Philadelphia—all those one-way streets mess me up. When I worked in the city I took public transportation."

"Don't worry—I told Carroll to meet us at the Society, and I can drop you back at your car when we're done."

"Sounds good."

"You ready to go?"

"I guess so. You have the letters?"

"I do, in an acid-free folder. No sense in exposing them to any harm now, after all these years."

"You're the expert."

The ride into the city was surprisingly quick. Nell pulled into the parking lot across the street from her building and parked. I saw a woman standing next to the door under the columned portico. "That's Carroll waiting for us," Nell said.

Nell got out of the car and I followed her across the street and up the steps. "Carroll, thanks for meeting with us on such short notice," Nell greeted her. "Let me disable the alarm and get the door open and we can go in and get comfortable. This is Kate Hamilton—she's the one who found the letters I told you about."

Carroll Peterson turned out to be younger than I expected, but Nell had said she was working on a graduate degree. I stuck out my hand. "I hope you can help. It's a kind of complicated situation, and the letters are involved in a weird way. I just wanted to make sure we know what we're dealing with, and also that they're safe."

Carroll shook my hand. "Hey, I was intrigued by what little Nell told me. And they're part of a murder investigation? That is so cool."

"I guess." I suppose I would think it was cool too, if I wasn't smack in the middle of it.

Nell held the door open. "Ladies, come on in. I thought we could set up in the old boardroom. There's a big table and good light. But I want to dust the table first. I'll get some cotton gloves too. Kate, why don't you explain the background to Carroll? I've already heard that part of the story."

"Happy to," I said. Carroll led the way to the ground-floor room, behind an imposing staircase. It was a handsome space, although it looked as if it didn't get much use.

"Sit, please," Carroll said. "So, what's the story?"

I led her through what little I knew about Henry Barton and his missing brother, and the possible link to Clara Barton. Carroll listened carefully.

"Wow," she said when I'd finished. "Sounds almost like a movie—the body on the steps, a slew of possible suspects who hated the victim, the unexpected discovery. Do you have any reason to believe anybody else knows about the letters? And whether there's anything else hidden in that attic?"

"It's our guess that the victim—Cordelia—was working with an accomplice, although whether she found the letters and told him or her—or whether that person suspected there might be something up there and sent Cordelia back to look for more is not clear. Either way, she was the kind of person who didn't like to get her hands dirty, but she probably would have liked the money if she could sell some unknown letters by somebody famous. Maybe she got greedy or threatened a bit of blackmail. We really don't know, but now at least we have the letters. Unless, of course, you tell us that they're fake."

"What did Nell tell you about what I'm working on?"

"Not much—we haven't had a lot of time to talk. She's the only museum professional I could think of on short notice, so I bolted out of town with the letters."

"Ooh, more cloak and dagger stuff. I love it! Anyway, I'm working on a degree in Museum Administration, and my primary research interest is the change of women's roles after the Civil War. Obviously Clara Barton jumps to the head of the line there, at least in terms of her visibility and ultimate success. She's still nearly a household name, which is more than you can say for a lot of Civil War generals and the like."

"I will plead ignorance. What do I need to know?"

"She fought hard to be allowed to help the Union soldiers on the battlefield—and I mean literally on the field. Seems like the North hadn't quite thought through what to do with thousands of sick and wounded—it's a depressing story. Clara stepped up, identified the most pressing needs, and set about organizing and collecting supplies and the like. She met with a lot of resistance from the military and the government, but she was a very persistent woman. She made a real difference. As you can imagine, as the war wound down she was kind of adrift, after years of intense work and effort, so she identified another need: finding what had happened to soldiers who had never come home, and there were quite literally thousands of them from both sides. So Abraham Lincoln authorized her to set up an office in Washington, staffed with women, and they spent a couple of years tracking down the missing men. She looked for something like sixty thousand in a very short time by any era's standards, and she managed to locate over twenty thousand of them. All this from a tiny third-floor office that's still there. It was only a couple of years ago people realized that, and now it's on the National Historic Register. I'm going to guess that the letters you found relate to your Henry Barton's request for help to locate his brother. It's just icing on the cake that Clara Barton may have been a relative."

Nell reappeared. "Sorry it took so long—would you believe I couldn't find the cleaning supplies? I've got some lint-free cloths here. Just dust off the tabletop and we can dig in—carefully! Did you explain your interest to Kate, Carroll?"

"I did, and her story—or her guesses—dovetails neatly."

We all started dusting. Funny how three professional women trying to solve a murder started out by cleaning house. "I don't mean to be crass, but are these particularly rare or valuable?"

"There's no simple answer to that," Carroll said. "Clara was a prodigious letter writer, even on the battlefield, so there are many around. The Library of Congress has a large collection. They come up at auctions now and then and sell well. From what Nell said, it might be that your letters—or rather, Asheboro's—cover a single investigation, from start to finish. I'd have to see if such a complete set exists somewhere else.

The personal connection might bump up the value more. But I hope that's not your primary concern?"

"No, except on behalf of the town. But I'd much rather see them installed as some sort of display relating to the history of the house and the town. I think it would be a terrific draw if we develop the house and the town as a tourist destination."

"Don't display the originals! Replicas, please!" Nell and Carroll spoke simultaneously.

"Gee, and here I thought I'd just tack them to a corkboard. Just kidding! Are we ready to look at them?"

"Put your gloves on," Carroll said firmly. "Then sort the letters by date, where possible. We can insert any undated ones later."

We spent a very quiet fifteen minutes arranging the letters in order—altogether they took up more than the length of the conference table. It was hard to resist the urge to read them, but I hoped that would come later. Right now the need to avoid damaging them was foremost.

Finally Carroll stepped back and said, "I think that's it."

"Are they . . ." I began.

"Original? They certainly appear to be. The paper and ink are right, and the handwriting looks like other Barton letters. Nell, I'm sure you can find someone to confirm that."

"Sure, no problem," she said quickly. "What would you suggest we do now?"

"Apart from putting them in a safe place and not telling anyone where they are?" Carroll smiled. "Not that I expect the mystery killer to track them down here and burgle the place, but it can't hurt to be careful."

"Are you, we, going to read them?" I asked.

Carroll looked pained. "I know you're curious to know

what they cover, and so am I, but I think we need to have a conservator handle them first. What is it you want to know about the contents?"

"Nothing that's urgent, I guess," I admitted reluctantly. "It's not like the whole remodeling of the town depends on whether Clara Barton spent the night there. And we're a long way from approving any plans, much less starting on them. But I would like to know what she found. Henry Barton is pretty much a mystery himself in the town."

"Do you know if that missing brother was ever found?" Nell asked.

I shook my head. "Using all the willpower I possess, I did not tear into the letters and look at each one. I didn't want to risk damaging any of them."

"Good for you! So here's what I'd suggest," Carroll said firmly. "Nell, you look after the physical preservation and conservation of the letters. Kate, you go back to Asheboro and comb the town records, and that attic of Henry's, and see what you can find out about the man and his family, including that brother. And I'll do some research on the Search of Missing Soldiers—the time line, the funding, the results—and see where your letters might fit. Does that make sense?"

"I was going to do the genealogy in any case," I told her. "I've already asked our local librarian to pull together any references she might have. Nell, maybe you can point me to some online resources I can use, if I come up dry."

"Of course."

I turned back to Carroll. "What do you think I should do about whatever else is in the attic? I mean, these letters were in the top section of the only trunk we looked at. There could be a lot more things in there, and I know there are a lot more boxes and trunks."

"How's your security system?" Carroll asked.

"Pretty pathetic. Nobody ever thought there was anything worth stealing. All the silver and artworks and any other valuables are in a vault in the town bank. I don't think anyone had looked in the attic for a long time, before Cordelia. But we now know or guess that somebody else knows something, and that person may come looking."

"Exactly. Did you mention a caretaker?"

"Yes, but he's an academic, not a guard. Henry left enough money to keep the place maintained, and the caretaker works in exchange for the use of the rooms over the stable or garage or whatever it was. Josh is pretty scrupulous about checking the perimeter, making sure things are locked and such, but that may not be enough now."

"What did you say his name was?" Carroll asked.

"Josh Wainwright. He said he teaches at Johns Hopkins, but he's been on sabbatical this year."

"Midsize guy, fortyish, glasses, beard?" When I nodded Carroll said, "I think I know him."

"This may sound ridiculous, but do you know him well enough to trust him?"

"I don't understand your question."

"Might he have any personal interest in pilfering whatever historic documents he might find up there? I mean, he has free access to the whole place, and there's no inventory at all. He says he's never been up to the attic, and the footprints in the dust back that up, but now that he knows what's up there, he might be tempted."

"Hmm, I see your point. All I can tell you is that he's well respected in his discipline, and I've never heard anyone say anything negative about him. But I don't know him well."

"Well, he has an alibi for the time of Cordy's death, but that doesn't mean he isn't involved in stealing documents. Although we came up with the whole theft theory together, and he suggested looking in the attic. Am I being paranoid?"

"You want us to come down and see what's what?" Carroll asked.

"You'd probably have a better handle on what questions to ask than I do. And I've got free use of Cordy's bed and breakfast, if you want to stay. Both of you. We can have a slumber party and read Clara's letters out loud." I must have been getting punchy—I sounded ridiculous even to myself.

Nell smiled and said gently, "Take a step back, Kate. You've been living with this for a few days now, right? You're stressed out, and you don't know where to turn. Why don't you go back, if you feel safe enough, and Carroll and I will go over what you've told us, and figure out what to do with the letters, and maybe then we could join you? But I don't think it benefits anyone for the three of us to go running around the countryside in a panic."

I took a deep breath to calm myself. "You're right. You know, it's a kind of weird feeling. I mean, Asheboro was my hometown, the place where I grew up. Now I realize there was a lot of stuff I never knew or even thought about. And I don't know who to trust. I'd like to think a peaceful night would help me see things more clearly, but it still troubles me that Cordelia may have had an accomplice who may also be a killer lurking around the town, and now through no fault of my own I could be in his sights."

"I can't say that I blame you, Kate," Nell said. "But I'm not sure what more we can do today. I would urge you to talk to the police who are investigating, especially now that the letters—which still seem to make up the only tangible proof—are safely out of reach. If your detective is a decent man, I'm sure he won't accuse you of obstruction of justice, or anything like that."

"I hope so. All right then. Carroll, thank you for your information. I'll keep it in mind when I start digging into the Barton family history. Nell, you said something about taking me back to my car?"

"Oh, right, of course. Carroll, I'll walk you out. Oh, wait—let me lock away those letters."

"You're going to keep them in this building?" I asked anxiously.

"Yes, and I won't tell you where I put them, just in case the bad guys kidnap you and try to force you to reveal their whereabouts."

"You are too kind," I said sarcastically. She'd just given me another reason to feel paranoid.

Nell disappeared up the stairs, leaving Carroll and me staring at each other in the lobby. "Bet you didn't think old letters could be so interesting," Carroll said.

"Can't say that I did. Oh, can I ask one favor?" When Carroll nodded, I went on, "Henry was said to have made his fortune in the factory he built in town, but I know next to nothing about the place, except that the building is still standing. I know Josh is looking into that, but if you have anything in your research that might shed light on any part of his efforts, industrial or commercial, could you share it with me?"

"Of course. And all you've got is Henry Barton who fought

in the Civil War, then moved to this small town in Maryland and bought himself a house, married someone named Mary, then built a factory and got rich, then completely remodeled his house, and left it to the town when he died. Have I got that right?"

"More or less. And could you start with what he made there? Lisbeth and I keep saying he made widgets, but they don't really exist, do they?"

Carroll smiled and shook her head. "Not specifically. Before the computer age they were usually some kind of small mechanical things that nobody knew or could remember the name of."

"Well, that fits."

24

O nce we had retrieved Nell's car and navigated the downtown streets, she asked, "Did that help?"

I shook myself out of my lethargy—I was suffering from a post-adrenaline slump now that I knew the letters were stashed away. "Goodness, yes! And thank you for getting Carroll and me together. It's a big weight off my mind to know that the letters are safe."

"Maybe you should make it known that you don't have them anymore," Nell said. "If you seriously think someone might come after you."

"I don't know what I think anymore. In the clear light of day it seems absurd that anyone would want to do me harm for a bunch of old letters. And then I remember that Cordelia is dead, and the letters are real. Not priceless, but worth something. And it's a town that's struggling to keep its financial head above water. No money in the bank, a declining tax base, no new people moving in. They as much as told me I'm their last best hope. And I really do want to help, but it seems to get more complicated with each day."

"Will you accept Carroll's judgment about Josh Wainwright?" Nell asked. "That he's one of the good guys, or at least that it's unlikely that he killed Cordelia?"

"I guess so. The detective accepted his alibi. It's possible he's in financial straits since his divorce, although I'm just guessing. He's doesn't seem like the type who would do something like this just for the money. And I really have to trust *somebody*. I can't do this all alone." Wow, I was beginning to wallow in self-pity.

"Well, when you see him, tell him you met Carroll and see how he reacts," Nell said firmly. "And tell him you met with me, so he knows that someone else knows . . . Well, you get the idea."

"Yes, I do. Thank you. And if we all get through this, I really would appreciate it if you, or you and Carroll, could come down and give me some ideas about how to revive the town by going backwards in time."

"I'd love that. A field trip where I don't have to give a speech and don't need to ask anyone for contributions? Heaven." She pulled up outside her house. "Keep in touch, will you?"

"Of course. Thanks for the ride, and, well, everything else. Thank James for me too, and let me know if he comes up with any insights. Must be handy to be in bed with the law."

Nell grinned. "It has its moments. We'll talk."

I climbed back into my car and turned toward Asheboro. I was still smiling. I'd done one thing right: I'd found some more allies.

On the way back I debated about stopping by and telling Detective Reynolds what I'd just done. I vetoed it because, one, I was afraid he would yell at me, and two, I wanted to know if there were any new developments in Asheboro—like something that would mean I didn't have to talk to Detective Reynolds. Besides, it was a long drive back. Maybe tomorrow.

I pulled into town about five thirty and headed for the B&B. I'd call Lisbeth from there, but first I wanted a shower and a change of clothes. I let myself in the front door, and then I kind of stopped. I wasn't even sure why. I thought I'd purged my paranoia on the drive back, but maybe I was kidding myself. Here I was walking into a large building that I didn't know well, and there was nobody else there. Right? I listened, but didn't hear anything beyond the creaking of an old wooden house as the temperature dropped for the evening. All normal. I'd been so proud of myself about letting Nell know where I was staying, thinking I was somehow protecting myself, but when I thought about that in practical terms, if I was found with my head bashed in on the floor here (after who knew how long?), why would anyone think to call a museum administrator in Philadelphia? How likely was that?

Lisbeth had invited me to dinner. To hell with the shower—I was going to head over there, where there was a warm, normal, chaotic family and light and activity—and I'd think about coming back to the B&B later. Or maybe never.

I turned myself around and marched out the front door, pulling it shut behind me and making sure the lock had engaged. Then I pulled out my cell phone and called Lisbeth. When she answered I said, "Hey, I'm back. Is that dinner invite still open?"

"Sure, come on over. If the kids get too noisy I'll just lock them in a closet—you won't call the cops on me, will you?"

"Of course not. They'd arrest me too, for concealing evidence or something. I'll be there in five."

When I parked in front of Lisbeth's house, I could hear the racket of children from the driveway. I led a quiet life, and much of my time over the past few years had been spent trying to ensure that our hotel guests *didn't* hear anything at all in their luxury suites. That much chaos coming from two less-than-full-size people was startling. It took a minute or two of determined knocking before Lisbeth finally opened the front door. "Kate! I thought I heard something. Where the heck have you been?"

"I told you—Philadelphia. Quick trip, there and back again within twenty-four hours."

"Do I want to know why?" Lisbeth asked.

"Probably not, but it was a useful trip." I followed Lisbeth into her kitchen, where every countertop was covered with assorted cooking utensils, both clean and dirty. "I'll give you the short version." At least I'd kept her safely out of the mess so far, and I didn't want to put her or her family at risk.

"Find a seat, if you can. Dinner's in half an hour, more or less. You want wine or something?"

"No, it would probably put me to sleep in minutes. I'm not even sure how far back to go in explaining."

"Keep it short before the kids descend like a swarm of locusts. If a swarm can be only two."

"Mom?" a voice came from upstairs.

"What, Melissa?" Lisbeth called back, loud enough to be heard upstairs.

"The cat's barfing on the bed."

Lisbeth sighed. "The joys of the domestic life," she said to me. "Which bed?" she yelled.

"Jeffrey's."

"Is your father up there?"

There was a silence of about thirty seconds. "Yeah. He was taking a nap."

"Well, tell him to clean up the cat barf. I'm talking with my friend." She turned back to me. "One more crisis averted. You were saying?"

Oh, what the hell. She was already involved in this. I took a few moments to condense the events and theories of the past two days into a very short version and then dumped it all on Lisbeth in a rush.

She didn't interrupt, but when I finished, or at least ran out of steam, she sat down across the kitchen table and said, "Wow. All this started in sleepy Asheboro? Not just murder, but also a possible theft of who knows how many historic documents worth who knows how much money, and you had dinner with an FBI agent and a museum president? Makes my life seem pathetic."

"No way. You lead a normal life. I seem to have wandered into some weird alternate universe."

"I notice you didn't mention our detective."

"Nope. I thought about updating him, really I did, but the theories Josh and I cooked up were so fragile that I thought he'd just dismiss us, or the letters would get lost or damaged in police storage. I know the letters are safe for now, and if I have to explain later, I'll cross that bridge when I come to it. At least we're pretty sure they're authentic. And Nell and her friend could be really helpful if this Victorian village idea goes forward. Anything new on that front?"

"Not really. Everybody got so flustered by Cordy's murder that they more or less forgot about it for now. I'm going to guess they'll schedule a regular meeting this coming week. You can present whatever you have then, or nothing at all—I'm sure the council members will understand."

"We'll see. But to tell the truth, the murder aside, I'm really getting excited about the potential for this project. Now that I'm back, the first thing I have to do is dig into Henry Barton's history, because he seems to be the key to all this. So come tomorrow, I'm going to vanish into the library and dig."

"Did Audrey come up with anything good?"

"I don't really know. I met with her once, and I kind of explained what I was looking for—the true version—and she pulled some good stuff together, but I haven't had time to go back since. Anyway, whatever I don't find in the local collections I can hunt for online."

"So you're sticking around Asheboro for a while longer?" Lisbeth asked, stirring a pot.

"At the risk of sounding pathetic, I don't really have any reason to go back to my place right now. I've got free board at the bed and breakfast, and a full kitchen there, so why not stay? Oh, did I mention that Ryan tried to put the moves on me?"

"No! Really? Are you, uh, interested?"

"In getting back with Ryan? No way. But I didn't want to burn any bridges. Actually I think he was just testing the waters, in case I was still into him, but I don't think his heart was in it. Which is fine."

Lisbeth extracted plates from a cupboard. "Dinner's ready— I'm going to go call the rest of the gang." She set the plates on the table and went out to the front stairs, where she yelled, "Dinner's ready! And we've got company, so be polite, kids!"

Lisbeth's husband, Phil, was the first to appear, and Lisbeth immediately asked, "Did you take care of the cat, er, stuff?"

"Hello, Kate. Yes, Lisbeth, I did; I gather the kids were playing with the cat and he got a bit overexcited."

"Thank you, Phil—you are a prince," Lisbeth said sweetly.

The kids came clomping down the stairs, battling over who could arrive first. "Wash your hands and say hello to my friend Kate, please. You've met her before."

"Hello, Kate," the children chimed in unison. Then Jeffrey said, "You the lady who's poking around that spooky house where the body was?"

I glanced at Lisbeth, but she only shrugged. "Yes, that's me." I decided it wouldn't be wise to mention that I'd found the body.

Jeffrey looked disappointed. "Was there any blood left?"

"I didn't look. Are you planning to be a detective or a vampire?"

"Can I be both?" he asked eagerly.

"I won't say no," I replied.

Lisbeth set plates at each place around the table. "Milk? Water? No soda."

"Aw, Mom!"

"You heard me."

Dinner progressed in what Lisbeth seemed to find a normal fashion, and as I watched I wondered if I was missing something by staying single. I'd had relationships, but none had really stuck. Was I too smart for the men I met? Too successful? Or just too boring? All I ever did was work, and yet here I was, out of a job. But on the plus side, I was, as Nell had noted, really excited about the idea of bringing Asheboro back to life somehow, and I was kind of intrigued that the whole town had somehow forgotten Henry Barton, who had in large part shaped the town. Why? Sometimes I wished I had taken a class or two on urban planning when I was in college—it would have come in handy more than once.

By the time everyone had cleaned their plate, I was beginning to droop again. I accepted Lisbeth's offer of coffee, since I still had to drive back to the B&B. She sent the kids off to bed, with instructions to her husband to make sure they brushed their teeth; and he should read them a story if he wanted any peace. Finally it was just the two of us in the kitchen.

"Welcome to my world," Lisbeth said softly to me.

"Go on, you love it," I told her. "I like your husband, and the kids are good kids. If you get bored, you can get a job or volunteer when they're a bit older. So don't you dare apologize for your life. Listen, if this village thing ever happens, I'd love to have your help on it. There might be money in it, although we're a long way from finding any, but at least you could set your own hours and have some flexibility."

"Let me think about that, because you're a long way from making it happen. But I do admire your enthusiasm. If it does go forward, would you stay around?"

"Probably. At least until it gets up and running."

"I'd like that."

I checked the clock on the stove. "I'd better head back—it's been a long day. Not that I have any idea what I'm doing tomorrow, beyond going to the library. But if I do that I need to be able to stay awake, so I'd better get some sleep."

"Let me know if you want to go play or something—as long as it's during weekday school hours."

"Will do. Thanks for feeding me."

"Happy to."

I walked out into the cool night and breathed deeply. That could have been my life in there, if I hadn't been so determined to get out of town and make something of my-self. I couldn't see myself in her place though. But Lisbeth seemed content, so I wasn't about to criticize. The world is full of choices—and roads not taken.

I drove home carefully and parked on the street in front of the B&B. It was only when I got out of the car that I saw a man sitting on the front porch. Damn, I'd forgotten to leave the outside light on.

I gathered up my courage and walked up the front path-way, until about halfway there I recognized Josh. "What the hell are you doing here? Something wrong?"

He stood up. "No. When I didn't hear from you, I got wor-ried."

"Oh. Well, come inside and I'll fill you in, if I can stay awake long enough."

25

I fished out my keychain from my bag and fumbled to get the key in the lock. And when I finally did manage it, I hesitated, recalling the weird feeling I'd had earlier.

Josh noticed. "Problem?"

"No. I don't think so. Well, maybe. I'm not sure." I was not exactly articulate.

"You want me to go in first?" he asked. I nodded mutely, so he reached around me and turned the doorknob. The door swung in smoothly, and the inside of the house was as quiet as when I had left it. He stepped around me and walked into the center of the hall, where he stopped. "Come on in—the water's fine."

"I am acting like an idiot," I said, as I closed the door behind me.

"Why were you scared? Did something happen?"

"No, nothing at all. I drove back from Philadelphia, and—"

"Philadelphia? Your museum friend?"

"Yes. I spent last night at her house. It was easier for me to go up there than to have her come down here."

"You're going to have to back up. You went to Philadelphia to talk to your friend. You took the letters with you?"

"Yes. All of them. And I left them there."

"And this is why?"

"Because the more I thought about, well, everything, the more rattled I got. You and I more or less agreed that there was somebody working with Cordy who was probably somehow involved with the letters, but I have no idea who, and I didn't want to put the letters at risk. So I just grabbed them and ran. To Philadelphia."

Josh took a deep breath. "I get the feeling that this is going to take more than a couple of minutes. Is there any of that wine left?"

"You mean, have I managed to drink up the whole supply of premium vintages in three days? Of course there's some left. You want some?"

"I think you need some. You fetch the wine, and I'll find some glasses."

He disappeared toward the kitchen, and I popped open the secret panel in the parlor. The wine was still all there. Unless somebody had swapped out all the bottles for something poisonous and then carefully replicated the labels and added just the right amount of dust to the bottles and . . . *Kate, get a grip!* I pulled out a bottle, more or less at random, and marched to the kitchen. "Here you go," I said, handing it to him. He looked at the label, and then he looked at me, but I didn't volunteer any information and he didn't ask.

Josh opened the bottle and poured two glasses. "I'm sorry it hasn't had time to breathe."

"I can live with that." I accepted the glass he offered me, and took a sip. "Nice. Too bad I can't get used to this."

"So, sit down and enjoy it now." Josh waved a hand at the table. "And fill me in."

"Where do I start? Oh, by the way, Carroll Peterson says hi." I watched his face to see how he reacted to her name.

He smiled, and his eyes lit up. "You met her?"

Nothing suspicious about his response, I decided. "She's a friend of Nell's. Nell's the friend I went to see, and she invited Carroll to join us. Carroll said your areas of research over-lapped somehow."

"They do, although she takes more of a feminist slant. It makes perfect sense that your Nell would think of her when she learned about the Barton letters. What did Carroll say about the letters?"

"I think she was really excited, but she tried not to show it. We laid out the letters in chronological order, and she said she thought it was the complete story of Henry's search for his brother, which might be unusual—having the whole series, I mean. Although there are plenty of Clara's letters around—apparently she wrote to everyone, all the time, even in the middle of battles."

"And where are the letters now?"

I wasn't going to share all the details, even if I trusted Josh. "Carefully locked away somewhere in the Society for the Pres-ervation of Pennsylvania Antiquities, or whatever the heck they call the place. And you are now the only person, other than me, Nell, and Carroll, who knows where they are. So the letters are safe."

"Are you sure we are?"

Funny that he should zero in on that particular point. "From our mystery murderer? I don't know. I worked myself up into a lather on the way to Pennsylvania, because I hadn't even thought about that earlier. Oh, did I mention that Nell's partner is an FBI agent? So he's heard our story too, and he knows about the letters."

"Did he have any comments?"

"Not yet, but I gather the FBI has some rules about not getting involved in somebody else's investigation unless they're invited, and only in special cases. He was deliberately very noncommittal."

I realized my glass was empty. Josh noticed and refilled it. His was still half full.

"So everything was fine in Philadelphia—no men following you or lurking in the shadows?"

"Not a one. I was beginning to feel stupid for worrying, but it all came back while I was driving back here. You might have noticed that I don't handle being scared very well. I got as far as this place, and I opened the front door, and I got spooked about being alone here, so I bolted to Lisbeth's house. I didn't want to put her or her family at risk, and I really hope nobody thinks I might have given her the letters to hold. Like you and I talked about. But she noticed I was pretty jumpy, so I ended up telling her everything. Josh, am I going crazy? You think *anybody* is at risk?"

Josh took a sip of wine before responding. "Frankly, Kate, I don't know how to answer that. We now know the letters are probably authentic, and that they have some market value. We know Cordy had one of the letters, and was most likely the person who removed it from the others in that trunk, as some sort of proof of something. We've made the leap of logic that she was working with someone else, since she didn't have the smarts or the contacts to sell them herself, and that person is quite possibly her killer. That person still doesn't know who else knows about the letters, and clearly no arrests have been made for the murder. So it's altogether possible that he is quietly looking for the letters now."

That did not make me feel any better. "Has anybody tried to get into the Barton house, or into the attic?"

"Not that I've noticed, but I don't watch the place 24/7. And if this person is careful, he could conceal the fact that he's ever been to the house. Or here. Do you want me to search this place?"

I was surprised by how much I welcomed that idea. "Could you? I hate it that I'm acting like such a wimp, but I guess murder makes me nervous. But I'm coming with you. No way are you leaving me here alone to listen to the house creak. Even with a good bottle of wine."

"Fine. Just stay behind me."

"Ooh, you gonna protect me, Mr. Professor? How are your martial arts skills?"

"Kate, I'm only trying to help. Just say the word and I'll go home."

"No," I said in a small voice. "Please don't. I apologize. I'm not myself these days. Damn that Cordelia—is she going to hound me for the rest of my life? Even when she's dead?"

"Apology accepted. You want to start upstairs or down?"

"I don't know. You decide. Oh, do you want a weapon?"

"What did you have in mind?"

"Maybe a fireplace poker, if there is one? Or a small frying pan? God, I am such a cliché. Is there a more modern version of impromptu defensive weapons for hapless females?"

"I'd go with the poker. Right there." He pointed at the fireplace in the dining room.

"Right. Thanks."

"I vote for starting downstairs."

"Okay," I said cautiously. "Right behind you."

"We know the kitchen is clear—unless somebody's messed with the lock on the back door. I'll check." He stood up and walked over to the door, then bent down and peered closely at the knob and lock. "Looks all right. No suspicious scratches. Now the dining room."

We must have looked like something out of the Three Stooges, tiptoeing in single file into the dining room, Josh leading, me carrying the sturdy brass-and-iron poker. "I didn't see anything out of the ordinary in the wine cabinet," I whispered.

"Why are you whispering? If there's someone here, he already knows we're here."

"Oh. Right. Anyway, short of dusting for fingerprints, I can't tell if anyone has messed with that cabinet."

"Okay. Then we should check the one in the library, where you found the first letter." He strode across the hall and turned on the overhead light from the wall switch next to the door. As soon as the light flooded the room, I grabbed Josh's arm.

"What?" he demanded.

"Look at the paneling there. The one where the letter was hidden. It isn't completely closed—you can see the crack from here."

"You're right. Are you sure you closed it when you removed the letter?"

"I think I did. I don't remember how tightly it fit, and as you know, there's no exterior latch. But there was nothing inside it."

"Let me take a look." He crossed the room and crouched by the panel and opened it with one finger. I clutched my poker with a death grip.

"Anything?"

"Not that I can tell. Inconclusive. Is there a cellar here?"

"Like I'm supposed to know?" I asked, a bit shrilly. "I'm a guest here, more or less. I have not gone down to the cellar to check on anything. Isn't that what gets someone killed in every slasher movie ever made?"

"Only if the person going down the stairs is wearing a skimpy nightie and clutching a candle. I suppose we can save that for last. Upstairs, then."

"After you."

He gave me a dirty look and started up the stairs. Several of the treads creaked, but I was expecting that. I tried to imagine our villain removing each tread to see if Cordy had hidden her finds under one, but that would have taken a lot of work, not to mention destroying the staircase. So very not like Cordy to find such a complicated hiding place.

Upstairs there were plenty of bedrooms, and I'd explored only the one I was using and had peeked in Cordy's. Everything in the other rooms looked untouched, even to the light coating of dust, which had not been disturbed, even by the police. I wondered if Cordy had tacked up the name of a local housecleaner somewhere, and whether Ryan would foot the bill for cleaning the place.

"Which room was Cordy's?" Josh asked.

"Oh, that's at the back. Very unlike her, but I guess she figured that the rental income was more important than her pride. Follow the scent of her perfume—it's that door at the end of the hall."

Josh didn't spend long back there. "All clear," he said as he reappeared through the door. "Although I'm pretty sure I'm allergic to that perfume, whatever it is." He fished out a handkerchief from a pocket and blew his nose.

"Is that a clue to anything?"

"I doubt it. Anyway, nothing looks like it's been touched back there. Did the police check it out?"

"I think maybe Detective Reynolds and his crews checked, but I left while they were here."

I got bored after the next bedroom, and sat down in the middle of the hall floor with my legs crossed, clutching my trusty poker, and listened to Josh move quietly around the rooms, opening and closing doors and apparently peering under beds, if the creaking of bedsprings was any indication. Victorian furniture didn't offer many places to hide, except for the beds and any armoires. I think he covered them all. He was certainly thorough.

Finally he emerged. "Nothing. You sure you didn't hear any odd noises when you came in earlier? Smell somebody's perfume or aftershave?"

"No, nothing specific. It just felt wrong when I walked in. Look, I'll admit it might have been just my paranoia. But I'm used to living alone, and I'm not usually like this. Of course, it's been a really odd few days."

"I get it, Kate. Attic?"

"What about it?"

"Is there one?"

"Please refer to the part about cellars. I have not gone into the attic since I arrived here. I have not opened the door to the attic. For all I know, there may be bats up there. Or squirrels. I am not in the mood to have a confrontation with a bat or a squirrel. Please feel free to investigate all you want. I will remain here and fend off attackers from the rear."

"That gives me great confidence," Josh said solemnly, and disappeared up the stairs. I continued to sit, listening to his footsteps moving around above my head and wondering what I would do if he met someone up there, or if someone tried to sneak up on me. I was kind of ashamed of myself: I'd worked for years in a hotel in a big city that had its share of crime, but I'd always been careful, and I'd relied on the security guards at the hotel for protection, even if it was only to walk me to my car in the parking garage late at night. I'd never taken a self-defense class in my life. My plan if I was accosted on a dark street was to run like hell and scream as loudly as I could. Right now that didn't seem like enough anymore.

I heard Josh coming down the stairs, and in the dim light I thought he looked concerned. "Is there something I need to know?" I asked quickly.

"No. And nothing appeared disturbed. Not even the dust."

"Okay, so I am now officially paranoid without any basis. Thank you for checking, anyway. I appreciate it."

"Glad to help. I have a stake in this too, you know. If something was taken from the Barton house on my watch, I might be liable in some way since I'm the official caretaker, and I think I signed some documents for the bank. The sooner someone goes through that attic there to see if there is anything else of value, the happier I'll be. Here, let me help you up." He held out his hand, and I untangled my legs and took it.

He must be stronger than he looked, because I was on my feet in seconds, and then somehow my momentum carried me forward into his arms. He looked as startled as I was.

"Did you do that on purpose?" I asked, noting that I hadn't moved away from him.

"Would that be a problem?" he said, with a slight smile.

"Uh, actually, no, I don't think so."

26

I woke up with the sun the next morning, with only a vague memory of the rest of the night before. I was willing to bet that Josh and I had finished that bottle of wine; I was a little less clear about whether we'd opened another one. Apparently the combination of stress, fatigue, and Burgundy, with a dash of relief after our search of the house, had done me in.

I heard footsteps on the stairs, but before I could panic Josh's face peered around the corner. "Oh, good, you're awake. What do you want for breakfast?"

"You're here," I said intelligently.

"Brilliant deduction, Watson. Coffee?"

"You spent the night," I said flatly.

"Yes. It was late."

"Did we, uh, do anything?"

Josh laughed. "No, we did not engage in any unseemly behavior. We did, however, polish off that bottle of very good wine—downstairs, I might add—and then it appeared unlikely that you could navigate the stairs, so I assisted you and tucked you in. Then I went looking for another bed because I didn't trust myself to drive. No one attempted to break in here while we slept the sleep of the just. Or do I mean the innocent?" He was still smiling.

And I was suddenly very conscious that I had been wearing the same clothes for two days without benefit of a shower and was suffering from extreme bed head. "Yes to the offer of coffee. Let me get dressed and I'll join you downstairs. You'll have to improvise as far as breakfast goes."

"Got it. See you soon." He disappeared down the stairs.

I had intended to spring out of bed and perform my ablutions, but I needed a minute to think about what had happened—or not happened—the night before. I had not been at my best, and that was before we opened the wine. I was unmoored, camping out in an unfamiliar place, with a murderer on the loose somewhere in the neighborhood, and an ex-boyfriend hovering around the edges, and I'd just lost my job, and . . . now I was wallowing in self-pity. *Focus, Kate!* This was not the time to consider a relationship with anyone. Or hop into bed with a man—that wasn't my style under any circumstances, whether or not wine was involved. Did I like Josh? Yes, well enough—he was mature, reasonably attractive, obviously intelligent. And single. But only yesterday—or was it the day before?—I had been wondering if he might be a killer or a thief. Potential mate material or combination killer/thief—I couldn't have it both ways.

All right: Get up, get clean, get dressed, and go find coffee and food. Everything always looked better with coffee. And I needed to find more clothes—I rejected the idea of rummaging through Cordy's wardrobe, even if we might be the same size, which left the options of making a fast trip back to my condo to pick up more, finding a local clothing store, or doing a very fast load of laundry. Oh, right, that might mean going to the basement. It couldn't be too bad by daylight. Could it?

I was downstairs in fifteen minutes, clean but not exactly glamorous, but why would I need to be? Josh wordlessly handed me a mug of hot coffee. Smart man. After a few sips I said, "Do we have an agenda for today, or are you going back to your regular work?"

"I should be working," he said, as he sat down across from me with his own coffee, "but I'll admit this whole Barton thing has got me hooked. I think a trip to the library is called for."

"I agree, and that was my plan for today," I told him. "But there are multiple aspects to that research, like Henry's family background, and whether he and Clara were connected and how closely. The building of the factory and the development of the town, and then of course, when the house was built, or rather, expanded, which was clearly some years after the Civil War ended, which tells you *when* he made his money. That side is more your department. I'd be happy to do the genealogy side of things, if you want to do the history and the local economics."

"That works for me," Josh said amiably. "But what about the criminal side? There's the murder, and there's the theft. Are they related? Or coincidental? Do we have any suspects that took part in both, or are we really dealing with two different criminals?"

"You are far too coherent for this early in the morning," I told him. "Besides, that's not something we're going to find at the library. You said something about breakfast?"

"Oh, right. Slim pickings, as you said."

"I wasn't expecting to stay here, if you remember. And

there hasn't been time to go food shopping. Are you saying you can't throw together a breakfast using only the ingredients you can find in the pantry and kitchen? May I remind you that until a week ago this was an operating bed and breakfast?"

"Is that a challenge?"

"If you like."

"Then I shall rise to the occasion."

"And I shall observe and toss in pithy observations while you work." Gee, this was kind of fun. The man actually appeared to have a sense of humor, in addition to his other sterling qualities. Plus, he might even know how to cook.

Josh appeared to have whipped up some kind of quick bread and was sliding it into the preheated oven when I heard a knocking at the door. "Can you get that?" he asked.

"Sure. You weren't expecting anyone, were you?"

"Uh, nobody knows I'm here, remember? So it must be for you. Or maybe a guest that Cordelia forgot to notify that she was dead."

"Oh. Right." I got up and made my way to the front door. When I pulled it open, I found Audrey standing there, with a tote bag full of books. "Hi, Audrey. I was planning to stop by the library this morning. What brings you here?"

"I thought I could get you started. I brought some published references over—signed out, of course, in your name. Any original documents can't leave the library building, so you'll have to stop in to see those. Are you going to ask me in?"

"Of course. Would you like some coffee? Something to eat?"

"I'd appreciate the coffee. Let me leave the books on the dining table." Audrey seemed to know her way around the place and went straight to the dining room, where she carefully set down the bag and one by one pulled out a stack of shabby bound books that looked fairly old. Then she turned and walked toward the kitchen—and stopped dead in the doorway. "Oh," she said flatly. "I didn't know you had company."

Oh, right, Josh was in the kitchen. "Hey, you're not interrupting," I assured her. "Sit down and have a cup of coffee, at least." Did she look pale?

"No, thank you. I need to go open up the library. I'll see you later." She turned on her heel and hurried toward the front door, and I had to scramble after her to open the door for her.

"Thanks for the books," I called out to her retreating back. She didn't reply.

I went back to the kitchen feeling puzzled. "What was that all about?"

Josh looked uncomfortable. "What, Audrey? Well, to put it delicately, she kind of has a thing for me. Do you know her story?"

"Lisbeth filled me in a bit when I first arrived. Unmarried, spent her best years taking care of her sick and aging parents, et cetera. Like Marian the Librarian in *The Music Man*, or maybe I'm thinking of Donna Reed in *It's a Wonderful Life*— the part with the lousy outcome. Poor Audrey is almost a caricature. I take it there aren't a lot of eligible men in Asheboro?"

"Not many under the age of seventy who aren't already married. I would have thought that once she didn't have to worry about her parents any longer, she could have sold the house and moved somewhere else, but maybe she believed it was too late. She has a niche here and she can't seem to dig herself out of it."

"And where did you come into the picture?"

At the sound of a timer, Josh retrieved the loaf of whatever it was from the oven and set it on a rack to cool. It smelled wonderful. "Let it cool for a few minutes before we cut into it," he said sternly. "So, back to Audrey. When I first arrived, some six months ago, I checked out the library, just to see what there was to work with there. We academics are always hoping to find some long-lost documents that will rock the scholarly world, but no luck. Just a nice small library, although the local history section is pretty decent."

"And? She saw you across a crowded room and sparks flew?"

"Not exactly. She's been professional throughout, but sometimes I've been in there and I've noticed her watching me. Trust me, I haven't encouraged her. I've never even had lunch with her."

An aging woman with a serious crush? "Josh, I'm sure she treasures every scrap of encouragement that she thinks you've offered. I feel bad for her—now she thinks we're an item."

"You want me to tell her we're not, or would you like to do the honors?"

"It might be less awkward coming from me, I guess. I can simply ask whether she might have misinterpreted what she saw this morning."

"Two fully clothed adults eating breakfast? Why would she jump to any conclusions?"

"Because, based on my thirty seconds of observation, I think she's got it bad for you. Just what we need—one more complication. It's not easy to get things done around here, is it?"

He looked like he wanted to debate what Audrey had really thought, but in the end he let it go. "I can't really say—I've spent most of my time out at the Barton place, and I rarely come into town."

"Smart man. Maybe I should have given Lisbeth a polite 'no' after my preliminary visit and gone on my merry way. Maybe I'm using this project as a diversion from the fact that I don't have a job and I don't even know what I want to do next."

Josh moved the bread to a trivet he had found in a drawer, and handed me a plate, setting one in front of his seat as well. He then retrieved butter and butter knives, refilled our coffees, and sat. "That's actually two problems, you know."

"Why do you say that?" I mumbled, my mouth filled with crumbs. "By the way, this is great."

"Thank you. I meant, the first problem was what to do about the town, which poses an interesting challenge. The second problem was the sudden and unexpected loss of your job. Your brain said something like, 'Oh, look, I have something that will keep me busy now that my job is gone, and I actually think it would be fun.' The issue is, do you want to take on this project? Are you really interested or are you only using it to distract yourself?"

"You sure you aren't a shrink? Those are very good questions, and I've already been asking them myself. And here's what I think: to the best of my knowledge, and after a few days of reflection, I really do think this project to take Asheboro back to an earlier era is very promising and could make a real difference to the town. Especially now that I don't have to worry about dealing with Cordy—not that I'd kill her just to avoid butting heads with her on the town council."

"I never thought you would." Josh grinned.

"Glad to hear that. Anyway, losing my job gives me the opportunity to *choose* whether I want to take this on for the town, while I sort out the rest of my life. You already know that the discussions are very preliminary and there's nothing like a plan in place. Even if I present the council with a glossy report with my recommendations, there's no guarantee that the council will accept it. Or the numbers might not work out. Right now it's only a couple of weeks out of my life. So, in case I haven't answered your question in all this rambling, it's not just a diversion for me."

"Got it. If I'm going to get sucked into it, I want to know I'm not just wasting my time."

He really did want to be part of this? "I promise I'll pull my weight. What you choose to do is up to you."

I realized we'd both stopped eating, so we turned our attention to the marvelous bread, and there might have been a second piece involved. "I'll clean up," I volunteered.

"Good. I'd better go back to my place and shower and change, and grab my tablet. Want me to pick you up here in, say, an hour?"

"No, I think I should go over alone and try to talk to Audrey woman to woman, without you lurking around. But if she's still casting yearning glances your way, it will be up to you to let her down gently."

"Fair enough. I'll be on my way then, and I'll meet you at the library."

After Josh had left I tidied up the kitchen—and thought. Had Cordy more or less shut down her own B&B operations to deal with the Barton letters or others? Then I wondered what, if anything, was happening or might happen between Josh and me. I was not looking for a romantic partner at this particular time. He was probably on the rebound from his broken marriage since he hadn't managed to find a long-term living arrangement yet. Put those together and you got a lousy situation in which to start anything new.

But . . . it had been a long time since there had been a man in my life. Maybe I didn't recognize flying sparks anymore. So why was I smiling as I washed the dishes?

I'd been telling the truth when I said I thought working on the town project would be rewarding and interesting. I had few doubts of my ability to carry it off, but I still wasn't sure I could sell my vision to the town. I would still need outside help from people like Nell, and the town would need an infusion of outside money, at least at the start. Both were potentially high hurdles, and I wouldn't be doing anyone a favor if I tried to downplay them.

But I thought it was worth trying.

27

As I prepared to leave for the library, I had to ask myself: How had things gotten so complicated? I had come back to Asheboro at Lisbeth's request to scope out what potential there was to use the Barton estate to generate some money for the town. Then that simple plan had ballooned to include the whole town. Now all I needed was the town's approval—and a big chunk of money.

Then Cordy was murdered. And in poking around trying to find out why, Josh and I had uncovered a significant theft, and we still weren't sure if it was an isolated incident or part of a larger scheme that had been going on for a while. I made a mental note to ask Nell to check auctions and sales over the past year or two, to see if any collections had shown up unexpectedly. But the question remained: Had Cordy died because of her involvement in this hypothetical theft, or for some other reason?

And that's where things stood. I was a hotel manager, not a detective. I'd been dumped into the middle of this mess purely by accident, unless I chose to believe in karma. I had no skills or expertise to bring to the crime side, apart from common sense and some insider knowledge of the town and some of its citizens that was years out of date. It was a bit more than Detective Reynolds had, as far as the town went, but he was a trained professional and it was his job to track down murderers. As for thieves? That was a little murkier, but I had faith that he could figure out the right person to handle that.

So what was I doing now, heading for the library? First: I wanted to soothe Audrey, for whom I felt sorry. I could understand her attraction to Josh, but he said he wasn't interested. But I was not the one to tell Audrey that. Besides, I needed Audrey's help to find the information I wanted.

Then I had to see exactly what information the library had on Henry Barton, and if there was any, to determine whether that shed any light on his role in Asheboro, both personal and commercial. Then figure out if this Victorian village project was actually viable, and talk to Mayor Skip about presenting a coherent plan to the town council to consider and ultimately vote on. Once I had their decision, I could either settle in Asheboro, at least for a while, or start job hunting aggressively. And last but not least, decide if there was any possibility of a longer-term relationship with Josh, and if I thought there was, whether I should see where it went, or nip it in the bud?

That seemed like a long enough list for one day: solve a murder and a theft, figure out my romantic life, and plan how I was going to spend my next six to twelve months. First on the list was Audrey. To the library!

I checked to make sure my cell phone was charged and tucked in my purse, then gathered up my laptop, pads, pens, pencils, and the keys to the B&B and let myself out. It seemed to be a nice day, so I decided I might as well walk to the library, which was only a few blocks away. After all, I had to work off that second piece of bread that Josh had made, which had been pretty darn good. As I walked I looked critically at the buildings I was passing. The B&B's location was well chosen for its current purpose: an attractive large old house, in good repair, close to town but not fronting on a busy, noisy street. If my plan went forward, it could still serve as a bed and breakfast, under new ownership. If my plan evaporated, there would be few guests, and Ryan might decide simply to sell the property as a home, or home plus office suite.

As I strolled toward the center of town, I paid more attention to the commercial buildings, and kind of let my imagination run wild again, visualizing what this approach might have looked like in 1900. Would Main Street have been paved? If so, with what—brick, stone, macadam? When did asphalt become the norm? The bank, the post office, the library, and a couple of churches anchored the center of the town, and they had changed little over time. There was a fire station, but set a block or two over. Had it always been there? Or had it moved from the main street to accommodate larger fire equipment, and what had filled its slot? It could be fun to have an old horse-drawn pumper truck—for display only, of course.

Stables. Had there been any in town? When had car sales begun? Had there been a tram or trolley that ran along Main Street, before automobiles had become widespread? I realized that I kind of liked this kind of fantasizing, and reminded myself to look at the library for old photos of the town—after I nailed down who Henry Barton was. And then I found I had already arrived at the library.

I peered in the window: Audrey seemed to be the only person inside, which wasn't surprising given that it was barely nine o'clock on a Saturday morning on a fine spring day. The door was unlocked, which kind of surprised me, so I went in. If Audrey noticed me, she didn't react, so I approached the desk and waited until she looked up.

She didn't smile—her expression was all business. "Oh, Kate. I left a batch of non-circulating materials for you on the table in the Local History Room. Remember, no pens and no photocopies."

So she was going to play it as though our earlier encounter had never happened. "Audrey, we should talk."

Audrey was shuffling papers in front of her, and she didn't look up. "Why? What's the point? He's a grown man, you're a grown woman. What you do is your business, not mine."

"You're upset." I stated it as a fact, not a question.

She didn't answer right away. "Yes, I guess I am. Stupid of me. So?"

"Audrey, please, can we talk? We don't have to take long."

Finally she looked up, not at me but at all the empty chairs in the library. "I'm not expecting many people this morning. You want to talk. So talk."

There was no reason to dance around the subject. "All right. I think you misread what you saw this morning. Josh and I are not involved, if that's what you're thinking. He stopped by last night because he knew I had gone to Philadelphia on a research errand, and he was eager to hear the results, and I got back late." That was true enough, even if it wasn't the whole story. "We had a couple of drinks and talked, and by then it was late so we went to bed—in separate rooms." Having covered the basic facts, I realized I had no idea where to go next. Apologize to Audrey for inadvertently encroaching on what she thought was her turf? How could I have known?

Audrey's expression was neutral with a tinge of grim. "You don't need to apologize to me. I have no claim on Josh Wainwright. I know he's not interested in me. I was just startled this morning because I wasn't expecting to run into him. Or anyone else," she amended quickly.

"Audrey," I began desperately. "You don't have to explain, or to defend yourself, whatever you feel. Look, I'm single. I've never been married, or even close to it. My job is more or less my life—I don't even own a houseplant. So I'm guessing we have something in common."

Audrey stood up abruptly. "You don't know the first thing about me!" she spat. "Oh, poor Audrey, still stuck in her old hometown—a librarian, of all things! What a pathetic cliché! Doesn't she have a life?" She snorted in a very unladylike way. "At least you have choices."

"And you don't?" I shot back. "You're not even forty. You don't have anyone holding you here. You can go anywhere."

"And be a librarian? Who reads books anymore? In case you haven't noticed, libraries are cutting their staffs, and in some cases they're closing. I'm not exactly a valuable commodity on the job market. And I haven't kept up on my computer skills, because I haven't needed them here. Those few high school kids who come in know more than I do about those little electronic toys, and they do most of their research from home now."

I debated saying something soothing and trying to cheer her up—but I realized she was right. She'd picked a career that was contracting, not expanding. She'd stayed in this town for personal reasons, but that added nothing to her resume, and she'd already waited too long. "She was kind to her parents" wouldn't look very impressive on a job application. Plus her personality was not exactly warm and welcoming. Maybe it had been, a decade earlier, but right now she'd kind of shrunken into herself.

I realized she was watching me, with an ironic half smile on her face. "I can tell exactly what you're thinking. I don't want your pity. I don't even want your sympathy. You got out. I didn't."

"I got out for one reason," I said.

"Cordelia. That bitch."

I was surprised at the anger in her tone. "Yes, Cordelia. You were a couple of years ahead of me in school, right? Did everybody know about what happened?"

"You and Ryan? Sure. She made sure everybody knew. If it happened today, there would probably be videos all over the Internet."

Ick. "But she was younger than you."

"Yes. I missed the first reign of Queen Cordelia—the high school years. But I had to move back to town, to take care of my parents, and then she moved back. She might have gotten away from here for a while, but she missed her adoring fan club, and she didn't do particularly well in college. She wasn't school smart, but she could read people well enough to figure out their weak spots, and she knew just how to stick it to them. You could almost admire it, unless you were her target."

"What the heck did she have against you? You never did anything to her."

"Didn't matter. She came back, she found her fan girls had moved on with their lives, and then she latched onto Ryan. When that didn't prove to be enough to keep her busy, she went back to her old ways. I was easy prey. I mean, here I sat in the library, day after day. Watching the kids I hung out with in school get married, have babies, find jobs. And I was stuck, watching my mother die by inches, and then my father. And she just couldn't resist twisting the knife. 'Oh, Audrey, you poor dear. How are your parents doing? Is there any hope for improvement? What a shame you had to give up your own life to take care of them.' If I'd had any guts I would have given her as good as she gave. 'How kind of you to ask, Cordelia. Have you had any guests at that little business of yours lately? It seem awfully quiet over there. Too bad you couldn't work things out with your husband—I hear his law practice is doing very well.'" Audrey sighed. "I could have, but I didn't. I let her get away with it. And I knew I wasn't the only victim. Sitting here in the library cuts both ways. After she and Ryan split, I watched her carry on with half the men in town, married or not. I'd see her on the street with the new man of the moment, or in the market—anyone could tell when she'd picked a new one. She'd be all over him, and then she'd drop him like a hot potato. The guy never saw it coming. That was how she amused herself—torturing other people. I don't think there are many in this town who will mourn her passing."

While I agreed with Audrey, I wasn't going to say so. "I think I'll start looking at the materials you put together for me, if you don't mind."

"You go right ahead. You won't be disturbed." She turned to sort a stack of papers on her desk, signaling our conversation was over. I escaped to the empty Local History Room, where stacks of books and folders were neatly arrayed, waiting for me. I took a seat facing the main room—somehow turning my back on it didn't feel right.

I'd barely begun sorting through the piles, trying to decide where I wanted to start, when I saw Josh come in. There still were no other library patrons, and he went straight to Audrey's desk and leaned toward her. I had to guess he was following my suggestion, but I had to look away. Poor Audrey—she simply couldn't catch a break.

A couple of minutes later Josh slipped into the Local History Room and closed the door quietly behind him. "You talked to her," he said.

"I did. What did she say to you?"

"I apologized if I'd misread any signals she was trying to send. She said she was used to that. I fled, like the clueless coward that I am, and here I am. Shall we get down to business?"

"Pick a pile. I've only just begun."

"Maybe we should talk more specifically about what we're looking for and where we're likely to find it," he suggested.

"You're the professional researcher—you tell me. No, wait—maybe there's something else we should be thinking about first. Like, who knew about the Barton letters, and when? Why did somebody decide to take them now? And we should verify that they really do belong to the town, even if they aren't specified in the will. That might point us to whoever had a motive to kill Cordelia."

"Making money from selling them isn't enough of a motive?" Josh asked, not unreasonably.

"Maybe. I'm sure there are plenty of people in this town who could use some money. And as far as we know, the letters aren't listed in any sort of inventory for the property, so if they're gone, nobody would know. Maybe that tells us the 'why now.' If the Grand Barton Hotel or whatever Cordy wanted to call it was going to be developed and opened to the public, the attic would be cleared out, and the letters—and whatever other goodies are up there—would be discovered. So the thief had a narrow window to make off with them. Maybe Cordy's partner was getting nervous, what with the council dragging its feet, and then me getting called in to suggest other ideas."

"If they knew about you, and it's not clear that Cordelia did. Although some of the other council members must have," Josh said. "But what you say makes sense. Somebody could have wanted to collect the good stuff sooner rather than later, and Cordy somehow got in the way. In any event, we'd better get started. We outlined areas of responsibility earlier. Do you want to change any of those?"

I shook my head. "I don't know any more than I did. I think we boiled it down to 'I do the people, you do the things.' And we don't have a lot of time. I've still got the books that Audrey brought over to the B&B earlier today," I reminded Josh. "I assume they aren't duplicates, and we can look at them later. So the new materials are here on the table."

We started searching through what Audrey had gathered. "Should we split this up, physically?" I asked. "I mean, you take this end of the table and I'll take the other?"

"Fine. Though I wish we'd had time to do some online searches before we start in, but I guess that's moot. You could do a basic genealogy for Henry and his family quickly on any of a number of websites, but we're here now, and there may be information in these documents that's not online. Cross your fingers and hope that there's something like a family tree lurking here. Plus, Audrey didn't have a lot of time to pull these together, so if we come up dry, maybe we can do a broader search in the library for anything connecting to any Bartons."

"Am I doing Clara?" I asked.

"Save that for the computer. I'm sure there's plenty available for her."

I looked at the sizable pile of materials in front of us, and I remembered the stack of books waiting for me back at the B&B, and I felt a surge of panic. "Josh, I hate to bring this up, but our thief may decide to move faster now, with so much outside attention focused on Cordy and her death. He doesn't know we have the letters, and he may double his efforts to find them. Do you think it's risky to leave the Barton house unprotected?"

Josh looked defensive. "I armed what pitiful alarms there are. I made sure everything was locked, including the gates. I wasn't hired as a security guard, you know—I'm just a caretaker, there to report if the roof caves in or the furnace explodes. Not to fend off desperate thieves and potential killers."

"I know, I know. I'm not saying you should put yourself at risk. And I'm not any better equipped than you are, if somebody decides to ransack the B&B. All I meant to say was that we'd better get this worked out pretty fast."

"I agree."

And so we began. After a while we each became so engrossed in our reading that we didn't notice whether anybody came into the library, and Audrey left us alone. I struck gold first, in the form of a lengthy obituary of Henry Barton from a local paper. "Got something," I said.

"What is it?"

"Henry's obituary. It says he was born in Massachusetts, and it gives the names of his parents and his surviving relatives. He was one of several brothers, two of whom survived him. The one Clara was looking for was named William, and he isn't mentioned in the obituary, so he must have been dead by 1911. In letters I saw, Clara had only just started looking for him. We still don't know if she found him."

"You didn't stop en route to Philadelphia and read them all, to see what Clara found?" Josh said, smiling.

"No, I didn't want to risk damaging them. And I wanted to get them somewhere safe. We did lay them out at in order in Philadelphia, and I'll admit I peeked to see who Clara was searching for. Carroll was going to go through them for conservation purposes, but I'm sure someone will send us copies soon enough."

"Wonder if she ever found William, or at least his remains?" Josh mused. "That is, if he's buried anywhere? I wish I had time to read up on how Clara went about tracking down people back then. There were no dog tags, and it was total chaos on the battlefields. What little I've read tells about body parts flying all over during the shelling, and then the bodies—and the pieces—were stacked in heaps after the battle. It's hard to imagine, isn't it?"

"I'd rather not." I suppressed that image, which wasn't easy. Then I had a sudden brainstorm. "That place where Nell works, the Society—they have one of the best genealogy libraries in the country. We don't have a lot of time. I think I'll call her and see if she can sic one of her trained people on it. I'm pretty sure it wouldn't take long for one of them to collect what information there is, now that I've got Henry's parents' names and his birthplace."

"Makes sense, if she's willing. What information do we want?"

"The official record of William's death, assuming he died in the war. Any wills the family left. Property records. When Henry arrived in Maryland. Military records. All that kind of stuff. Might as well go straight to the top. The worst Nell could do is say no."

Josh nodded. "And we work here with the original records for the house and the town and the factory that are not available there and also not online."

"Exactly."

"So call her!"

I got my cell phone out of my bag and retreated to a corner so I wouldn't distract Josh. I called Nell, crossing my fingers that she wasn't out to lunch or something inconvenient like that. I almost wept when she actually answered.

"Hey, Kate. I didn't expect to hear from you so soon. What's up?"

"I have another big favor to ask."

"All right—tell me."

"Josh and I are at the local library now, and we're trying to figure out more about Henry—who he was, where he came from, how he made his fortune. And did his older brother, William, ever show up, or was he really dead? We're going through local records, but I would be eternally grateful if you could find someone at your place to look up all those family history details. I know they're available online, for the most part, but I don't have the skill or the time to do it. Can you help?"

"Sure. It would probably take only a couple of hours to collect the basic information, so I could get it to you tonight or tomorrow."

"Thank you! I hate to sound like such a wimp, but it really bothers me that whoever may be looking for the letters is still at large, and may decide to wrap things up sooner rather than later if he sees his chance slipping away. He could be desperate. I'd certainly rather not find out."

"Believe me, I understand. Tell me what you need, specifically."

I read off the pertinent details from the obituary, and listed the questions Josh and I wanted to answer quickly—the rest could wait. Maybe someday the Barton House would attract guests from all over, and my staff (ha!) and I could put together a glossy pamphlet outlining Henry's career, but that was for later. Maybe.

"Got it," Nell said at last. "I've got your email so I can send you the results. Oh, and Carroll is over the moon about the letters. She's already scanned them. I'll have her send you copies of them. Same email?"

"Sure." I could always call them up on Josh's computer—he must have a printer in his rooms at the estate. "I can't thank you enough!"

"Don't worry—I'll find a way for you to thank me. Happy hunting, and I'll be in touch later."

Josh looked up expectantly when I returned to the Local History Room. "What did she say?"

"I was right—someone who knows what they're doing can get what we need in a couple of hours. She thinks we may have the information by tonight. And she's sending scans of the letters. Have you found anything good?"

"I've been putting together a general time line, with a lot of guesses. We know Henry fought in the war, and we'll probably find out which unit he fought with, and which battles he took part in. I'm going to guess that it was somewhere around here, since he didn't go back to Massachusetts. Clara Barton was hunting for the lost soldiers for a relatively short time, before she went on to other projects like the Red Cross, so, based on the addresses on the letters, Henry must have contacted her shortly after the war ended. By the way, the addresses don't tell us much—they were to Henry Barton, Asheboro, Maryland.

Presumably it was such a small place then that anyone would have known where to find him."

"I'm with you so far. What else?"

"We'd have to look at county records to find out when he did buy the property. What we do know is that the factory was up and running by 1870."

"What did they make?"

"Shovels. Don't laugh. Shovels were important then. And after a couple of years it looks like he graduated to plowshares—bigger metal items. And so on, for the next forty years or so. At its peak, the factory employed almost every male in town who wasn't a farmer or a shopkeeper."

I pondered. "So Henry buys a property outside of town, and we're guessing that it was a pretty simple place then—your basic farmhouse. He starts up his factory in town, and it does well. Somewhere in there he marries. He's getting richer, so he builds his grand mansion—based on the style that has to be 1880 or later. How long did the factory keep going after Henry had died?"

"From what little I've seen, probably until the Depression."

I nodded. "And it was well on the way to becoming a ruin when I was growing up here. So, what else do we need to know?"

"How did he fund building the factory in the first place? That would have taken some money. Of course, it could have been family money, although New Englanders preferred to keep their money close."

"I hate to say it, but I think we need to look in the attic again. There may be a lot of answers up there, like factory records."

"True. But it's getting kind of late today."

I looked at my watch. He was right—it was past four. Where had the day gone? "I suppose we should adjourn and pick this up in the morning. We might have Nell's information by then."

"I, uh, I'm not sure how to say this," Josh began awkwardly, "but I think it might be best if we stayed together. For protection. The thief doesn't know if Cordy hid anything at the B&B, and he'd probably target the mansion first. So I think we should stay at the Barton place tonight, just in case."

"That makes sense," I said. I hadn't thought about staying alone at the B&B overnight, alone. "Can we stop by the B&B so I can pick up some stuff? And we should think about food, since we missed lunch completely."

"Sounds like a plan."

28

We left the library with no more than a nod to Audrey, who was busy with an older woman with a stack of mysteries. Josh drove me back to the B&B.

It was frustrating not knowing who Cordy might have roped into her moneymaking scheme—or by whom she had been roped in? I doubted she had the brains to plan such a theft, but she did have access and she wanted money. And she had (or believed she had) the charms to wheedle some man to do what she wanted. Maybe that's why I kept thinking of Cordy's accomplice as a "him"—her track record with female friends was kind of pathetic. It was still possible that she was being used, but she was going to get paid for it. Too bad she didn't live to collect that fee.

Everything at the B&B looked peaceful, but that could be deceiving. Maybe the Bad Guy had gotten keys from Cordy and was inside even now, rummaging through drawers and closets and such.

"You want me to come in?" Josh asked quietly.

"Damn it, how do you keep doing that?" I demanded.

"Doing what?"

"Reading my mind."

"It's not hard—you have a very expressive face. I hope you don't play poker."

He'd actually been watching my face? I didn't know whether that pleased or alarmed me. Something to think about later. "I don't have the time. Would you please come in with me? I'll admit I'm nervous."

"No problem."

He followed me as I unlocked the door and stepped into the hall. Nothing had changed, except that the air was beginning to smell a bit stale since the place had been closed up for a few days. "Wait here," I told him, and scurried up the stairs. Nothing had changed up there either. I pulled clothes and some underwear from the dresser I'd been using, picked up my toiletries, stuffed them all into my bag, and hurried back downstairs. "You have food at your place?"

"Some. I wasn't planning on entertaining," Josh said.

"Then we're going to have to stop somewhere and pick up some."

"Fine."

I set the alarm system and locked up.

When Josh started the car and pulled out, he headed toward the supermarket just outside of town. While he drove, he said, "What kind of food places do you envision for this Victorian town of yours?"

"A grocer, of course. Maybe a butcher–slash–poultry shop, although I have mixed feelings about that. It's appropriate to the time and place, but I doubt a lot of tourists are going to stop and buy a chunk of stew beef or a dead chicken. A dry-goods store. A tearoom. Are you trying to distract me?"

Josh smiled without turning his gaze away from the street. "Maybe. What's for dinner?"

"You're asking me? It's your kitchen."

"Kitchenette at best."

"Does it have a microwave?" I asked.

"Yes."

"Then you're good to go."

At the store we stocked up on a mish-mash of quick and easy microwavable foods and left quickly. It was already getting dark.

"Too bad I didn't think to snag a bottle of that wine from the B&B," I said.

"I've got some at my place."

"Do you have a printer?"

"I do. All the comforts of home. You're thinking about printing out Henry's history?"

"Of course I am. And the scanned letters. You know, if all this goes forward, I'm going to have to bone up on Maryland history. And the Civil War."

"There are worse problems to have," Josh said wryly. "Do you think you'll do the project? Not just the proposal?"

It was a fair question, but I hadn't really made up my mind. "I don't know. This past week has been such a disaster that I haven't really had time to think of any of the details, much less any long-range plans. I need to put together a written plan for the council, with financials, if we have any hope of raising money."

"You said 'we.'"

"Did I?"

"You're identifying yourself with the town now. Dead giveaway."

Maybe it was, again—I hadn't done it consciously. Something else to think about. That list kept growing.

"Do you know how much money is available from the funds Henry left?" Josh asked.

"Actually I don't. I can ask the bank president—he's on the town council, so he should be willing to help."

"I would think so. What would it cost to pretty up Henry's house?"

"If it were a modern rebuild, I'd have a better idea. Henry's house is a challenge. I'm guessing a lot of the interior details came straight from the Tiffany Studios, which is a big plus. But on the minus side, some of it is a bit shabby, just from age, so it becomes a question of restoring it or replacing it, and if the latter, with what? And what about the infrastructure—plumbing, heating, wiring? Nobody's looked at that for a while."

"Despite your protestations, you *have* been thinking about it," Josh said.

"Yes, I guess I have."

We had arrived at the front gate, which was locked. Josh got out to unlock it, drove through, then locked it after us. "No point in making it easy," he said.

"Heck, if I were a thief, I'd come in the back anyway, although it really doesn't matter from which direction they come in because there's nobody to see. Think Cordy has been replaced as an accomplice?"

"Don't even go there!" he said firmly.

Josh parked in front of the stable, and we unloaded the bags of food. He went up the stairs and unlocked his own door, and I entered after him. The place was Spartan, to put it politely, but at least it was neat.

"Cute little place you've got here. Mind if I use the computer while you cook?" I asked.

"Oh, now I'm cooking?" he protested.

"Well, it is your place, so technically you're host. You do know how to use a microwave, right? Is the computer password protected?"

He slipped past me to the other side of the table where the computer sat. "Here, let me." He typed in a few commands then stepped back. "All yours."

I logged into my own account. As promised, Nell had delivered the information. Her cover email said only, "Piece of cake. Let me know if there's something more you want."

"Josh, do you have a blank disk or a thumb drive? I want to save this stuff before I mess with it."

"Thumb drives in that box on your right," he said, intently reading the microwave instructions on the food we'd bought.

I fished out a new thumb drive and inserted it in an empty port, then went back to Nell's attachments. There were quite a few, but as I downloaded them I saw that most were only a page or two long. Except for the file folder of Clara's letters. I decided to start with those. "Mind if I print out the letters?"

"You have them all? That was fast. Sure—the printer's on but in sleep mode. Just open the files and print."

"Thanks," I said. As I knew, there were some thirty letters from Clara to Henry, but I'd never seen them fully before. I downloaded them then started sending them to the printer, one at a time. I wrestled with myself: read those letters right away, or be responsible and download all the other files and print them out as needed? Sometimes being a responsible adult could be a pain. "Do you want to read them together? I can finish downloading while you cook."

"Cooking at this point consists of pushing about three buttons on the microwave. But go ahead and finish downloading and printing—we might want to compare the information in the other items to what's in the letters."

"Good point." I returned to downloading, saving, printing, rinse and repeat. Actually it didn't take all that long, and by the time I'd finished Josh had filled two plates with food.

"Let's eat first," he suggested. "It's been a long time since breakfast, and we should be clear-headed."

Again, he was right, but he was driving me crazy. Was I the only person in the room who was eager to see what Nell had collected for us? "Okay. What is it?"

"Some kind of chicken, some rice and a veggie that came in a plastic bag. Real gourmet stuff."

"It's food—it'll do."

"Wine?" he asked.

"Let's save that for later."

We dug in. After a few bites, I said, "You know, I feel like a kid on Christmas morning. We've got some facts here about a guy who lived over a century ago, in the very place we're sitting now. He was a big part of this town in the nineteenth century, and then he was kind of forgotten, and now we're talking about bringing him back so he can save the town. How cool is that?"

Josh smiled. "It is officially cool."

We finished eating quickly and cleared off the table, wiping it down to remove any grease.

I was getting very antsy to get started. "Oh, I do have one suggestion. I said before that we could read the letters first, but it occurs to me that we should look at his family tree, and check whether Henry and Clara are related, and if they might have known each other apart from the war."

"Good point. Have you got that?"

I called up that file and sent it off to the printer, which spit it out thirty seconds later.

Josh picked it up and set it between us on the table. As best I could see, it looked like Henry and Clara were less than twenty years apart in age, but somehow that came out to two generations. Which didn't necessarily mean anything. If I was reading the tree right, their lines came together four generations back for Clara, six for Henry. Both families had lived in the central part of Massachusetts, but that didn't guarantee that they had crossed paths. So for practical purposes it might be safer to conclude they did *not* know each other, but somehow Henry had heard of Clara's efforts to find missing soldiers immediately after the war, and he had contacted her. And that should be reflected in the letters.

It was time to turn my attention to them. As I'd told Josh, in Philadelphia we'd sorted them chronologically, and then Carroll had taken them away to scan them by archival standards, to avoid damaging them. I needed to know more about Clara's history with the search for missing soldiers, and where these letters fit with that, but right now I just wanted to see what she had written to Henry. I stacked the copies up by date and started reading.

It didn't take long. While I was looking at only one side of the correspondence, from Clara to Henry, the outlines were clear. Henry was the second child in his family, and his older brother, William, had not come home from the war, while the two younger ones had, only somewhat damaged. Henry must have heard about Clara's efforts and reached out to her. Her first response acknowledged his letter as well as their kinship, which I'd suspected. His first letter must have been a brief inquiry, because she asked for additional information, which apparently he had provided in a following letter. There were a number of letters from Clara after that, confirming receipt of his letter, and then providing additional information about her search. They were short and polite, but businesslike rather than familiar.

As I read I found myself wishing that I knew more about the war. I tried to imagine Clara taking on the huge task of trying to track down literally thousands of men who remained unaccounted for. I'd read that soldiers had taken to carrying some form of identification on their persons for such eventualities. But reading about the horrific carnage that had taken place, I had to wonder if something as fragile as a slip of paper with an address could have survived. And much of the time the commanding officers were wounded or dead, so they couldn't account for all their own men.

Which often just left personal correspondence, during or just after the war. Clara had made a name for herself by the end of the war, and she was a rather manic letter writer. I was going to guess that she had looked up enlistment records, eliminated the known dead, read individual regiment reports, and then started working her way through the survivors searching for any news of the soldier she was looking for. It must have been largely hit or miss, trying to find the survivors or their kin, but clearly it had worked some of the time.

By the time I reached the end of the small stack of letters, I knew that Clara had found out what happened to William Barton, Henry's brother. But she didn't reveal it in the letter. Instead she asked Henry's permission to call upon him and convey her findings directly. So she had in fact visited Asheboro to meet with Henry.

And the correspondence ended there. I might have snarled.

29

Josh looked up from whatever documents he had been immersed in. "What?"

"Why was I snarling? Because there's a cliffhanger here, in the last letter."

"Which is?"

"Clara Barton found what happened to Henry Barton's older brother, William. But instead of just writing to him, she decided to come visit and deliver the news to him personally."

"Here?" he asked.

"Or wherever Henry was living in Asheboro at the time. And there's nothing after that."

"What was the date on her last letter?"

"March 1865—the day is kind of illegible. Why do you ask?"

"What do you know about the Office of Correspondence with Friends of the Missing Men of the United States Army?"

Couldn't the man give me a straight answer instead of another question? "You mean, her Missing Soldiers Office? Only what I've learned in the past few days, which is not much. Why? I mean, I know why it's important, but why does the date matter?"

"President Abraham Lincoln appointed her to take on the search for missing prisoners of war on March 11, 1865. She recruited a few volunteers, including her own family members, and set up the organization in rented space in Washington and started collecting inquiries. She spread the lists of names as widely as possible for those days, in newspapers and post offices. Veterans could check the lists and send her any information they had. The group logged in over sixty-three thousand letters. The practice was carried over to the Red Cross years later. She was the first woman to run a government bureau, and she received payment through congressional appropriations. She made a final report to Congress in 1869, when she told them that maybe forty thousand soldiers were still unaccounted for and were most likely dead."

Josh wasn't finished yet. "The Treasury back then was reluctant to hand out back pay to the families if there was no evidence of death, or a date. Clara proposed to change that, to help the widows and orphans."

"Josh, this is a wonderful story, but what's it got to do with our Henry Barton?"

"Bear with me. There are a couple of key points. One, look at the timing. That March Lincoln had barely created this group, and there was little money to be had in the government at that point in time. The President may have promised support, but Clara had to fund things at the beginning with her own money or contributions. Keep that in mind. Two, the Treasury didn't want to pay out if no one could prove a soldier was dead. I don't know much about William, so I can't say if he was owed anything, but the fact got me thinking. Henry was the second son. The first son, William, was missing. Henry was eager to find out what happened to William. What if his parents' will specified that their estate would go to their eldest son?"

"Interesting logic, but we don't even know if the parents were dead in 1865."

"We can find out," Josh shot back.

"Okay. We don't know what's in their will."

"We can find that too, assuming there was one. Look, I've got a pal in Massachusetts who can access all this information and answer exactly these questions."

"What if there wasn't a will?" I protested.

"Then he can look up the laws for inheritance without a will as of 1865—maybe it was split evenly among the surviving children. And it might depend on which state they lived in. Again, easy enough to look up."

Now he'd finally gotten excited by our research, just as I was about to dissolve into a lump. "Josh, it's getting late. What's your point?"

"This is just a theory, mind you. What if Henry needed to know what had happened to William because he needed the money, and could only inherit if he could prove that William was dead? Either all of it or a one-third share rather than a one-quarter share, assuming both of his younger brothers survived?"

"Needed it? Or wanted it?"

"Does it matter? Look, we know Henry moved here after his service in the war and was living here when Clara was writing to him in 1865. We don't know how much money was involved, but say he was already thinking about his factory, and that it was the perfect moment to start up a new business in this area. Property might have been cheap, and there would be a lot of returning soldiers who could use a job. He needed a good chunk of change to take advantage of the opportunity."

"And you can check local history for references to the start-up date," I said, almost to myself. "Or ads. Or patent applications."

"Exactly!" Josh said triumphantly. "But there's one more thing. Clara Barton had approval from the President to start up her search group, but little or no money. Once she could show that William was dead, and Henry received his inheritance, what if he gave part of it to Clara, who then used it to start up her organization?"

"So you're suggesting that Henry might have offered to provide the seed money for Clara's work if she could prove that William was dead?"

"It's possible, isn't it? Providing we can find something like evidence. But a lot of her papers have survived. Think she was good at keeping accounts?"

I sat back and rubbed my stiff neck. "Oh, Josh, don't tempt me. You've just put together a scenario based on a lot of wild guesses and maybes. I'd love to believe you—it would be such a great hook to draw people to this house and the town, because it puts Henry and this place into the mainstream of the Civil War. But it has to be true for us to do that. So we've got more work to do. And I hate to burst your bubble, but we really need to find Cordelia's killer before we go chasing pretty theories. Right?"

Josh looked disappointed, but I knew I was right: murder first, nineteenth-century history later.

"I know," he said reluctantly.

God, I was tired, and I couldn't think straight. "But one other point: Where does the theft of the letters fit in this? Was it coincidental, and all it meant to the thief was a juicy payday? Or was there something darker behind it? Who else would have an interest?" I asked.

"That I can't tell you—yet. Maybe things will look better in the morning. Look, like I said earlier, you need to stay here tonight, and maybe beyond, until we get this sorted out—there's still that killer at large. You can take the couch."

"Gee, what a gentleman!"

"Don't worry, it's comfortable. I've fallen asleep on it plenty of times. The bathroom is through the bedroom. I'll hunt down some pillows and a blanket."

I went one way while he went another. The bathroom was surprisingly clean for a guy who lived alone. Right now we were partners in anti-crime, with a working theory about who had killed Cordelia, although we were kind of lacking a name for the person. Now if we could just nab the thief, maybe we could hang up a shingle as investigators.

I went back to the main room, and Josh retreated discreetly to the bedroom and shut the door. I checked the time—I hadn't realized how late it was. I had no idea what I or we would be doing tomorrow.

I lay down, pulled the blanket up to my neck, and turned off the light. Wow, it was dark here. I should have thought about that. This was the country. There was next to no traffic on the road, no sounds of ringing phones or loud music. No lights, either on the house or along the road. I wondered what the electric and heating bills were like. Had Henry liked it out here? I wasn't familiar with where he had come from in Massachusetts. Was it like this? Or more of a town?

Since it was so dark, it occurred to me that I ought to take a look at the stars, something I seldom had a chance to do where I lived—too much light pollution. Not that I had a lot of time for stargazing, but I should indulge in it while I could. I tossed back the blanket and padded barefoot across the floor, carefully feeling my way around the table in the middle of the room where we'd laid out our documents, to look out the nearest window, one that looked toward the house. The house loomed like a big black hulk, only slightly darker than the space around it.

Except for one small light, moving from room to room on the second floor. Either it was another pair of hormonal teenagers, or our letter thief was back.

I darted across the room to Josh's door without stumbling over the table, and crept in quickly. If the light snoring was any indication, Josh was asleep, so I put a hand on his shoulder and shook him gently. And then not so gently.

He finally woke up with a start, "Wha? Oh, Kate. Bad dreams?"

"There someone with a flashlight inside the big house."

Suddenly he was alert. "Who? No, scratch that—stupid question. Did you hear a car?"

"Nope, and I haven't been asleep."

"The gates are locked anyway, so whoever it is had to walk in from the road. He must have assumed I was alone, since only one car is here, and I'd turned off the lights. He doesn't know you're here."

"What're we going to do about it?"

Josh took a moment to think. "If we call the cops, he'll hear them coming and clear out on foot before I can get the gates unlocked. I'll have to go over and check him out."

"Are you, uh, armed?"

"You mean, do I have a gun? Of course not. I'm a history professor."

"So you're going to sneak up on a possibly armed intruder in the middle of the night and ask him politely, 'What are you doing here?'"

"Look, lady—you've vetoed the cops and you just vetoed me. What's left?"

"We sneak up from two sides at once? One of us is bound to surprise him, since he's only expecting one person."

"You want to go with me?" he asked, incredulous.

"It sure beats sitting here and worrying."

What little I could see of Josh's face in the dark radiated dismay: he didn't want to take me along. Heck, I was pretty sure he didn't want to go himself. In his shoes, I probably wouldn't either. But here we were, two intelligent people. We were stronger together, weren't we? We should be able to out-smart one white-collar criminal, shouldn't we? "I'm going to put some clothes on," I whispered. "Maybe you should too."

He looked down at himself—we were dressed pretty much alike, with ratty T-shirts and baggy pajama bottoms. Not the right outfits to confront a thief. Who might also be a murderer.

Josh disappeared into the bathroom, while I pulled on what I'd been wearing earlier in the day. Josh emerged a minute later, and I almost giggled because our "stalking the thief" outfits matched as well as our earlier ones: shirt, jeans, sneak-ers, and a dark windbreaker. "Just for the record," he said, "I think this is a bad idea."

"Duly noted. By the way, what do we do when we get there?"

"Split up, for a start. You made a good point, about him

looking for only one person, not two. I guess from there it depends on who it is. If it's someone we know or recognize, that's one thing. If it's a stranger, that's different. If the guy is armed, either way, I think we should back off and call the cops ASAP."

"State or local?" I asked.

"My first reaction is to call Reynolds or his office, But I think local has jurisdiction over thefts, and they're closer. Ready?"

"I want a weapon," I said, sounding pathetic even to myself.

"I don't have one," Josh said, sounding testy.

"I know. I don't mean a gun—just something to whack the guy with, to defend myself. Or you."

"I think there's an old shovel downstairs, outside the door—it's heavy. Will that do?"

"I guess."

"Fine, we'll pick it up on our way out. Don't drop it, drag it, or trip over it."

"If we don't get moving, I may use it on you. The guy's going to be in DC fencing the goods by the time we get there."

"So let's go."

30

I hadn't brought a flashlight because I hadn't packed one, but Josh had a small but efficient one in his jacket pocket, or so he told me. We didn't dare turn it on yet. We tiptoed down the stairs, and he pointed at the shovel leaning against an outside wall. I had to wonder why we were tiptoeing, if, as we guessed, the thief was rummaging through the attic, looking for one last haul. But better to be safe than sorry, and we needed surprise on our side. We tiptoed across the rolling lawn until we reached the house. I mimed unlocking the door, and Josh nodded and pulled a key ring out of his pocket. Turned out it didn't matter—the door was already unlocked—not a good sign—and it opened silently.

I tried to figure out how to mime "when do we split up?" There were a few details we should have covered back at Josh's place when we could actually speak, but we were kind of new at this game. I tried to review what I knew of the house. There was only one door to the attic, if that was where our guy was currently, and it was on the second floor. So unless he jumped out a window, we could trap him up there. If he was on the second floor, he had more options, and I thought I remembered a back stairway, for the servants, of course.

I leaned close to Josh and whispered in his ear. "Can you hear him now?"

"Only faintly—I think he's still in the attic," Josh whispered back.

"Can we lock him in before he hears us?"

"Maybe. Can't say how long the old lock would hold."

"There are two stairs from the second floor to the first. Our prowler might not know the back stairway to the kitchen is there, so maybe you should cover the main stair and I'll take the other one. Ready?"

We tiptoed up the grand staircase, single file, placing each foot carefully. The higher we got, the more clearly we could hear our thief bumbling around the attic, believing that nobody was paying attention to him. Under ordinary circumstances he'd have been right. At the top of the stairs, Josh pointed to me and then to the door to the back stairs. I took a firmer grip on my shovel and retreated to stand guard, pondering which end of the shovel would do more damage. Josh's shadowy figure advanced toward the attic door, with the key already in his hand.

And that's when our plan went wrong. As Josh was preparing to insert the key in the door, we both heard footsteps clomping down the attic stairs. Definitely male, I thought irrelevantly. Before Josh could react, the door swung open, shoving Josh back against the wall. The shadowy figure said, "What the hell?" and pulled the door away to confront Josh, who was armed only with a bunch of keys to defend himself. Luckily, as I had predicted, the guy from the attic was focused on Josh and had no idea I was there, lurking in the shadows. Before either of the men could react, I gave the loudest roar I could muster and rushed toward them with my shovel raised—and brought it down as hard as I could on the guy's head. He toppled over onto the floor, and for a brief moment I wondered if I'd killed him. Apparently not, since he started trying to get up.

"Now what?" I hissed at Josh, and then remembered we didn't need to whisper anymore.

Josh kept his eye on the guy as he said, "You keep your, uh, shovel cocked, and I'll take off his belt and tie his hands."

"Good plan. I'm ready." Now I was holding the shovel handle like a baseball bat.

The guy on the floor didn't protest when Josh stripped off his belt, rolled him over to pull his wrists together, and secured them with the belt. "Lights?" Josh said to me.

"Oh, right." I fumbled for the nearest light switch—a classic push-button kind—and managed to turn on the overhead hall light, whose single bulb gave off a feeble glow. Then I turned to take a better look at our captive and did a clichéd double-take. "You? You're behind this? Josh, you recognize this guy?"

"Uh . . . damn, I do. This is the bank president, Arthur Fairchild. He's the one that had me sign the contract when he picked me to keep an eye on this place. He's come by a couple of times since to see how things are going."

"Alone?" I asked, trying to convey the rest of the question: was he with Cordy?

"As far as I know," Josh said. "He might have made visits when I wasn't around."

Inconclusive. "I met him at that town council meeting when I first got here. Oh, shoot—he's the one in charge of the Barton trust that pays for this house. He could come and go any time he wanted—he controls the keys. The plot thickens."

"It certainly does."

"Can I sit up?" Arthur wheezed. "You two scared the living daylights out of me."

"We'd be happy to let you sit up, as long as you don't try to make a break for it," Josh said. "And you can tell us what's been going on here?"

"What do you mean?" Arthur asked, trying to sound innocent. He failed. He was a lousy actor.

Josh pulled his cell phone out of a pocket. "I'm calling the police."

"Wait, no, please!" Arthur protested. "I can explain."

"I'm sure you can," I told him, "but I have a feeling that the police will want to hear your story. Let's let them decide what to do with you." Now Arthur looked like he wanted to cry.

Josh had turned away to make his brief call then turned back to us. "I called the local department. They're sending someone over now. They can decide whether to turn this guy over to the state police. I'll have to go unlock the gate. Kate, are you okay staying here with him?"

"Sure, I'll be fine. After all, I have a loaded shovel. Go!"

Josh loped downstairs and out the front door, leaving me alone with Arthur. I wondered what the law would say if I asked a few pointed questions, just to satisfy my own curiosity. I decided to try a test question. "How many letters?"

The poor man was leaning against the wall, and he sort of collapsed into himself at my question. "Clara's? Or others?"

Bingo! He'd been in on it. "Start with Clara's. By the way, they're all safe, including the one that Cordelia had. Were there any others taken?"

Arthur shook his head vehemently. "No! We picked that batch because we thought there'd be plenty of interest in them. Then Cordy . . . died, and I figured people would be paying more attention to this place and I'd better move fast. That's why I was here tonight, to get the rest of the letters."

And probably anything else that looked tempting and easy to sell. "So you and Cordy were working together?"

"That's hard to answer. We had a . . . thing awhile back, and when it ended, she threatened to tell my wife unless I helped her."

"Who found the letters? Who knew about them? Are they included in the inventory of this place?" I was on a roll, and I wasn't sure how much time I would have.

"No, or at least, not specifically. The inventory says only 'trunks and cases with papers.' It was Cordy who got curious when she was scoping it out for her so-called investors, and she started poking around in the attic. Seems like nobody had looked up there for a very long time. I can't tell you what all she found, but the name Clara Barton rang a bell. So she took one letter out and brought it to me and promised that there were a lot more like it. She said she'd checked on eBay and they were really popular, and we could make a lot of money by selling something that nobody in town knew existed."

I suppressed an urge to strangle him. "That's theft, you know. Maybe some bigger fancier title once the market value of the items is determined."

"But we never stole them! At least, I didn't, and Cordy took only the one. Borrowed, I mean. So she could verify what it was. I could say I authorized her to take it, which I can do because I'm the custodian of record for this place." Arthur was working hard to cover his ample derriere.

He could have a point. "Are you sure?"

"Well, that's what she told me."

"Let me get this straight, Arthur. You've lived in Asheboro most of your life, and you knew Cordy way back when. I speak from experience when I say that she was not a very nice person. How the heck did you get sucked into her plan?"

Arthur couldn't meet my eyes and looked down at his knees. "Dunno." He sounded like a kid at school who had swiped some other kid's lunch.

I decided to switch tactics. "Did you have a buyer lined up for the letters?"

"I don't think so. I was going to let Cordy handle all that. I mean, in the beginning, I was the only person in town with free access to this house, and I could come and go without anyone questioning me. Then Cordy got this crazy idea about turning the house into something else, and she wangled a key for herself so she could show it off. Since the town owns the building, and she's on the town council, she could go in unsupervised. And I guess she could take whatever she wanted."

Once she'd wrapped poor Arthur around her little finger. Now for the fastball. "Did you have anything to do with Cordy's death?"

"Me?" Arthur's voice almost squeaked. "No! No way! I'm not a killer."

I wasn't sure that I believed him. "What was Cordy doing here the day she died?" I snapped at him.

"I don't know. Maybe she'd decided to collect the letters while she still had a chance. She knew the town council didn't like her plan for this place, and she might not get too many more opportunities."

"Who might have wanted her dead?" All right, I was being cruel to the man, but I figured he deserved it.

"Who didn't? She'd made a lot of enemies here."

As I knew only too well. "But you stuck by her and this crazy idea about the letters?"

"I was just waiting for the right time to end things. I figured when she sold the letters, I could say that we didn't want anyone looking too hard at us and we should end our, uh, collaboration. It might have worked."

Maybe, unless Cordy had made off with the letters or other loot and pocketed all the money. I wondered if she would have stayed around, if she had been successful. I thought it was a possibility: she could think to herself smugly that she had a secret and she'd pulled one over on the whole town. She would have enjoyed that. But I had a feeling she had been aiming higher than Asheboro.

"Arthur, why were you planning to take the letters? Because Cordy wanted money and leaned on you to do it? Because you could? Because you thought autograph letters from Clara Barton belonged to the nation, and shouldn't be hidden away in a trunk in east nowhere?"

He stared at his knees again. "I needed the money."

"Why? Doesn't the bank pay well enough?"

"No." Now he looked up at me, with tears in his eyes. "Do you realize my salary hasn't gone up in the past five years? Business is down, but that's not my fault. Nobody needs mortgage loans around here anymore. Savings accounts have all but disappeared. The bank's in trouble. I was getting desperate."

Then I was slammed by an unpleasant realization: the Barton fund or endowment or whatever they called it around here was the single largest account at the bank. Heck, maybe the only large account. And Arthur controlled it. "Arthur, were you taking money from the Barton fund?"

"Yes." He looked away again.

"How much?" I demanded.

"About eighty thousand dollars," he said grudgingly.

Ouch. There were so many things I wanted to say, most of them obscene. There were so many other things I wanted to ask, like what the hell he had done with it (I hoped with all my heart that Cordy hadn't gotten her hands on any of it).

I could hear the sound of cars approaching: the police had arrived. Shucks—I wouldn't get the chance to pummel Arthur to a bloody pulp for what he'd done. Just as well—I couldn't afford an arrest or worse on my resume if I needed to start looking for a new job.

I heard voices outside. The door opened. "Kate?" Josh called out.

"Upstairs," I called out. "Right where you left us."

He took the stairs two at a time. "Everything all right?"

"Just dandy. Arthur has been explaining a lot of things. I'll fill you in later."

"Great. I told the cops as much as I knew, and they're going to take him in for questioning. And hand him over to Detective Reynolds, if that's appropriate."

The cops followed a bit more slowly. Apparently Josh had had time to explain the basic story to them, so they simply hauled Arthur to his feet and told him they were escorting him to the police station for an interview. He didn't protest. He didn't even comment. Apparently it had never occurred to him that he could get caught for larceny and embezzlement. Had Cordy really had that kind of power over men? That reduced them to blubbering idiots?

Josh and I promised we'd show up at the police station in the morning to give our statements to yet another law enforcement agency, and the police took off with their suspect. That left Josh and me alone in the Barton house.

"You okay?" He asked. Not very original, but I appreciated the thought.

"I really don't know," I said to him.

Josh didn't reply, but he didn't argue with me. "We need to get some sleep if we're talking to the police in the morning."

"You've got that right. What time is it?"

"Somewhere between two and three. You want to go back to the B&B? It's probably safe now that Arthur is in custody."

"No," I said quickly. "Back to your place. I don't want to deal with this alone. I'll probably crash when the adrenaline stops flowing."

"Okay," he said gently, without asking any questions, and then he led me out the back door, and we walked across the dew-wet grass to his door, and then I kissed him, or he kissed me, and things got kind of blurry after that.

I could think about that in the morning.

31

Somewhere far away a phone was ringing. I refused to open my eyes, even though I could tell through my eyelids that the sun had risen. Wasn't my phone, nope. That was somewhere else. Wait, where was I?

I grudgingly opened my eyes. First observation: I was not at my home or the bed and breakfast or the Barton mansion. My sluggish memory began to rake up fragmented memories for the night before. Police. Darkness. A shovel? Arthur? By a brilliant process of deduction I concluded I must have stayed over at Josh's place, even though whatever risk there might have been from the thief (Arthur? seriously?) was gone. So where was Josh?

Behind me, struggling to get his ringing cell phone out of his jeans pocket and cursing. Quick readjustment in my head: yes, I was at Josh's place. Apparently I had slept on the sofa I had originally planned to sleep on before we went off to catch a thief. Somehow Josh had ended up sleeping on it too. A quick check verified that we were still fully clothed. Well, it had been a rather difficult day, and apparently neither of us had had the energy for anything romantic.

The phone had stopped ringing. I attempted to roll over to face Josh without falling off the sofa, and said, "We have to stop meeting like this."

He snorted. "Whatever. The phone call was for you. Sounds like your pal Lisbeth is freaking out, although I don't know how she found my number. You'd better call her before she sends in troops."

"Oh, right. What time is it?"

"About eight, I think. She's awake even if you're not."

"She's got kids—she has no choice. All right, all right—I'll call her." Lisbeth would probably understand why I hadn't called her already when she heard how we'd spent the last—goodness, less than twenty-four hours. I managed to get my feet under me and staggered off toward the bathroom. I'd now spent two nights with Josh, and they were quite possibly the least romantic nights I had ever spent with any man. Well, it had been a really nice kiss at the door, from what I remembered of it, but we'd both been so strung out on adrenaline and exhausted from the stress of hunting thieves and killers that neither of us had managed to pursue whatever sparks we'd struck. Hmm . . . maybe we needed to work on that.

On the other hand, our crime-solving relationship was going really well.

Marginally clean and combed, I returned to the main room and rummaged through my bag for my cell phone, which I had conveniently turned off. I turned it on and called Lisbeth. She started shrieking before I had even had time to say hello.

"Where the hell have you been? The police arrested Arthur Fairchild for embezzlement."

"I know," I said in a calm and soothing manner.

It didn't soothe Lisbeth. "What do you mean, you know? Where have you been?"

"Well, Josh didn't think it was safe for me to stay alone at the B&B, so we came back to his place. And then we captured Arthur in the Barton house in the wee hours, where he was trying to find the rest of the letters that Clara Barton wrote our Henry Barton, and we handed him over to the local police to be charged with embezzlement of funds or something." I deliberately didn't mention the murder. "It was a busy day, so we just crashed for what was left of the night."

Apparently I had finally stunned Lisbeth into silence. In the end she said, "You have a lot of explaining to do, and talking on the phone will not be adequate. Lunch?"

"Sure, if I've got time, after we give the local police department our statements about Arthur. Where?"

"If what you have just told me is true, I would recommend not eating in town because everyone is going to want to know the details. The hotel?"

"Fine. I'll meet you there at noon."

"Fine." Lisbeth hung up.

Josh handed me a cup of hot coffee, and I took it gratefully. "Well," I said, and stopped. I had no idea what to say.

"Exactly," he replied. "Sit." He waved at the table.

I sat, across from him. "That was a very interesting day. Unique, I might say."

"It was," he agreed. "Can we summarize what we think happened? Because we were both kind of busy. Then you had a chat with Arthur while I was guiding the police, and you promised to fill me in."

"Ah, yes. Do we need to write this down?"

"I'll do it," he said, hauling a lined pad from a pile of stuff at the other end of the table. "Speak."

"I don't think Arthur killed Cordelia."

Josh didn't sputter or protest. He studied my expression for a moment then said neutrally, "Why?"

I sat up straight and laid my hands on the table. "Arthur told me a whole lot of stuff about what he and Cordelia were doing, and about the money and the letters, and most of that made sense, or it made other stuff make sense. Arthur needed money for personal reasons. He'd already gutted the Barton trust and who knows what other accounts at the bank, and he was desperate for money. He didn't get around to telling me if Cordy was involved in looting the bank accounts, but the bank records should show how long it had been going on. You and I figured that he and Cordy joined up to steal Clara's letters, again for money. But Cordelia had gotten what she wanted and was more or less dumping him, but she could use black-mail at any time—you know, tell his wife, tell the town, get him fired—and she was mean enough to do it. I'll admit that gives Arthur a motive. But the bottom line is, I think he's too much of a wuss to bash a woman in the head with a rock."

Josh thought for a while before answering. "I think that makes sense, Kate," he said calmly. "From what little I know about the man, I can't see him killing Cordelia in a fit of rage." He paused before adding, "I'm sorry."

That confused me. "For what? You didn't do anything wrong. You just walked into this idiotic drama by accident."

"But this wasn't your fight either, Kate. Are you worried about what will happen to the town's project?"

He'd hit the nail on the head. "Well, yes. I know, so far it was mainly a figment of my imagination. Now I'd have to go back to the town council and tell them there's no money left because Arthur stole it, and there's little hope of finding any more money, so the project is dead and Asheboro is going to fade quietly away."

"There are still Clara's letters—they can be sold on the open market, if the town approves," Josh pointed out. "And there may be other letters or valuables in the attic. I'd suggest getting a reputable dealer or expert in to find what actually is up there."

Suddenly I realized something else. "I don't want to sell those letters! They are so intimately linked to Henry Barton's personal history and to the town. They belong here. We need to find something else to sell, something less personal."

"Spoken like a true historian. You know, you've really gotten invested in this. Maybe you were kidding yourself about your life," Josh said.

I glared at him. "Damn, stop doing that. How do you know what I'm thinking?"

"I told you, it all shows on your face. Look, I don't know you well. But from what I've seen, you came here to help a friend. You agreed to help out the town, without asking for anything in return. In the midst of all this you were told you were fired from your day job, but I haven't noticed you grieving a lot about that."

"I've been kind of distracted by murders and thefts and things like that," I mumbled.

"But you never talked much about hotel management, and I never saw you excited about it," Josh pressed on. "The only enthusiasm that you've shown has been for this historical project. Which leads me to think that matters to you."

I was afraid he was right. The hotel job had matched my skills and paid enough for me to live quite well. Maybe once I'd entertained vague hopes of moving to a hotel in some exotic foreign location at some point, but I hadn't done anything to make it happen. And it had taken only a week in Asheboro to divert me from what I had thought was my life plan.

"Is there a cure for that?" I asked feebly.

"You tell me. You can still walk away from Asheboro. Now you've got the perfect excuse—someone took all the money. You at least will be covered with glory because you caught Arthur, and you can leave with your head held high, the thanks of the grateful citizens ringing in your ears."

"Don't be patronizing."

He gave me an odd look. "I'm not, and I'm sorry if it sounded that way. You came back to help a friend, and you ended up solving a crime that nobody even knew was happening."

"I already knew the history of the town. That helped."

"Yes, it did."

"Why did you become a historian, Josh?" I asked.

He looked bewildered by my abrupt change of subject but decided to answer anyway. "Simple. I liked history. I excavated my parents' garbage can when I was five. I wanted a profession that let me focus on history, paid reasonably, and gave me a certain flexibility. Academia fit. And here I am. Obviously investigating murder and theft in this small town wasn't part of the plan, but both of those came about because of events that happened in the past. I came here to study regional industrialization. Turns out Henry Barton was a leading industrialist. But the more you and I poked around, the more we both realized that there was a personal element to his role, by way of his lost brother. And what he did in 1865 or 1880 led to the theft and the death in the here and now, separately or together."

That actually made sense to me. "But the story included a dose of luck. Don't forget that."

Josh cocked his head. "What do you mean?"

"If Lisbeth had invited me a month or so later, Cordelia might have already sold the letters and moved to Palm Beach. If Henry Barton hadn't fought in a battle around here and lost a brother and contacted distant cousin Clara, this town might not have survived into the twentieth century. Those are only two examples of that luck. Do you see what I'm saying?"

"In a sense, yes," Josh replied. "But to get back to the present, you know what we have to do now."

It was a statement, not a question. "Yes—find out who killed Cordelia." Which was somehow the part of my personal history.

"Exactly." I helped myself to more coffee, mostly to give myself time to think. "We agree that Arthur didn't kill Cordelia."

Josh nodded once.

"Good. So who's the next suspect?"

"Ryan?"

I shook my head. "I may be biased, but I think Ryan was over Cordy, both emotionally and financially. He seems to be making good money as a lawyer. He never had any interest in history. So what's his motive? And why would he choose the Barton house to kill her?"

"Fewer witnesses?" Josh suggested. "Maybe Cordy invited him out there, to ask him to invest in her project for the house. Or maybe she tried to use her physical charms to do it—it had worked before—and Ryan got so fed up he simply grabbed the first thing he could find and bashed her. Every man has a breaking point."

"Creative solution, but I'm not buying Ryan as a killer. Who's next?"

Josh sat back in his chair and looked at me. "I'm not an expert on Asheboro, but it's my impression that a lot of people disliked Cordelia—including myself, based on limited exposure—but I'd guess that few people hated her enough to kill her. I don't really have any other suggestions."

I returned his look. "I know what you mean about Cordy. She made my life hell for a time, and I've spent years getting past that, but I still can't imagine killing her myself. Or even hiring a hit man. Or woman. Let's go back to Arthur. Does he have a wife? Who might have found out about the affair? That could have made her angry enough to go after Cordelia."

How many motives were there for killing anyone, I found myself wondering. Hate—but that could come from so many sources. Revenge? Jealousy? I had to believe that a brutal, unplanned murder like Cordelia's had to come from emotion, not calculation. Who in this small town had hated her that much?

And then an unlikely thought crept into my mind. I turned it over and around, studying it. It was improbable, but was it possible?

"What about Audrey?" I said carefully.

"Audrey?" Josh stared at me incredulously. "As Cordelia's killer?"

I had to admit that the idea of the patient drab librarian killing the town bitch Cordelia seemed ridiculous, but we were running out of candidates. What could Audrey's motive have been?

Jealousy. Audrey had fixated on Josh as her last best hope for love, or at least for escape from Asheboro, perhaps even knowing how unlikely it was that he was attracted to her. But the heart wants what it wants, and love is not rational. At least that's what romance novels said.

If Cordy had sensed Audrey's yearning, she would have pounced on it like a cat on a mouse. She would have tormented Audrey just because she could. And she wouldn't have let up. So Audrey would have grown angrier and angrier.

Would there have been a trigger incident that could have pushed Audrey over the edge?

"Josh?" I said slowly. "You told me awhile ago that Cordelia had made a play for you. Did Audrey ever see you and Cordelia together?"

"That's an odd question," he said.

"Just tell me—did she?"

"Probably. Every time Cordelia and I crossed paths in town, she was kind of all over me—you know, the whole girly standing too close, touching me, et cetera. I didn't encourage her, but short of shoving her away there wasn't much I could do. I suppose Audrey could have seen us any one of those times and jumped to conclusions."

"And Cordy would have played it up, if she had an audience," I said, almost to myself. "Did Audrey ever come out to the Barton house?"

"Rarely. But there was one time when she said she wanted to check the condition of the books, and she came out and spent some time in the Barton library. That was about the same time that Cordy was in and out of the house with her so-called investors. They could easily have overlapped."

"Any reason why Audrey would have been there on Sunday?"

"Kate, I don't like where you're going with this," Josh warned.

But I would not be diverted. "Did she come out to see you, or to deliver something to you?"

"No. I wasn't around for much of the day. But . . . Cordelia might have asked Audrey for something, asked her to bring it to the house. Let me get this straight: are you really saying you think Audrey might have killed Cordelia?"

"I think it's possible. Do you?" I shot back.

"I . . . don't know." Josh looked troubled as he wrestled with the question.

I stood up. "I need to talk to Audrey."

"I'll come with you," Josh volunteered quickly.

I held up a hand. "That's not a good idea. This will be hard enough without you there. If I'm wrong, she doesn't need to know that you know what I'm thinking."

"If she's killed once, she might go after you."

I really couldn't picture that. "You can wait close by, or peer in the window. But I can't see her attacking me."

"I don't like it," Josh muttered.

"Do you have any better ideas for the killer? Like, maybe a random stranger wandered into the estate and bashed Cordy because she happened to be in the wrong place at the wrong time?"

Josh sighed. "No, that doesn't seem likely. But then, none of the other possible suspects, which would be half the people in town, seems likely."

"Then let me eliminate Audrey from the list, if I can. If I've guessed wrong, I'll admit it. I kind of like her, and I know I feel sorry for her."

"Kate, it's Sunday. You think she'd be at the library?"

"I do. She really has nowhere else to be. Sad, isn't it?"

"It is. So let's do it—try to talk with her. At least it will move this mess one step forward. But I'm not letting you walk into this alone."

32

Josh drove us into town and parked a block or so from the library. "What do you plan to do?"

"Just talk to Audrey. I don't intend to accuse her to her face. I hope I'm wrong, you know. She's not a bad person."

"Good people do bad things all the time," Josh reminded me. "Be careful, will you? I'll be waiting outside."

It hadn't even occurred to me that the library might not be open on Sunday, but I knew Audrey had nowhere else to be. As I walked the block to the library, I remembered what Audrey and I had talked about earlier. I could understand Audrey feeling trapped by the demands of her family. But Cordy's veiled insults and contempt would have made things worse. Plus Audrey was not the type to stand up to Cordy. If I believed Audrey, she'd never responded to Cordy's taunts, which I was pretty sure must have pushed Cordy to go even farther.

When I reached the front of the library building, I peered through the windows. There seemed to be no one except Audrey inside, and I was relieved both because I'd found her and because there's be no one to overhear what promised to be a very awkward conversation. I pulled myself together and opened the door, and then strode over to the main desk. "Audrey, I need to talk to you."

She looked up without smiling. "All right. What's this about? Henry Barton again?"

I shook my head. "There's no easy way to say this, and you have every right to be angry with me and refuse to say anything, but I hope you'll give me an answer."

"Get to the point, will you, Kate?" Audrey folded her arms across her chest.

"You told me you were, uh, interested in Josh Wainwright. Did Cordelia set her sights on him?"

Audrey studied my face, and I wondered if she was trying to make a decision about how much to say. "What do you think? New in town, attractive, intelligent? Of course she did."

"Did that make you angry?"

I was surprised when she actually answered my tactless question. "That's not exactly easy to say," Audrey said. "Did I honestly expect that Josh would ever even notice me as a living, breathing woman? I knew perfectly well that he wasn't interested in me. That was a bit too much to hope for. But I guess I had dreams, or fantasies. Helps pass the time. But then Cordy spied him. You know, he was staying in that big place outside of town and he didn't come into town often, except to the library for his research now and then, so it took Cordy awhile to notice him at all, but when she did it was right here in the library. 'Who's that?' she asked me. I gave her a short answer—'He's the caretaker at the Barton house.' But he was fresh meat and attractive and breathing, so she moved in. I got to watch the whole thing. To his credit, he was polite but he didn't take the bait. But you know how persistent Cordy could be."

"I do, unfortunately." And then I waited, because I was pretty sure there was more.

Audrey looked past me, and I guessed she was revisiting her own memories. "Then the town bought the Barton property, and Cordy decided to get herself involved with it. And, from what I hear, she thought the town wasn't moving fast enough with its plans to use the place, so she went out looking for other people to step up. And found some. She thought she was on her way to dumping her tacky little bed and breakfast and moving up in the world, or at least in the Asheboro universe. Of course she was out at the mansion a lot, showing the place off to investors and the like."

I could see it. Cordy would sometimes by out there by herself. And she could just happen to run into Josh.

It was time to go all-in, and I knew I had to ask the question. "Audrey, did you kill Cordelia?"

Audrey almost smiled. "I wondered when you'd figure that out."

We stared at each other across the book-strewn desk, but she made no move to threaten me. There were plenty of times during high school that I had fantasized about killing Cordelia, or at least torturing her—a lot of spiders and worms figured in those daydreams. But I'd left town and moved past that. Audrey had had to live with Cordelia just popping in at the library on a regular basis and saying snide things. And it seemed that Audrey had finally had enough.

"What happened, Audrey? Would you like to explain? Or,

wait—maybe I should go lock the door. I don't think this is the time to deal with people looking for books."

"You're right." Audrey reached into her pocket and fished out a heavy ring of keys, then handed it to me. "The big one is for the front. We'd better stick up a sign, or people will start pounding on the door."

I waited silently while Audrey made a sign with a broad black marker, reading CLOSED DUE TO PERSONAL EMERGENCY. Then I scurried to the front door and made sure it was locked, and taped the sign to the glass of the door. Josh was indeed waiting outside, near the street, and I gave him a quick thumbs-up so he wouldn't come barging in. Then I went back to the main desk where Audrey was waiting. I had now locked myself in the library with a woman who had just admitted to being a murderer.

Now what? Part of me really wanted to call Detective Reynolds and tell him to get his butt over here and pick up his suspect. But I felt I owed it to Audrey to give her the chance to tell her story before the inevitable process of police procedures took over. I found a stool and pulled it behind the desk, so that Audrey and I could sit face to face.

"What happened?" I said quietly.

Audrey cocked her head at me. "Look, Kate, let me say now, don't feel bad about ratting me out, which I know you're going to do. I probably would have turned myself in anyway. Even if I wanted to run, I have nowhere to go."

I couldn't think of anything to say to that. "Audrey, why were you at the Barton house that day?"

Audrey sat up straight on her stool and raised her chin. "Cordelia asked me to meet her there. She wanted to know what to do with the books—I don't think a stuffy old library fit into her grand plans for the place, but thank goodness she knew better that to toss them all in a Dumpster. I'd seen some valuable volumes there, and I wanted to make sure the town got a good price for them—the town owns them, you know. I wish we had room for them in the library."

I nodded. "So what finally pushed your last button—that was because she was making fun of you, right?"

"Yes. Nothing I hadn't heard before, but enough was enough."

I knew how she felt.

Audrey interrupted my thoughts. "Listen, I know you wanted information about Henry Barton, how he came to live here, who his family was, all that, and I put together all that I could find on that rolling cart over there. Once I'm arrested, I'm not sure whom they'll get to run the library—they might even just shut it down. If it makes any difference, as one of my last official acts I give you and Josh permission to use whatever you like here, whenever you like. I doubt the town will object. There's a spare set of keys in the drawer here."

Audrey was a librarian to her bones—I hadn't even thought of that. She went on, "You know, I haven't done a lot of research myself, but you'll find that Henry Barton was a very interesting character. There was more to him than you might think at first. But he was a private man as well, so you have to hunt for the trail."

"I'm just beginning to realize that. Look, Audrey, I'm sorry I figured out that it was you. You've had enough troubles in your life without this."

Audrey smiled ruefully. "Some people seem to be cursed, and I think I'm one of them. I'm proud of you, though."

"Me? Why?"

"Because when Lisbeth called you to help Asheboro, you could simply have said 'sorry, no thanks,' and left it at that. Okay, maybe you didn't know then that Cordelia was still in town. But once you found out, which I'll wager didn't take long, you could still have told the town that you didn't think you could help and walked away."

"I could have, I guess, but that's not me. I needed to be a grown-up here in Asheboro and deal with those old issues. And I do think the project is challenging and worth following up on." An errant thought struck me. "You didn't kill Cordelia just to get her out of the way to make sure I'd stick around and save the town?"

Audrey smiled ruefully. "You give me too much credit, Kate. It wasn't planned at all. No, it was pure fury, distilled for years. And you know what? It felt really, really good to admit to myself how angry I was, and to act on it. I didn't think it through—I just snapped. I grabbed a rock from the garden next to the door and hit her as hard as I could. Had I been in a rational state of mind, I could have plotted something much more subtle. But in the end, on her way out the door she said something like, 'I'll leave you to your dusty old books. If you see Josh Wainwright, tell him I want a word with him, will you?' And then she sashayed out the front door, turning her back on me. And that was it—I'd had enough. She'd twisted the knife one time too many. I followed her to the front, and when she heard me coming she turned around. That's when I found that convenient rock in the garden next to the steps. I picked it up and raised it over my head"—Audrey closed her eyes for a moment, but she was smiling—"and I brought it down on her head, hard—wham. And I looked down at her then, lying on the steps, bleeding, and all I felt was triumph. I'd finally taken charge of my own life."

"Oh, Audrey, I'm so sorry it had to come to that."

I needed to do something. But what? The clear and obvious answer would be to tell the state police, right now.

Or I could tell someone else and share the misery. Someone like Josh, who I could see approaching the front door of the library at that very moment. Audrey noticed at the same time. "Oh, crap," she muttered. "You brought *him*?"

"Can he come in?" I asked.

Audrey smiled sadly. "Why not? It's all over anyway."

I went over to the front door and unlocked it. Josh looked past me at Audrey, still seated behind the main desk then looked at me. "Yes?" he asked quietly.

I could only nod.

"Then I should go and call the detective." Without waiting for my response, he turned and walked toward the road until he was out of sight from inside.

Audrey looked up at me after Josh had left and I'd carefully locked the door behind him. She looked oddly serene. "He's calling the police now, isn't he?" she asked.

"Yes, he is. Do you want a lawyer?" I asked.

She sighed. "I suppose I should have one, but the only one I know around here is the one who handled my parents' estates. He's about eighty, and I don't think he could deal with a murder trial."

"There's always Ryan, although I don't know if he handles . . . big things like this, and it probably wouldn't be appropriate anyway. But he could recommend someone at his firm. Actually, you might do better to save him for a witness—he could testify why Cordy was such a pain in the ass. You could plead temporary insanity, or something along those lines."

"Good point."

Josh came back, and I let him in again. "He's on his way," he told me. "I'll wait out front for him."

33

Audrey and I sat in uncomfortable silence—what was there to say? Twenty minutes later I looked up to see Josh leading Detective Reynolds and a couple of uniformed cops to the front door, so I hurried over to unlock it again. As the police walked into the library, Audrey remained where she was.

"Kate," Detective Reynolds said then turned to Audrey. "And you're Audrey Perlaw? The librarian?"

"I am. And you are?"

"Detective Reynolds of the Maryland State Police. I understand you have something to tell us?"

"I do. Please, sit down. This may take awhile, and I'd like to tell you the story in my own way."

"Fine." The detective glanced at Josh and me. "Please wait outside." Josh and I didn't argue. Besides, I'd already heard the story, and I could fill Josh in.

Once outside we sat numbly on a bench in front of the library. I had no idea what to do. I watched as a number of people strolled by after church, then slowed, then tried to peek inside. It must have been the police car parked in front that had attracted them, but now they kept looking at Josh and me too, as if trying to put the pieces together.

Josh leaned toward me. "We can sit in my car if you want."

I shrugged. "Why bother? Is the detective going to want to interview us when he's finished with Audrey?"

"I can't say—I haven't been part of too many murder investigations. In fact, none."

"Same with me." I took a breath. "Look, Josh, Audrey explained what happened, and it's pretty much the way we guessed. She didn't think you treated her unfairly."

"I suppose I should be happy to hear that, but that doesn't make me feel much better."

"I know what you mean. Poor Audrey."

After a while I said, "Do we need to tell the police about the Barton letters?"

"I think not," Josh said. "Audrey's motives for attacking Cordelia were purely personal and had nothing to do with the letters, and I think the local police will handle Arthur's thefts, so Reynolds won't be involved. I think we're safe in leaving that door closed."

I nodded. "That's what I was thinking. I don't think Audrey knew anything about them, and I doubt she'd mention them if she did."

Time slowed to a crawl. The detective took his time interviewing Audrey, and when I got up to stretch my legs and just happened to glance through the front window, I saw the two other officers sitting mutely in the corners of the back room, taking notes. Audrey stayed calm and answered all of Detective Reynolds's questions, as far as I could see, so apparently she hadn't asked for a lawyer. I went back to the bench and sat again. Josh and I waited, and then we waited some more. Finally after an hour or so, one of the uniformed policemen came out of the building, and I went to meet him.

"The detective wants to talk to you next, then your friend."

"Fine." Inside, Detective Reynolds rose to meet me.

"Kate, this is not a formal statement—we can deal with that later." He turned to one of the guys in uniform. "Jenkins, please take Miss Perlaw out to the car."

He talked to me first, and I explained what little I'd learned before he arrived. The he sent me out to tell Josh to come in, and I went back to what seemed to have become "our" bench, and sat staring into space. When he had finished talking to Josh, the two men came out to join me.

Reynolds said quietly, "I understand you have keys to the library?"

"Yes, Audrey wanted us to have them, to continue some research we'd been doing. Is that a problem?"

"I don't believe so," Detective Reynolds said. "I think we can trust you."

"What happens now?"

"We take Ms. Perlaw to our offices and arraign her. I'll be in touch with you two about giving an official statement. And thank you." With that he turned and left.

Since I had no better ideas, I sat down on the bench again, and Josh joined me. The small crowd had vanished. "Poor Audrey," I said to him. "That could have been me, if things had turned out differently in my life. What do we do now?"

"Are you forgetting Henry Barton?" Josh asked.

"You mean our research, and where Clara's letters fit? We do have the keys to the library, thanks to Audrey. Are you seriously thinking of doing research right now?"

Josh looked down at his shoes. "It might be better to use the library resources while we still can—Reynolds or the town could change their minds and we won't be able to get back in."

"Audrey told me that she thought Henry Barton was a very interesting man. Maybe she was hinting she knew something. I think she'd expect us to follow up."

"Definitely."

So we went back into the library, locked the door, leaving the sign taped in place, and assembled all the files Audrey had collected for us, sat down at the long table in the Local History Room in the back, and got back to work.

The next time I looked outside, it was already getting dark. The afternoon had vanished while Josh and I sat in the empty library immersed in nineteenth-century Asheboro history and Henry Barton's life. I had stopped reading only because my brain was no longer accepting input.

I stood up and stretched. Josh looked up and said hopefully, "Quitting time?"

"I vote yes." Then I stopped. It was time to leave, but where would I go? The B&B, I supposed, although I could certainly go back to my Baltimore condo, only an hour away. But I didn't want to go back to Baltimore tonight. I wanted to stay and celebrate in Asheboro . . . with Josh. Except I didn't know how to ask, exactly. There had been so many misunderstandings lately—Josh missing Audrey's signals, Cordy completely oblivious to anybody else's signals, and so on. I didn't want to mess things up. But what did I want?

Oh, grow up, Kate! I thought there had been some electricity between me and Josh, and it would be better to know now rather than play silly games. "Want to come back to the B&B with me? We can pick up some dinner, and I know for a fact that there's more of that good wine. Maybe we could exorcise Cordy's ghost from the place."

"If we drink a bottle of that stuff, I probably shouldn't drive back," Josh said carefully. His unspoken question hung in the air between us.

"Then why don't you plan to stay over?" I said.

He smiled. I smiled back. No mixed signals here.

We went back to the B&B, stopping along the way to pick up an assortment of Chinese food. Maybe it didn't go well with fine wine, but we didn't care. The wine was perfect for other activities.

Morning found us tangled up in the sheets of the big bedroom upstairs. As I rolled over to look at Josh, the irreverent thought flitted through my mind: maybe if we tried this in the master bedroom at the Barton mansion, it would put to rest any bad memories of that awful moment with Ryan, when Cordy and her army of giggling friends arrived with cameras flashing. Worth a try, anyway.

"Hey," Josh said. His eyes were open now.

"Hey, yourself. Are we okay?"

"More than okay," he said, smiling.

Sometime later I asked, "What day is this?"

"I'm not sure. A weekday, maybe? I'd guess Monday."

"I hope so. I have to call Lisbeth and explain and apologize and all that stuff. And then I have another call to make."

"Town council?"

"No, Nell Pratt, in Philadelphia. She's going to help us sort out the treasures in the Barton attic. I want her to see them sooner rather than later, so I know what to tell the council."

"So you've figured out what comes next?" Josh asked.

"What part do you mean? For the Barton house? For Asheboro?" *For me?* "I've got some ideas. And I'm willing to present them to the town, in rough form, when the dust settles. This week or next. If they reject my solution, I need to know that up front."

"There's something else I could add, I think . . ." He seemed to be struggling to find the right words. "This is really speculative, but as we've been looking at the materials that Audrey assembled, and also checking out Internet sources, I'm beginning to see something that could be really interesting."

"Are you planning to share this with me?"

"I'm not ready to, but let's say it falls within my area of academic expertise, which is to say, commercial history rather than personal."

"Why do you bring it up now?"

"Because if I'm right, it could be really important, both historically, which benefits me, and financially, which could help you—*us* save the Barton mansion and the town. Assuming you don't mind hanging around and working on the project for a while longer."

"I confess I've been thinking along the same lines. If Nell can find someone qualified to assess both the Barton letters and whatever else might be in the attic, it could provide some seed money for the project. And if it works out, I'd like to be a part of it, going forward. But don't you have a day job, when your sabbatical is over?"

"Yes, I do. But if you look at a map, Kate, you'll notice that my job is not far away. And what I have in mind fits quite neatly with the research I've been doing for a while now. I'm sure my department would understand."

I laughed. "We really are a pair! After last night—which was great, by the way—here we sit kicking around ideas that might turn things around and help the town save and promote the Barton house. And we both seem to be on the same page about giving it its rightful place in history. Have I got that right?"

"I think so."

"Josh, do you think we have a shot at pulling this off?"

"I think it's worth trying," he said. "I hope so."

34

Nell's train pulled into Baltimore's Penn Station on time, and I was there waiting. I was happy to see she was carrying a small travel bag—so she was staying? goody, goody—more time for me to convince her of the potential significance of the town project, including the Barton house, and to pick her brain on how to make it work. I pulled over to the curb and opened the passenger door for her. "Welcome! And thank you for coming. I hope I didn't sound too crazy."

She buckled her seatbelt and turned toward me. "Don't worry—I was ready for a field trip anyway, and you've certainly got me curious. Leading with those letters was a good strategy—you sucked me right in."

"I'm glad to hear that. And there's a lot more to talk about."

"Like crime solving?" Nell grinned at me.

"Exactly." As we drove from the station and headed west, I filled her in on the house and Audrey and the louse of a bank president and the quandary the whole mess had put everyone in. When I finally ran out of steam, she said, "Wow, you make my job look tame. Although I did find one body in the stacks. Welcome to the sisterhood of accidental sleuths."

"Before you make any judgments about the project," I said, "I really do want you to see the house—it's fabulous. It's as if it's preserved in amber. But it's still a big step to finding money to preserve it—that's where finding anything of value that the town could sell becomes important."

"And you're hoping what's might be in the attic can make a difference?"

"I can hope, can't I?"

"So you really have no idea what's up there?"

"No. Josh and I don't know where to start. We figured we'd leave that to the experts."

"Josh?"

"Long story. He's going to stay involved." I proceeded to tell Nell the story as we drove back to Asheboro.

When I'd finished my G-rated summary, she said, "It sounds as though he could be a real asset to the project."

"I think he's hooked. The Barton stuff dovetails beautifully with his own work."

"Selling the Clara Barton letters should be no problem. That market has held up well."

"That's good to know. But in a way I'd like to keep them and weave them into whatever story we put together to market the Barton place. Selfish, I know. If we have to sell them, so be it, but I'd like to know if there are alternatives first."

"I understand, believe me. We've done our share of de-accessioning at the Society, and it hurts me every time."

We reached the outskirts of Asheboro by mid-afternoon, and I told Nell, "I'd like to take you by the house first, because that's the centerpiece of the plan, if not exactly the physical center. It won't take long to check out the town after that. Have you been to this part of Maryland before?"

"Not often, and not lately. It's rather lovely, isn't it? Although I hate to think of what it must have been like during the Civil War."

"As far as I know—and I'm no expert—I don't think any important action took place here, just all around. And I assume there would have been regiments of soldiers and supply trains and, yes, medical tents and supplies and personnel tramping through. From what little I've had time to read, it sounds like such an awful war, although all wars are, aren't they?"

"That they are," Nell said quietly.

We arrived at the property. Josh had left the front gate open for us, so I passed through it and drove slowly toward the house, still concealed in its dell. When we came over the crest of the hill, when the house first became visible, I heard Nell say quietly, "Oh, my."

I stopped the car and let her admire the view. Finally she nodded once, and I drove slowly forward to the front of the house, where I parked. "You haven't even seen the inside yet."

"I can't wait. All the furnishings are intact?"

"They are."

"Be still, my heart," Nell breathed.

Once we went in, I wasn't sure I'd ever get her out of the building. At one point she asked, "Can I touch things?"

"Why not?" It was getting dark when I finally managed to tear Nell away from the building. We walked out the front door and admired the unmarred landscape in front of us.

"Wow," she said finally, in a reverent tone. "I get it now,

why you were so excited. It really is rare to find a place so untouched by time. And I wouldn't change it, apart from any necessary safety issues."

"But where's the money going to come from?"

"We'll find it. I promise."

READ ON FOR A LOOK AHEAD TO

KILLER IN THE CARRIAGE HOUSE—
THE NEW MYSTERY
BY SHEILA CONNOLLY,
AVAILABLE SOON IN HARDCOVER
FROM MINOTAUR BOOKS!

Remind me again why I said I'd do this?" I whispered to Lisbeth, who knew me better than almost anyone in the world, except maybe my parents. I kept my voice down because we were waiting in the wings of the high school's stage, watching the good citizens of Asheboro, Maryland, come in and find seats, so they could listen to me telling them how I thought we could transform the sleepy town into a place that tourists and historians would want to visit—and leave some of their cash behind. If that didn't work, the town would probably shrivel up and blow away, and I'd get the blame.

"Because you're the best person for the job," Lisbeth whispered. I knew she had my back, because she was the one who had called me and begged me to come help the town, and I'd been foolish enough to say yes. She was also standing behind me so that I couldn't turn and run away.

"You know I hate talking to crowds of people," I whined. She'd seen me botch my one stab at taking part in our high school debate team, in this same auditorium. Come to think of it, that was the last time I'd spoken to more than a dozen people at one time. I'd forgotten how terrifying it could be.

I checked my watch: ten of eight. Still time for even more people to drift in, ready to throw rotten tomatoes at me. This year there was a bumper crop of ripe tomatoes.

This was a special event for Asheboro, maybe even unique. While town meetings happened occasionally, seldom in my memory had there been one that affected the future of the town and all its residents. It sounded melodramatic to put it that way, but unfortunately it was true: if I couldn't help the townspeople find a new source of revenues for this struggling town, it was doomed. I knew I couldn't use dramatic words like "doomed" because people probably wouldn't believe me, but somehow I had to get them to believe that things in Asheboro really were that serious. If I could.

Over the last month or so I'd come up with a general proposal, but there were still a lot of holes in it, the largest ones in the budget. I could probably spin a good story about what could be done to transform the place, but I couldn't begin to tell them how to pay for it. The fact that a major storm had swept through recently and damaged a lot of the buildings along the main street, and then the bank manager had embezzled most of what little cash the town still had, didn't make my job any easier.

Lisbeth tugged at my jacket. "You might as well get started. A lot of these people have kids at home and will want to get back. Just tell them the truth, and keep it simple. Now, go!" She gave me a gentle push toward the stage.

Since I couldn't recall ever attending a town meeting here, although in my own defense I'd left for college and never looked back, I had no idea what kind of reception to expect. Stony silence would not have been my first choice. But here I was, and I had to move forward.

"Thank you all for coming tonight. I know you've got busy lives, so I'll keep this short and to the point." I swallowed, as many pairs of eyes stared blankly. "If you've lived here for any length of time, you may remember me. I'm Kate Hamilton, and I grew up and went to high school here. Until about three years ago my parents lived in the same house they always had, before they moved to Florida." The crowd still looked like it was made up of zombies. "All right, how many people in this room have lived here for most of their lives?" A few hands went up. "Twenty years?" A couple of dozen hands. "Ten years?" About the same number—which was telling me something: nobody seemed to have any reason to move to Asheboro, and that had been true for a while.

"Let me be honest with you. When I finished high school, all I wanted was to get out of town." Several people laughed at that. "I went to college, and then I found jobs in other places. I never planned to come back, especially after my folks left. So why am I here now?" I waited for a response that never came.

I pushed on. "Because my best friend back in those days— Lisbeth Scott—came to me to tell me that the town was broke and things weren't going to get any better unless something big happened. And she told me flat out that the town was desperate, and I was the only person she could think of who could help. And here I am."

Finally someone spoke. "Why'd she think that?" said a guy near the back of the room.

"You'll have to ask her that, because I'm still wondering. Look, how many of you know what kind of shape this town is in?"

"Physically? Financially?" the same guy said.

"Physically, all you have to do is walk down the main street. It looks shabby, tired, like it got left behind while the world moved on."

"Why is that?" someone else asked.

"Please, don't throw things at me. I grew up here, so I can say what I see and what I believe. This is and always has been a good town, with good people living in it. But the only industry was the shovel factory, and that closed long before most of us were born, and nothing came along to replace it. We're too far from Baltimore to make it an easy commute. The train line passed us by a century ago. There was never any kind of important battle or big historical event here. It's pretty and peaceful and quiet, but you can't pay the bills or send your kids to college on that. So people have left, and nobody's replaced them. And Asheboro has just drifted along the way it always did, until very recently."

I scanned the crowd to see if I had their attention. At least no one had gone to sleep yet.

I went on, "And then the town council found some gumption and decided to buy the Barton estate and make something out of it. Which took all the money you had. I applaud the courage and the hope it took to do that, but it's not enough to have a house, no matter how gorgeous, without any other reason to come to this town. So you people really have only one shot at thinking outside the box and saving the town."

"And that's where you came in?" a middle-aged woman closer to the front spoke. "Why are you qualified to do anything about this mess?"

I focused on her, because it was a valid question. "I don't claim to be an expert, in city planning or in finance. The biggest project I've ever managed was a Baltimore hotel, and one in Philadelphia before that. But nobody else seems to have stepped up, and all I've agreed to was to try to come up with a plan that might work. And in case you're worried, I'm not getting paid for this. I just don't want to see the town die."

"And you think you have some ideas to fix this?"

"Maybe. But it's going to take some cooperation from the

people in this town, particularly those who have a business in the center of town."

"And money? Higher taxes?"

"I know there's no money, and how could anybody raise taxes here when salaries and revenues are in the tank? I may be inexperienced, but I'm not naïve. Just hear me out. You don't have to vote on it or support it in any other way, at least, not yet. If you have any suggestions, I'd love to hear them. But let me say one thing: to make this work, you all have to commit to it and work together. If you can't do that, it's over."

I could see that the natives were getting restless. So much for the big build-up. Time to get my Big Idea out there and let it sink or swim.

"Settle down, people—I'm just getting to the good stuff. I propose that we turn the central blocks of Asheboro into a Victorian Village, as authentic as we can make it. And an extension of that would be the Barton Mansion outside of town. In case you don't remember your local history, Henry Barton was the owner of the factory on the edge of town, and easily the richest man, and his house, if you haven't seen it, is a magnificent example of high Victorian architecture *and* it's in good condition. It wouldn't take much work or money to make it shine. The challenge is to bring the rest of the town up to that standard."

"When you say make this place a Victorian Village"—the speaker made air quotes—"what the heck does that mean? Level it and rebuild the whole thing? With what money?"

"Have you taken a look at the buildings on Main Street?" I challenged him. "Since the storm? Well, I have. And what I discovered—and I'll admit it surprised me—is that most of the buildings that date back to 1900 or even before, are still there, under a century of siding. Believe it or not, the village is still there. Now, many of you who kept your insurance paid up will probably get a small settlement for damages from the storm. If you were going to repair your shops, you'd have to peel off the newer stuff anyway, so you can put that money toward repairing what's underneath. Maybe replace some windows with older models, and patch up the roof. Then you gut the interior and rebuild it to look the way it would have been in 1900, which would probably be cheaper than going modern with it."

"What about stuff like lighting and plumbing?"

"As long as what you see looks authentic, what's behind the walls and under the floors can be up to the minute—and probably would have to be to meet local building codes."

One woman who I recognized from the town council said thoughtfully, "I'd like to see some more detailed costs analyses for this. And what about people who hate the idea? It sounds like everybody would have to be on board to make it work—you couldn't have a Starbucks on Main Street because then you'd lose the illusion."

"You're absolutely right. That's why we'd need some true cooperation to make this work. But let's think optimistically. If you gag at the idea of running a candy emporium or a corset shop on Main Street, it's altogether possible that someone else might want to, and would buy you out at a fair market rate." I took a deep breath. "Let me tell you, nothing has to be decided tonight. I want you all to go home and think about the idea, and then we can meet again and you can say what you think. You love it, or you hate it—you have a right to your opinion. Talk it over amongst yourselves. Take the time to walk around town and really *look* at it—at the way it is now, and at the way it could be. But if you want to go on living here, raising your children here, retiring here, something has to be done. Thank you for listening."